The Lost One

Naemi Tiana

The Lost One

Cover Design: Vixen Designs
Editor: One Love Editing
ISBN: 978-3-9824943-2-6

Content Warnings

This story contains content that might be troubling to some readers, including, but not limited to, cutting and self-harm, substance abuse, childhood trauma, anger issues, foul language, and domestic abuse. Please be mindful of these and other possible triggers, and seek assistance if needed.

To those who can't see how *fucking* lovely they are.

The Lost One

Prologue

Emily

HANDCUFFS SLICED INTO MY SKIN, AND I GASPED FOR BREATH. The taste of stale sweat and worn leather coated my tongue, making me nauseous. My pleas for fresh air mingled with the police sirens blaring in my ears. *I have to get out of here . . .*

I whirled around, but the burning pressure on my wrist robbed me of control, leaving me trapped in the back seat of the police car.

"Nein . . ." *No . . .*

My breathing accelerated as I felt the gradually mounting panic in my chest. I kicked my feet against the front seat. "Let me out!"

The policeman, long past his prime, covered in wrinkles and grizzled hair, shot me a sour look through the rearview mirror.

"Shut up," he spat.

"No!"

I kicked harder and harder, battling my instinct to surrender. But the seats didn't even budge; I couldn't fool myself. I was weak. *Pathetic, even.*

"You can give up, little girl." the policeman mocked and triggered this new rage. I balled my fists, fueled by that flicker of hope in my heart. *A fight isn't lost until it is over; this one has one round left.*

"Stop. Calling. Me. Little!" I screamed, attempting to squeeze my hands out of the cuffs. The policeman slammed the brakes at the red light, and my head crashed into the passenger seat. My vision morphed into a vignette filter, and my body fell silent.

"There's more if you don't keep your annoying mouth shut!" With my flickering sight, I squinted at the police officer twisting in his seat. "I know exchange student brats like you! They come to America, want the high school movie experience, but take drugs because . . . agh, I don't even know why!"

He slapped the armrest and pointed at me. "You're just like everyone else, so don't think your story will have a happy ending. You'll never get to come back to the US after the stunt you pulled tonight!"

I gulped so hard my throat hurt but gave a slight nod. He shifted his focus to the now green light while I tilted my head so he couldn't see that he had hit me where it hurt the most. Searching for comfort, I let my eyes wander over the night streets of Boonville. Seeing teenagers run into the secured shadows of the woods, fleeing from the scraps they had left behind in their haste not to get caught by this police car.

But I was caught because I'd given my heart to the wrong person. My lips trembled as a fresh tear rolled down my face. *Goodbye, America . . . it was nice to meet you.*

Chapter 1

Again and Again

Emily

One month before . . .

My body was scalding hot as a massive weight pinned me into the varnish of the bed. I braced my upper body when hands traced unexpected lines from my arm up to my collarbone, meeting my cheeks—cupping them.

Paul Shields.

The boy I had chosen was the lovely one I had shared the bed with ever since. I shouldn't have been surprised by this gesture, but my body froze. We had been aloof for the past two weeks. Not because I didn't want to be close to him but because something was standing between us. *Or rather someone.*

I wrenched my eyes open and sought to see something, but my eyelids felt like weights had been placed on them. The feeling of his fingertips caressing my skin now made my body tremble with anticipation, followed by a short gasp for air. A scent of smoky charcoal with a hint of musk filtered through me. He must've been smoking because this was not the usual fresh breeze I perceived on his breath. I rested my palm on his chest to feel his heartbeat; it always eased my mind. But the throbbing against my fingertips was faster than I had ever felt.

"Your heart..."

His finger applied slight pressure to my lips without a single sound escaping his throat.

"Okay," I breathed with conviction. He bent to my neck and nourished my skin with his lips. He sucked, licked, and teased so greatly that a thrumming sensation flowed through my veins. I craned my neck into the pillow and breathed in the moist air flavored by our increasingly sweaty skin. Every moment, every decision, every step I had taken in the last few months—this maze I'd been trying to figure out—this elation reassured me that it was all worth it.

His tongue traced a circle behind my ear, and a soft moan surprised my dry throat. I slid my fingers into his hair and yanked him up by the roots, eager to finally kiss him, to feel him as closely as possible, longing for his flavor like my lungs for oxygen.

My actions had always been about wanting to fulfill my list...

I had found my adventure by him opening the door to his world for me. *Check.* I had found my voice through his challenging behavior. *Check!* And experienced true love... *Check?* But now, having checked everything off, I suddenly didn't know how to proceed. My path felt like a dead end, yet returning was no longer an option. I'd already taken too many turns, leaving me... *lost.* Too drawn to ocean eyes, too magnetized by recklessness, naked by my anxieties, stuck with no way forward or backward.

His sharp yet playful tongue finally entered my mouth and dragged me out of my controlled thoughts, followed by an invigorating tingle wandering through my stomach as our tongues united at a rapid speed.

"Hmm..." I breathed into his mouth. It was like throwing a match into a hay field; I burned within seconds and let my impulses devour me. I deepened the kiss by opening my mouth further, letting him explore every corner. It suddenly didn't matter that no plan existed for me. The consequences of my actions were out of sight, and I could enjoy the desire and dive into a parallel universe. A universe in which I transformed from a shy little doll into a strong, confident woman. Addictive moments like this... with *him.*

I squeezed his shoulder harshly when his head wandered between my thighs, kissing them like a treasure. My back arched up, and my body, which felt heavy seconds before, suddenly felt like it was trying to fly up to the ceiling. But then he pulled away, and all I had left was my frantic breathing begging for more.

"Why did you stop?"

"Because this is not the choice you made . . . *Little German*."

In a split second, I sat straight, and the exciting thumping in my chest transformed into aching stabs.

"Jon . . .!" I coughed, unable to breathe.

"You thought Paul could make you feel this way? Oh, please."

Jon's face moved a bit back until his cocky smirk was highlighted by the moonlight entering through the window that I could've sworn wasn't there minutes before.

"Of course he can!" I winced, guilt running through my veins. Jon raised his brow, and his fingers traveled back down my stomach, creating goosebumps of unwanted delight. I had chosen Paul and sworn to myself that this was it . . . *but Jon* . . . I let out a soft breath. He lingered in my thoughts like a forbidden fruit.

"We can't do this . . . Paul is your best friend and my . . . *boyfriend*." The last word felt heavy on my lips.

"Did that ever stop you?" he coaxed, stroking the inside of my thighs again. I whimpered when his hand found my panties, playing with the elastic. Feeling Jon so close to me was like a rush, his surprising manner keeping me on my toes. But just the thought of losing Paul again—like I thought I had lost him by the lake—was like losing a part of myself. Paul had saved me. Whenever I was with him, I felt protected and appreciated. Like he brought my home to me. What was between Jon and me was toxic. A trap I'd sworn I'd never fall back into. Yet here I was . . .

The moonlight now lit up the entire room.

"Jon, we've got to think about—" I turned my head to the left, trying to hide my tears, looking straight into ocean-blue eyes. *Paul's eyes.*

"Paul!" I squealed. He was lying on my right side only centimeters, or inches, as he would say, away, giving me a soft face. I screeched and covered my mouth with my shaking hands. *Paul saw it all.* Promptly, I forced Jon away, but he refused to leave, kneeling between my legs.

"Why do you want him to stop now, Babycakes?" Paul asked, resting his forehead against mine gently.

"Because I chose you . . . We're together." I bolted, my gaze shifting back and forth between his ocean-blue eyes and Jon's chocolate-colored temptations.

"Your head chose me, but your heart is still holding on to him." Paul smiled tiredly and brushed his lips onto mine, not going in for the kiss yet. My nostrils flared as his crisp and mellow essence blew away the smoky charcoal.

"That's not true . . ." I quivered and stretched my neck to connect to his slightly parted lips. But the more I tried to reach him, the more he drifted away.

"Why are you pulling away . . .?"

"Because you haven't made your decision yet, Little German." Jon pulled the focus back onto him with a winsome frown. Then, blinking twice, I found his head resting on my stomach, unusually cuddly.

"I chose Paul." I covered my ears with my hands and squeezed my eyes shut, rocking my body back and forth. "He's the one I want!"

"Then why did you let me kiss you? *Again . . . and again?*" Jon's words were like an echo in my brain.

"It was dark. I had no idea it was you," I whimpered, still not daring to open my eyes.

"You didn't recognize my scent? The difference in the way Paul and I kiss?" His voice grew louder and louder. "You still want me. You always wanted me . . . you liked me first. Remember?"

I shook my body so much that my head hurt.

"Nooo!" I shouted, and my eyes flew open. As I woke up, the weight from my eyelids was lifted. Gasping for air, I glanced all around me. I was still in Paul's bed, the moonlight lighting up the basement, but I couldn't see Jon anymore. I quickly peeked below the bed. *Nothing there.* I threw my head back into the pillow while trying to calm down my bursting body. *That felt real . . . too real.* I wiped the ice-cold sweat from my forehead.

"It was just a dream," I whispered so my heart would finally catch up.

I rolled over, hoping for Paul's comfortable chest, but instead, I fell into the hollow he had left on his side of the bed. *Where is he?*

With still-trembling thoughts, I swung my legs out of bed—I had to find him. To know that I didn't mess up the best thing I'd ever had . . . *again*. Praying that I hadn't said Jon's name while sleeping, I stretched my legs until I was on my feet. The freezing air instantly formed goosebumps on my skin. I reached for my phone, seeing my usual sunset background. *1:20 am*. I sighed, grabbed one of Paul's Mizzou sweaters from the ground, and wrapped myself in it. Paul's heat usually kept me so warm at night that I only slept in a short-sleeve shirt and my underwear, even though it was December already. When his crisp smell hit my nose, my heartbeat slowed down.

"It was just a dream. You didn't hurt him again."

I walked over to the window and positioned myself on tiptoes to peer outside. Although it was night, it was as if the full moon illuminated the world. It was hanging so low that, as a child, I would've believed you could touch it if you ran up to it. Just like this man running . . . *wait, that's Paul!*

Dressed in shorts, he ran past a streetlamp, the light reflected on his sweaty skin, headphones plugged into his ears, the sweat of exertion running down his toned back. I bit my lower lip and soaked up his handsome image. He was doing high knees now. For a moment, I considered heading outside. I wanted nothing more than to hug him, feel him, and replace this image Jon had created in my head. But what the hell was I going to say? *Hey, I dreamed that your best friend was about to sleep with me, so I think* we *should do this instead?* Not the best idea after what happened down at the lake. Because even though two weeks had passed, Paul still went jogging in the middle of the night as if he couldn't bear to lie next to me.

"Emily?"

Gena's soft voice pulled me out of my thoughts, causing me to jump back.

"I didn't mean to scare you, but I heard screaming." Gena extended an arm toward me, going unusually slow. I looked to the side, seeing my reflection in the window. Dark circles dug into my skin, and my eyes were bloodshot and coated with a glittering haze. Gently, Gena squeezed my arm, and I turned back to her. She was wearing a blue nightgown in which she appeared cute and cozy. Nothing seductive, but knowing Henry, he would say that she was the most beautiful woman no matter what she wore.

"Are you okay?"

"Had a bad dream. It's a full moon." I tried to shoot her a smile, but my thoughts were not entirely in my reality yet. As I said, the only person who could ground me was Paul. *Or Jon?* My skin shivered again.

"Come here, honey." She pulled me into a motherly hug, ignoring that Paul wasn't in his room. I hesitated at first but then swung my arms around her body lightly. She might not be Paul, but she carried a part of his caring genetics, and I was more than thankful to have her as a shoulder to lean on.

"Dreams can be our escape, but they can also be our prison. Don't let them shift your reality," Gena said and patted my hair.

"Uh-huh . . ." I peeked out of the window again. Paul's body was drifting away from my sight until he only looked as big as a bobby pin. *Too late.*

Chapter 2

Good Guy Incoming

Paul

"SHE LIKED ME FIRST."

Jon's voice blared in my head even louder than the drums coming from my headphones as my feet flew across the concrete. My foot throbbed so hard I knew I should slow down, but I didn't.

I used to be a pro at running. With my long legs, I was always faster than everyone else in my class. It was effortless. At least back then. Now, it was more like torture for my still-healing foot. Yet it was the only thing that helped when I heard her sobbing at night. I ran across a crosswalk without looking. The streets were empty anyway.

It always felt natural to be the best version of myself for Emily. I finally had a purpose, a passion for what I was good at, and I could let go of a dream far from the past. I finally didn't feel *lost* anymore——at least, until now. All I could do now was run, and the cold air hit me like a whip. My lungs ached from the cigarettes I usually only smoked at parties, which had now become a daily habit. *Fucking tobacco. I should quit this shit again.* My former coach would've scorned me if I had even gotten close to inhaling. After all, I'd been his best quarterback until the accident changed everything. The accident caused by none other than my best friend.

The song reached the heavy metal chorus. The anger in the music made my brow furrow. *Shit,* I could forgive this dude for fucking up my foot and my future career, but with my girl . . . I set off for the final sprint, coughing and feeling water forming in the corners of my eyes from the cold wind. The way her sometimes more greenish, sometimes more bluish, eyes looked at him with such care made me pick up the pace. Prompted by that image of their lips touching, my strides lengthened. The way their mouths were glued to each other made my body channel the last energy left in me. And I ran so fast that I passed several front yards within seconds. She had enjoyed the kiss. I was not an idiot.

"Ah!" I screamed out loud, not slowing down. That fucking asshole who used to be my best buddy was causing a war in my head lately. And I was tired of feeling that war. To be the good guy who always forgave him no matter what shit he pulled. I was only human, after all—*damn it.* I made mistakes too, but compared to him, they tore me apart. So much that I wished I could go back in time and undo them, while Jon even had the gall to ask me if I would come over to chill tonight.

Well, I'm coming over now, but not to chill.

I flew through the air and landed face-first in the frozen grass with a dull thud. I snorted as I turned around to get the missing oxygen back into my lungs, wiping a few blades of grass and dirt from my completely drenched hair. I reached for my watch to turn off the music when the screen turned black. *Battery dead.* I shoved my headphones into my pockets, exchanging the loud static for a peaceful winter breeze. The twinge in my lungs felt strangely pleasant as my eyes watched the bright stars above me. It was a clear night, and the full moon hung so low that I reached out, pretending to touch it. I laughed like a madman when I sat up and realized where I was. The big maple tree to my left rustled in the wind. Jon and I used to play in it when we were kids. Now it taunted me, reminding me of when Jon told me to climb up to the top. I didn't want to be a loser, and I did, but I fell and got this one scar on my right knee. I'd had to get five stitches, but that didn't stop him from wanting to do it again a few weeks later. And that time, I did it and was rewarded with a view of the entire street.

"Damn memories," I hissed and spat out some saliva that tasted a little bloody. I had fucked my body with that run, but it was my best time. I guess I could thank Jon for that as well.

"Ironic," I growled to myself. It was like Jon had always been the source of my pain. But then the pain made me stronger, and I wasn't sure if I should be grateful or furious about that. I took off my left shoe because my foot was pounding. When I removed my tennis sock, I saw that my foot was already turning blue and yellow in places with scars. I should get it checked out.

"Paul?" a melodic voice breathed. I craned my neck to confirm who that voice belonged. *Kiki*. Jon's never-ending on-and-off girlfriend with a heart too big for her own good.

"Kiki, what are you doing here?" I quickly slipped my sock and shoe back on and picked myself up off the grass. My legs were still weak from my run. She watched me silently as I hobbled up the driveway toward her.

"I don't even know myself, dude." Her puffy acorn-brown eyes wandered to the moon, letting me see the red veins in them. "What about you?"

"Just finished a run." I shrugged and dusted the remaining leaves off my torso.

"At almost 2 *am* on a school day in December?" Kiki raised her eyebrows.

"Yeah, now that you say it out loud, it sounds shitty." I raised my shoulders and tried to lighten the mood with my usual sunny-boy demeanor.

She smiled softly to herself. "We're all a bit fucked-up, aren't we?"

She pulled out her phone, the electric-blue light destroying the mystical atmosphere around us.

"I have to go home . . . Could you . . .?" She turned her screen off again and glanced over her shoulder. "He's there, but he's not feeling well."

"What is he on?"

"Some stupid pills, weed, alcohol, I don't know. I came because I had to make sure he was okay . . . but I can't do this anymore, Paul. He took it too far this time. It's too much."

The tears welled in her eyes, and she put her hand to her cheek to stop them from flowing. I couldn't bear to see her break down, so I put my hand on her shoulder and held her tightly so she wouldn't fall over.

"Please, you have to take care of him. He can't lose both of us." She fixed her gaze on me, her eyes pleading with all the dignity she had left.

"Kiki, it's difficult. . ."

"I know." She exhaled loudly. "But if something happened to him, I'd never be able to forgive myself. But if I stay . . ." Her light tears turned into sobs. "I will hate myself for it."

I pulled her into a loose embrace to avoid bringing my sweat to her forehead. But she didn't care and pressed herself against my chest. This girl has been through so much shit with Jon because she had a way-too-good and patient heart. But now she was broken, and I could only add that to the ever-growing list of things Jon had fucked up.

"I'll keep an eye on him." I had no choice but to agree. If anything ever happened to Jon, I wouldn't be able to forgive myself for that either.

"Thanks." Her sobbing subsided as she broke away from my embrace. She gave me a hesitant wave before running down the path to her Mini Cooper. I took a deep breath after watching her get into the car. My intention of coming here to tell him to fuck off was gone with this disturbed girl. I limped through the gate into the garden. We used to sit for hours on those white, run-down plastic chairs in the good old days. We got millions of mosquito bites, which we didn't care about because we were philosophizing about God and the world. But now, I couldn't remember the last time we sat here.

As expected, Jon was perched in one of the chairs, his head craned back, and a bottle of rum was about to slide out of his hand. His lips had already turned blue from the cold as he was only wearing a leather jacket. I was freezing too, and I'd probably catch a cold if I didn't put some clothes on soon.

"Hey, man," I said, taking the bottle from his hand. He jerked up, blinking several times as he looked at me like a ghost. I reached into a garden box and pulled out the usual Dragon Ball blanket that had been mine since we were little kids.

"What the hell are you doing here?" he growled. I rolled my eyes as I dropped into one of the chairs, wrapping myself in the blanket and bringing the rum to my lips to take a hearty swig.

"Being your friend," I pressed out as the burn of cheap alcohol spread through my chest. He looked at me with empty eyes, and I wasn't sure he even registered my words. Suddenly, he snorted and went to reach for the bottle, but I held it away from him, causing him to grunt. Annoyed, he leaned back in his chair, and his eyes locked on me in annoyance.

"You remember I kissed your girl, don't you?" A flicker crossed his face. He enjoyed provoking me, and God, it was so fucking hard not to throw that bottle in his fucking shitface. I gritted my teeth, took his Newport pack off the table, and pulled out a smoke. Jon tossed me a lighter, and I inhaled the nasty-tasting herb against my impulse to quit again. It burned like hell as it traveled down my throat.

"Shit happens," I said as I exhaled, mustering all my strength to pretend I had long forgotten. Jon and I hadn't spoken for the past two weeks because I'd sworn I'd never talk to him again. And here I was, getting reminded of why I wanted to break off contact.

"Seriously? Won't you give me more crap about it? Just *shit happens?*" Jon was grinning, probably high on weed and other counterproductive pills. He was always like that when he combined everything, like he wanted to push everyone around him away. I knew the best way to deal with him was to pretend that his behavior didn't bother me, even though my core was exploding to do the opposite.

"Yeah, let's forget about it and move on."

We all have our parts to play. Jon was the one that destroyed everything he touched, and I was the one cleaning up the chaos he left behind. I was the good guy, whether I liked it or not. I threw the cigarette on the ground and stomped it out. *I'm better than him . . . for Emily.*

For the lovely girl I'd left in a cold bed to sit next to the guy who had destroyed our perfect little world. Kiki was right. We were all a little fucked-up.

Chapter 3

Game Not Over

Jon

MY HEAD WAS THROBBING LIKE SHIT. I GRABBED FOR THE water bottle Kiki usually placed on my nightstand together with aspirin whenever I went on another, as she called it, "self-destruction mission." She came over last night. I knew she would. Her taking over when my mind stopped working was one of the few things I could count on.

My hands only grasped air in my fist. *Fuck!*

It was dark, and the toxins from the alcohol surged out of my pores. I smelled like a fucking homeless person. My fist punched the empty air several times until I realized my usual helper elf hadn't come to my rescue. Or had she? I couldn't remember, and I didn't care.

"Hmm!" I growled as I straightened my torso. Every inch of my body felt like I'd been at the gym for hours. The only difference was that my eyes hadn't seen a gym since the last time I'd decided to go to AP, which was ... *Ugh, who cares.* I flipped the switch on my lamp, shielding my eyes from the burning light about to flood the room.

"Shit." My head throbbed even more, and my bottom lip trembled as that sickening aftertaste settled in my throat. *If Kiki wasn't here, how the hell did I get into bed?*

My dad had stopped doing so months ago, quoted in his words, "I don't want to support your stupid behavior." It was better he didn't. The days he carried me to bed as his little boy with dreams for his life were long gone. It made me sick to see how naive people crawled through life. I preferred to numb myself. It was easier that way. Honestly, I could probably even be happy with this lifestyle if I turned eighteen. I wasn't sure I wanted to grow old like that. People would be better off without me anyway, especially—

"Paul, fuck!" I had taken my hands away from my eyes, and after blinking twice, I noticed a huddled Paul on the couch. The corners of my mouth curved upward as I noticed he was wrapped in his stupid Dragon Ball blanket. Him and his traditions.

"Turn off the light, man." Paul cursed and turned around so I could see the twitching muscles on his back. Paul was always more ambitious when working out, but I did not need to impress anyone. The only way to make me sweat was boxing . . . or sex, but that was about it. I ignored his request and shuffled into the bathroom with a slowly growing rotten feeling in my stomach. *Why is this asshole even here after all the shit I did to him?*

After gulping down a gallon of water and wetting my neck and hair, I gazed at my reflection in the heavily soiled mirror.

Been worse.

Some of my curls hung low to my eyes. A little longer and I could hide my heavy eye bags with them. My now puffed-up face warned me that I was about to vomit. While leaning on the sink to keep from falling over, I pulled out my phone to distract myself from the shitty feeling in my stomach. The default wallpaper greeted me, and as my facial ID unlocked the screen, I lost hold of the sink. It was a preview of a message from *Little German.*

Little German: Hi. . . I don't want to annoy you, but

I regained my balance and rubbed my eyes, questioning whether this was real or if I was still sitting high in my backyard. I hadn't gotten more than a view of her hairline in US History in two weeks. I tapped twice on the message, only leading to my phone loading for a ton shit time.

"Finally." I cursed and held my phone closer to my face.

> **Little German:** Hi. . . I don't want to annoy you, but is Paul with you?

I snorted. Even texting, she sounded insecure. Her words were carefully chosen as if they could make or break her. A grin spread on my face—I still had power over her. The sickening feeling returned to my stomach, causing me to lose my grip on my phone. With the screen down, it landed with a loud crack.

"Shit!"

I tried to squat down to pick it up, but the pills were still doing their thing. It wasn't the cheap shit but the good stuff from Marna, which I could only afford at the beginning of the month. I would feel high for at least a few more hours. I rolled onto my back, grabbed my phone, and leaned against the filthy bathtub. I glided over the crack with my finger, feeling how those little crystal shards bored into my skin.

. . . is Paul with you?

I stared at the split screen with furrowed brows. Suppose she didn't know where he was and was so desperate that she texted me at four in the morning—*hell, who cares.* It was easy to play with this girl, just some stupid cliché lines, and I had her, for example, at Halloween.

"What are you doing to me, Little German?"

Fuck, I deserved an Oscar for that. But it had caused me more problems than expected. It was supposed to be a game: *Who can fuck the new girl.* If I had known how she would mess with my friend's head, I would've never asked Breana to bring her along to hang out with us. But then again, it was fun to tease her until her face turned crimson or the way she tried to fit in and gave me her challenging eye roll when I reminded her she was different. Which I never claimed as something bad, but she interpreted it that way. Plus, her apple shampoo was always refreshing and so strong that it masked my alcohol smell from Mr. Harrison, which made my life easier. I kind of appreciated having her around. But then again, she did choose him. But if he was here, maybe the game hadn't reached its final round. After everything, I knew he hadn't even properly fucked her. I could never be as patient as he was, but then again, I'd never been asked to be patient by someone before either.

I quickly typed my response and hit Send before my eyes fell shut again, and my bathroom floor turned into my bed of life. *Kiki should've brought me that fucking water bottle.*

Chapter 4

Too Many Questions

Emily

GENA HAD STAYED WITH ME A LITTLE LONGER, BUT I ASSURED her I was okay. As an elementary school principal, she was working overtime—I didn't want to be added to the list of kids who needed to be saved. *At least not again.* I still struggled to grasp that she'd let me move into her house.

But when the wooden basement door closed, my chest rose and fell faster than before. *Where is Paul?*

With a tense lower lip, I examined the message I had sent to Jon. For every second without a reply, I could hear my heart thumping louder and louder in my eardrums. *Did I really ask the guy who had gotten me into this mess for help?* I slammed my phone back on the nightstand and screamed into the pillow. There was no way Paul was still jogging. It was only 4 Celcius, 40 degrees, outside; plus, it was 4 am on a school night.

"Where are you!" I punched the pillow with my fist, my face crushed into the cotton to silence my scream. We had gotten stuck in this spiral of mistrust out of betrayal. I had kissed Jon twice, and he'd slept with Jamie once. I tried not to hold that against him. I mean, how could I? I had told him explicitly that we would never date that night, yet this picture of Paul disguised as a doctor kissing the mouth of a slutty superwoman didn't want to leave my head. My upper body shot up, and a sharp pain ripped through my chest.

"What if he went to Jamie ...?" I gasped, talking to myself like the crazy person I was turning into. "He could've done that, right? He's been distant since."

I jumped up and paced around the room. I stubbed my toe against one of Paul's football trophies, covered by a pile of clothes, and let out a painful squeak. "Ouch!"

I jumped on one leg while clutching my toe with the other. The stinging pain made me grumble and curse in a way I usually never would've. Paul and I never even mouthed their names again. Too bad that didn't make them go away. They were present, killing the lightness we used to have.

"We should've talked about all this," I whispered under my breath. Once again, my inexperience made me question whether I knew how to be in a healthy relationship. My parents didn't talk either, and I should've known sweeping it under the carpet wasn't the solution.

With my fingers spread, I tore through all the clothes and shoved them into a basket. Paul could be so messy sometimes, and it drove me insane. After I was done, pictures of a worst-case scenario returned.

"That's enough!" I lunged for my phone to dial Paul's number for the fourth time. I pressed it to my ear and bit my nails until they broke.

"C'mon, Paul ... pick up," I pleaded, hoping that if I said it aloud, the thought might transfer to his brain wherever he was. On the third ring, I turned my head back and caught a glimpse of light from the laundry basket. I almost toppled over my legs and rummaged through the laundry like a lunatic until I held Paul's phone. Without thinking, I slid the screen up and typed in codes that could have meaning for him. 0119, his birthday, no success. 1026, the day Mizzou had last won. Neither. Frustrated, I pinched the spot between my eyebrows.

"Think, Emily, what could be his code ..."

I'd been using the code of my departure date since I'd gotten here, but I'd changed it the last month ... no! He wouldn't use this one. *Or would he?*

"I'm in!" I marveled as I typed in the date of the day we met: October

3. Except I typed it 0310—in Germany, you say the day first and then the month. My heart leaped, knowing that this date had as much meaning for him as it did for me. Quickly, my index finger moved to the message icon, but I halted before tapping it. His background picture was us sitting around a campfire in Hannah's backyard. The blazing flames surrounded us in a warm, peaceful scenery. This composition screamed Breana.

Paul looked at me, enamored, with the little wrinkles he always had when discussing environmental science or football. But at that moment, they were caused by none other than me. And I looked . . . I held my breath. I'd never seen myself so happy in a photo before. My puffy cheeks had a red blush, and my grin was so wide that my full mouth appeared flat. I lowered the phone. I wouldn't turn into one of those jealous control freak girls. Or at least I didn't want to be in a relationship like that. In a healthy partnership, you shouldn't feel an urge for control. You should feel at peace. And peace wasn't pacing around in the middle of the night, freaking out because of a dream. I sighed and dropped back onto the bed. It wasn't too late to fix this. It just needed some glue . . . and lots of cuddles. I put Paul's phone back into his pants and crawled under the blanket. Looking up, I saw the spot on the wall where it said BABYCAKES. My breathing evened out, and my mind went quiet. My place was by Paul's side. The boy who took me into his home after barely knowing me, the guy who protected me from anything sketchy, and the one who told me he loved me in the middle of a small tornado in Oklahoma. Neither Jon nor Jamie should have the power to change that. I had to find a way to control my heavy emotions because they were my strongest weapon. With the slight difference that they were here to destroy me, not protect me. I felt my phone vibrate next to my ear, the first rays of sunlight rippling through the window. Within a split second, I sat straight in the bed with my phone back in my hand. Jon had replied. So much for peace.

Arschloch: Yeah, he's here

I drew in a breath. He wasn't with Jamie. *But what is he doing at Jon's?* This one question alone kept me from falling asleep again. And against me fighting it, I created stories in my head for a reasonable explanation, each one crazier than the other. But at least it was the only question to worry about.

I had replied to the others by having trust—too bad that trust could be crushed with one nasty thought.

Me: You are not lying to me?

And send.

I had just finished rinsing out my apple-scented shampoo when there was a loud thud at the door.

"Paul!" I gasped and accidentally choked down some water. I hastened out of the shower and quickly wrapped myself in a white towel adorned with red roses. *Two more knocks.*

"I'm coming!"

I double-checked that the towel was knotted tightly and looked at myself in the steamed-up mirror. The shower had helped a little, but my eyes were red like I'd been smoking weed. I sucked in through my teeth when I noticed a pimple that had grown above my left eyebrow. I yanked open my drawer. No matter how relaxed Gena and Henry had been about Paul and me sleeping in the same bed, they insisted on us using a different bathroom. It didn't make much sense, but I didn't object. I covered the pimple the best I could, dropping the concealer twice before applying it, yet it only helped a little in taming this beast.

"Arrrg . . ." I growled at myself like a provoked dog. Another knock, but this time, it was more like a bang.

"I can't change it anymore . . ." I turned the door handle.

"Finally, you took forever in there!"

Zack hopped from one leg to the other while placing his hands over his bladder.

"Zack!" I screeched, clutching the towel tightly. "I thought you were—"

"Paul? He's outside with Jon," Zack explained, not stopping the dramatic body language that he had to pee.

"Oh." I clung to the doorframe as Zack passed me. Paul had come home, finally. And he was with Jon, which meant he hadn't covered for him. But then again . . . *why was he with Jon?*

"Um, can you leave me alone now?" With his fingers at his sweatpants, Zack laughed loudly, ready to go in for the pull.

"Yes, hold on!" I flew out of the bathroom and shut the door. I already had walked in on Zack once, and I didn't plan for it to happen again. I gripped my towel tightly and hurried across the hall to my room. Nothing had changed here since I'd moved in. My clothes were neatly hung up in the closet. The bed had been untouched, but I had picked up some books. My last read was *Harry Potter.* Basic, but reading something I already knew calmed me down for some reason. I pushed the door to the side, moving hanger after hanger. The jumpsuit Paul had bought for me on Black Friday caught my eye. I hadn't worn it since, and it was ripped from when I got stuck on a nail at the lake. I quickly moved through all my clothing options. I was amazed by American closets. Having them integrated into the wall and hanging everything up gave a better overview of what you owned. My organizing self already imagined how I could find a way to do this in Germany. Just thinking about my departure, I shivered. *Six more months aren't enough. . .*

I threw on a pastel purple sweatshirt and hesitated between light denim and ripped black jeans. After a brief moment, I went for the darker option. All dressed, I walked out into the hallway and looked toward the bathroom, hoping that Zack wouldn't occupy it much longer when . . .

"Emily."

His soft voice hit me like a lightning bolt.

"Paul!" I whirled around with my soaked hair, causing a few drops to fall onto the wooden floor. Paul looked at me seriously before he rubbed his head uncomfortably. I grabbed the threads of my sweatshirt and let them roll through my fingers, sensing his tense manner.

"I hope you didn't notice I was gone last night?" he asked with pressed-together lips. "I didn't mean to stay out, but Kiki asked me to, um . . . watch Jon, and I forgot my phone."

I ran up to him so fast that he had to catch me so I wouldn't fall over my feet. He didn't go to Jamie's place and didn't hear me talk in my sleep. This scenario was the one I had expected the least, but it happened, and I squeezed him tightly to show him how relieved I was that he was back by my side.

"I missed you," I breathed into his neck as his arms pulled me even closer.

"I missed you too," he finally whispered after a long pause, and I pressed my lips to his. His crisp scent tasted better than before, and I promised not to let us create this distance any longer. When our lips parted again, I nuzzled my nose against his chest once more to catch a fresh breeze of his scent . . . but it didn't smell like him. It smelled like smoky charcoal. His chest tensed as I plucked at his shirt, which I recognized from Jon's black shirt collection.

"What's up, Little German."

"Jon!" I pulled away from Paul, turning on my heel. He was standing there with my favorite cup in his hand, the one covered with cats in different colors and eyes that looked like they'd rested even less than mine. His skin was stained with red spots, and his hair was messy. But not the perfect mess they used to be. Jon looked terrible. Paul's hand moved to my hip and pulled my back to his chest. My eyes traveled over to him, and the glare he gave Jon gave me goosebumps.

"Why don't you wait outside while I get changed, man?" Paul suggested to Jon with a harsh tone I wasn't used to from him.

"The couch looks comfier than the cold." Jon shrugged, but Paul's eyes narrowed, and he let out a loud breath through his nose like a bull ready to attack. I quickly placed my palm on his stubbled cheek. He hadn't shaved in a few days, but I liked the stubble. It made him look much older, and I was drawn to that.

When his gaze met mine, his look softened. "I don't want you to be alone with him . . ."

"I need to get ready in the bathroom anyway," I soothed him to avoid further drama, even though I understood why he wouldn't feel comfortable with me being alone with Jon. I wouldn't either.

"Okay then." He gave me a tired smile and cupped my cheeks for one more kiss, a hint longer than a normal *see-you-in-a-minute* one. I heard Jon snort, and even though I knew he was the reason for our struggle, I didn't like shoving it into his face. In the end, we did share this moment in which I believed what he said. Even though I knew now that it was all a lie . . .

I backed off toward the bathroom when Paul took two steps to get down to the basement, but Jon stopped me by pulling at my elbow. The only thing missing was the bell that opened the hunt.

"Here."

I turned my head to see how he held the cup of coffee in my direction, smirking in his usual cocky manner.

"I'm good," I said, taking a further step toward my escape from him.

"Gena told me to bring the coffee to you, saying you would need it."

My hand froze on the handle. *Gena, such a sweet gesture but delivered by the wrong person . . . It gives it a bitter aftertaste.*

"You look like you need it more than I do," I said as coldly as possible, pulling at the door but realizing it was still locked. *Ugh, Zack!*

"Okay," he said, and I was surprised by his breath on my neck. "But just for your information . . ."

I drew a sharp breath as Jon placed his fingertips on my neck, softly brushing my damp hair behind my shoulder. Out of my face, just like he liked it.

"There's no need for me to lie to you, Little German. You have already made your choice. Remember?" His voice darkened, causing my neck to tingle, thinking about how he had sucked my skin and playfully bit it in my dream. My eyes shut as I felt the control slipping away from me. His palm traveled above the fabric of my sweatshirt until he reached my hip bone, running small circles over it. "Or haven't you?"

The turn of the bathroom lock made me jump as Zack swung the door open. I twirled around, Jon leaning onto the staircase railing as if he hadn't just stood right behind me. *Is my mind playing tricks on me?*

"What's up, Jon?" Zack greeted with a yawn.

"Not much, buddy," Jon smirked and took a sip of *my* coffee while Zack slinked back into his room. Jon's cocky grin hit me. Last night, even though it was just a dream, I had gotten another taste of what playing with fire felt like, and I didn't intend to get burned again.

Following Danielle's advice, I stumbled and grabbed the coffee cup out of his hand, causing it to spill a bit. He looked at me with wide eyes, still swallowing his sip.

"Thanks for the coffee," I spat and threw him a fake smile, not even trying to hide the sarcasm. "You can leave now."

When the bathroom door was finally closed behind me, I let out my breath. *I should've let Paul make sure that he leaves the house. . .*

Chapter 5

Down by the Lake

Emily

Two weeks ago . . .

"I WON'T MAKE THE MISTAKE OF WALKING AWAY AGAIN," HE said. "I love you too much."

In my soaked jumper, my heart exposed, I stood in front of Paul on the dock in Hannah's backyard. Against all the odds, he hadn't left me behind. He'd even helped me get out of the lake, and I smashed my lips onto him, feeling my mind calming down from this climax.

"I love you too." I smiled while kissing him, but I could tell how a piece of me was still drowning in the water. But that piece wasn't good for me, Paul was my lovely one, and I wouldn't dare to risk removing the checkmark off #3 again.

"I will walk away, though."

A soft voice interrupted our moment. I searched for her with water droplets all over my face, arms, and legs. Then I saw cherry-red lips and amber eyes surrounded by smudged mascara, and I realized I had caused more than one heartache tonight.

"Kiki . . ." I winced and covered my mouth with my hands. Standing next to a tree, she must've seen and listened to everything. The entire conversation in which Jon admitted he liked me right from the beginning, the kiss he surprised me with, and the fight that caused the boys to fall into the lake. I twirled around to see how Jon would react. He had crawled out of the lake and stood there with dripping clothes and pale skin, not saying a word. His eyes were empty, not showing one hint of emotion, as if he couldn't care less that Kiki had seen us kissing.

"Jon, say something!" I screamed at him on Kiki's behalf, but as I spoke, I heard Kiki's footsteps hurrying up the stone stairs. I immediately made to sprint after her, but Paul grabbed my hand. I wanted to shake him off, thinking he would try to stop me as he'd tried with Breana, but he surprised me when he said, "Let's go together."

Hand in hand, we rushed after her, but we quickly lost her in the crowd of people decorating the backyard. The candles gave barely enough light, and everyone's shadow covered people's faces. But Paul was taller than I and could peek above their heads for Kiki's shiny hair.

"She's leaving." He pointed to the garden gate. I picked up my pace and let go of Paul's hand to squeeze myself through the people with my petite figure. No one noticed our wet clothes or Paul's bloody cheek. The gate was still open when I slid through it.

"Kiki, hold on!" I screamed as she opened the door of her Mini Cooper. She had played beer pong with us not long ago; letting her drive would be irresponsible. She slammed the door again with so much force I reeled back a bit.

"Don't you dare, Emily!" she spat at me with tears falling down her face.

"I'm so sorry." My nails pushed into my palms. "I never meant for this to happen!"

"Sure, you didn't . . . It was him . . ." Kiki's voice broke, and she covered her face with her hands before dropping onto her knees. I rushed down to her but hesitated. We had never shared close contact before, and I didn't know how she would react to my affection. I kept my hands off her.

"I promise it will never happen again. It was the last time, I swear. I only want Paul." I spoke with a trembling lower lip while sitting in a squat position. Kiki's face shot up, and her amber eyes bored through mine, burning this picture of her pain into my brain.

"This wasn't the first time you kissed?" Her tone had changed. It was calm in between the sobs. As if she had escaped the spell Jon had put on her.

"I . . ." My shaky legs gave in, and I fell onto my butt. My palms rescued my fall, but a sharp stone dug into it.

She didn't wait for my reply and processed it with a loud sigh. "If you believe this is over now, you're naive."

I gasped. "What do you mean? It is over!"

She let out an exhausted, almost scary-sounding laugh while shaking her head. Then her eyes glared back at me. "Jon has this ability to get under your skin. Once he crawls in, you won't be able to shake him off. I've been trying to do so for years."

I sat there in silence while she wiped her face.

"Can we talk, Kiki?" Jon's husky voice went like a shiver down my spine. I turned around, seeing Paul offering me a hand to get up. I took it wordlessly.

"We talked enough, Jon," Kiki hissed, ice-cold. Jon's jaw tightened, and he lowered his look onto the concrete.

"Can you two do me a favor?" she then asked us.

"Anything." Neither of us hesitated.

"Please don't tell anyone about this. I'm embarrassed enough as it is." She glared above my shoulder at Jon. The hate in her eyes was still coated with some care.

"We won't," Paul promised, alone this time. "But please don't drive tonight, Kiki. You had too much to drink." Paul grabbed her keys out of her hands. She nodded silently before walking back to the backyard with her shoulders down and her arms hugging her body. Jon took a swig from a bottle I hadn't noticed with him till now. *Did he seriously grab some alcohol before coming here?!*

Anger returned to me, but I struggled to look at him. Something about Kiki's words marked me.

"Well, you should thank me, if you ask me," Jon slurred to Paul while taking out his pack of Newports and shaking it as it was drenched with water. "Fuck, I need new squares."

"Why the fuck should I be thankful to you?" Paul growled.

Jon raised an eyebrow and looked at us with a devilish grin. "Because now—" He paused, taking another large sip, his face grimacing. "Because now you know she wants you. The game is over. *You won.*"

He held the bottle in Paul's direction, who ignored it and glared at him with furrowed brows. Jon waved us off, rolled his eyes, and trudged down the street. Away from the party, away from us.

"A game?" I pressed out with an odd feeling in my stomach while watching him leave. Paul laid an arm around my shoulder.

"Everything is a game to him, Emily . . ."

He stopped his sentence and tilted my chin so I couldn't watch Jon's retreating figure. Paul's eyes were the usual calm ocean in the middle of a storm. I leaned into him.

"That's how Jon is. And he isn't used to losing."

I harshly swallowed as I let that sink in. He'd tested me again at the dock, just like he had tested me when we'd worked on the project together. I lost trust in every word he ever said to me. Every moment we shared. I didn't even know who he truly was . . . Jon was a stranger.

Chapter 6

Little Things

Paul

I RAGED THROUGH THE BASEMENT LIKE A CATEGORY-THREE tornado—winds of 111 to 129 mph, a harrowing storm that smashed everything around. I had torn off Jon's stupid shirt and slammed it into the corner when I blew through the door. She had noticed his scent on it. I could tell by the way her sweet nose wrinkled. I smashed open my closet and fumbled for a sweatshirt that wasn't dirty or so wrinkled that it looked like I'd picked it up off the floor. A while back, after Emily had done her laundry and organized her entire closet, she told me about the difference. I found that the German style suited me better than it did her.

"Then you should come and live in Germany," she chuckled, yet I couldn't help but see a glint of hope in her eyes. Since then, I'd been gathering little facts about Germany. She didn't make it easy, though; each time I talked about her home, she suddenly became interested in the most random crap. For example, the cupboard with mushy carrots and old beans. "Oh, what a combination—beans and carrots."

I had just taken a bite from an apple pie and almost swallowed it the wrong way when she remained serious.

"Beans and carrots?" I cackled out loud, struggling not accidentally to spit out some apple pieces. "I asked about your mother's boyfriend, Babycakes."

But she kept her focus on the cans. "Hm, we should make the beans soon, or they will go bad. It must take so long for canned food to go bad. Can it even go bad? I'm not sure. I should look it up. Ah, my phone is in the basement. I'll be right back!" She pointed in the air and rushed out of the kitchen. I lowered my fork because I suddenly had nothing to laugh at anymore. The more I pulled at her door to Germany, the more she pushed. She had a secret, and whatever it was, she hid it in her hometown. I huffed, returning from that memory and making even more of a mess in my closet. I raked my hands through my hair, but still no sweater.

I should clean up my room; if I did, I would have been a fuck lot faster to get back to my girl and make sure Jon didn't get into her head. I knew how good he was at this shit, especially when there was a prize to win. I froze, thinking back about the time we had bet on who could get her first. He'd never admit it to me, but I knew the hunt had attracted him to Emily. They had shared too many moments, moments I didn't even know about yet. A queasy feeling crept up my throat—imagining them working on this project together in his room, listening to music in his dad's car, laughing as they strolled down the school hallway—

"Fuck it!" I grabbed the only thing I could find. I hadn't worn this orange sweatshirt in ages because it was a little tight on my arms and shoulders. Oh, and because Jamie had given it to me when I couldn't get out of bed a few weeks after my accident. I had lost so much of my muscle then.

"An outstanding brand," Jamie told me when I had peeked at it with raised brows. We had been together for over a year, yet she kept forgetting how much I disliked orange. After pulling it over my head, my hair was a mess, so I brushed it quickly with my fingers, thankful that I had taken a cold shower at Jon's. I returned to the middle of the room and looked for the pants I'd worn yesterday, guessing my phone would be there. I picked up one piece of clothing at a time, but my brain was stressing about returning upstairs that I couldn't remember what I had been wearing.

"Ahh!" I cursed as I stubbed my injured foot on one of my trophies and made a mental note to finally clean after school. *I hope Emily will like that.* As I held my foot with pressure on the sore spot, I heard light footsteps coming from upstairs and moving down the hall. I dived into the first jeans I could find. Emily should be ready by now. She never took long to get ready. Her look was always natural, a little concealer and mascara, that's it. I liked how the black lashes accentuated her light eyes, shining as brightly as the stars—

I shook my head as I tried to tuck in the boner that had grown in my pants, not letting it get jammed in the zipper. *What in the world is this girl doing to me?* With Jamie, I never noticed the little things, but with her . . . I wanted to know every little detail about her, no matter how small and unimportant it seemed. And I was getting horny as hell just thinking about them. I cursed at the ceiling, waiting for my blood to rush elsewhere. A few pictures of rotten fish and other turnoff stuff later, I grabbed my way-too-light backpack. It probably only carried a notepad and a nearly empty pen. This time, I took three steps at a time and flew up the stairs. I would search for my phone later.

My gaze quickly darted around the living room, but Jon was no longer in sight. I pushed aside the curtains, and my alarmed heart finally relaxed. Jon was leaning against my car, smoking a cig, busy writing in his little black book. My brows furrowed. I always thought that I was the one who had the most power over Jon, but I could be wrong. Perhaps she was the one who could help him escape this madness, but I would never risk him dragging her down with him. She didn't know half of the shit he was doing, and I'd rather leave it at that.

I backed away from the window as I heard her footsteps coming down the hall. Emily had only recently entered my life, but ever since she had, everything was better. My chest was lighter, and I felt motivated and happy about each day coming. I pulled my shoulders back. I had to find a way to make this work. Be friends with Jon without this fear of losing her due to it.

"Paul." Emily's sweet voice snapped me out of my warring thoughts. I turned to face her, and a big grin spread over my face. She looked exactly as I had imagined, but she hadn't tied her hair in a bun as it had been for the past few weeks. Instead, it fell in small waves over her shoulders, stopping right above her chest. The golden shimmer dancing on it made her look even more angelic.

"Oh, dear lord . . ." I felt my blood flowing back into my cock.

"What?" She looked behind her. *It's so cute how she doesn't even realize this huge effect she has on me.* I walked up to her and let my fingers slide into hers as I gave her a soft kiss.

"Nothing. You look perfect, Babycakes."

She giggled, just as she had the first time I ever complimented her. Then she placed two fingers around my sweater. "Don't you hate orange?"

"I fucking do."

Another kiss.

"We're finally going out tomorrow!" Brandon's dark voice was higher than usual as he told us for the third time about his first date with Hannah. Emily turned to give him the positive energy he had claimed. "When did you ask her out, Brandon?"

"At the bonfire after Thanksgiving!" Brandon's already wide grin grew even wider. Emily quickly moved forward, and I could see her blushing behind her hair.

"Oh . . . at the bonfire?" She shuddered. I put my hand on her thigh, and she grabbed it immediately. Then, glancing in the rearview mirror, I saw Jon slumped over in the back seat, having eyes only for his little black book again. I gave up trying to read it about two years ago when he even rejected tacos in exchange for a little peek. And he loved tacos.

"I was so drunk I don't even remember asking her!" Brandon seethes. "I only have the messages we had written each other that night."

He lightly punched Jon in the arm. Jon looked up. "What?"

"Do you remember how I asked Hannah out, man?"

I hit the brakes at full speed at a crosswalk for an old granny taking her sweet time. Jon caught my gaze.

"I was down at the lake. I wouldn't know," he huffed, not breaking eye contact with me. Emily squeezed my hand tighter.

"I can't believe you finally had the guts to ask her out, Brandon." I backed away from the fight. I was going to keep Kiki's promise. Emily bit her lower lip; I think she struggled a lot more than I did. Maybe I should talk to her about it after all . . . but god, just thinking about it made my hands clutch the steering wheel so hard that the white of the bones on my knuckles showed through.

"Fuck off, dude." Brandon flipped me off. "Oh, do you think it's a good idea to go for sushi, Emily?"

Emily and Brandon chatted about a perfect first date while my attention returned to the road. My feet lowered, and our pace increased. I'd always been a big fan of speed. I felt so powerful holding a steering wheel in my hands. I felt the control I had lost after the accident. Emily noticed my rush, and she smiled at me in return. This speed was certainly nothing compared to what she had experienced on the German Autobahn, yet she appreciated it just as much as I did. I imagined the two of us alone in the car and how she would let me into her world one day. Because, damn it, I would follow her with maximum speed. *And I will.*

Chapter 7

Full-Throat Laughter

Emily

I CHEWED ON THE INSIDE OF MY CHEEK AS I WATCHED THE TOMATO soup bubbling full of life right in front of me. I reached over to my cutting board to grab more herbs. The smell of sweet tarragon and aromatic basil filled the air, along with the dense heat from the stove. My gaze fell to the steel kitchen surface, and I cringed when I saw my swollen red eyes. I struggled to understand why Paul was talking to Jon again. He hadn't even looked at him in the school hallway for two weeks, ignoring his calls, let alone driving him around. It felt so awkward when Brandon mentioned the bonfire. I slowly moved the wooden spoon into the gradually thickening liquid to mix in the herbs. Something must've happened last night that completely changed Paul's mind. *But what?* I drew my eyebrows together and pressed the bridge of my nose.

"I didn't mean . . . but Kiki asked me to watch Jon . . . forgot my phone . . ."

My eyes widened as I remembered chunks of his words. Kiki had asked him for help, but why was help necessary? Was Jon worse off than I thought? Had something else—

"Emily, your pasta is ready!" Danielle tapped me on the shoulder.

"What?!" I plucked the spoon out of my soup and squirted some right in Danielle's face.

"Really?!" she squealed, pulling her head back. Her eyes were still laughing, nevertheless.

"I'm so sorry!" I ran over to her with a napkin and wiped her face. She laughed and took the napkin from me.

"That's what I get for pulling you out of your thoughts." She gave me a gentle look, set the napkin down on the countertop, and placed her hands on my shoulders. I stared at her fingers.

"I can tell something is going on. Where are you with your mind lately, Emi?"

I paled when she used my brother's nickname for me. Lucas wasn't the type to talk on the phone, even though we talked every day at home. I missed his laugh and the excitement in his voice when he told me his latest story. He always added a touch of extra drama to make it more entertaining for the listener. My brother was a performer, a natural in the spotlight—and I was behind him, his shadow at every family gathering, his open ear to every sorrow, his mind when he couldn't think straight. A huge grin spread on my face. Gosh, I missed him.

"Um, hello? Are you still in this kitchen, or did you fly to another planet?" Danielle raised an eyebrow at me.

"I was thinking about my brother. He always called me Emi as well."

"Oh!" Danielle showed her perfect white teeth, removing her hands from my shoulder. "Tell me more about him!"

I took my spoon and tasted my sauce. "His name is Lucas, and he's about four years older than me. So confident and rich in opinions. Sometimes he can be exhausting, though."

"How so?" Danielle rested her chin on her hands, leaning onto the steel table. I gave my soup an approving nod and turned off the heat. It was done.

"Sometimes when he came home at night, he sang in the kitchen, waking me up with a greasy toast to eat in my bed to watch a show together. Even when I had to get up early the next day."

"That sounds cute. All I get from my brother is the leftover bones from his chicken." Danielle snorted.

"Yeah, my brother is lovely. His girlfriends always get carried on his hands." I wanted to have a relationship just like theirs. The behavior that my father or my mother's boyfriend displayed was nothing like his. They could be charming, but only if they got something in return.

"Get carried on his hands?" Danielle pretended to hold something in her palms. "A German saying again?"

"It means that he treats her like a queen." I nodded. Sometimes I forgot that using German sayings didn't work in the English language.

"I like that! So, just like Paul carries you on his hands?" Danielle drew a shape of a heart in the air

"Kinda." I pulled in my lip. I hadn't noticed the similarities between Paul and Lucas until now. Her smile faded, and she looked at me dead serious.

"Kinda?"

I looked down. Two weeks ago, I would've agreed with her . . . but right now, I felt a bit alone in our relationship.

"Is everything okay with you and Paul?"

My grip around my spoon tightened. I wanted to tell her so badly, but I made a promise to Kiki. If one way to make up for it was to keep my mouth shut, no matter how much my heart clamored for it, I would do it.

I put on a smile, my cheeks feeling heavy. "Everything is perfect with Paul."

Danielle bit her lip doubtfully. "Well, your brother sounds great. You must miss him a lot."

"I do." It'd only been a few months, but I would do anything to hug him again.

Breana came sprinting out of the cooler. "Girls, you won't believe it. Leni is taking me to an art museum this weekend!" she shrieked, her phone still in her hand. Chef Sayle showed up behind her, reaching for it.

"You know the rules, Breana. No phones allowed in the kitchen."

"That's a stupid rule." She rolled her eyes but gave it to Chef, who walked away with it. Then she jumped between Danielle and me, throwing her arms around our necks.

"I'm so happy, you guys." Beaming with euphoria, she pulled us closer. "I just had phone sex in the cooler!"

Danielle twitched her shoulders, and I tumbled back. "Weren't you afraid someone might come in?!"

I was half-shocked, half-impressed by her bold move.

"That's the fun part, Emily." She winked at me and dipped her finger in Danielle's soup.

"*Ew!* Not with your dirty fingers!" Danielle nudged her away.

"I didn't even think of that!" Breana covered her mouth with her hands and suppressed a laugh that made her head even redder than the soup. But I couldn't keep it in and laughed uproariously while holding my stomach.

"Oh, you think that's funny?" said Danielle half angrily but grinned a second later. "Try it, then!" She smeared some soup on my face as well.

"Oh shit!" Breana roared as Danielle targeted her next. "Noo! My makeup!" She tried to dodge, but Danielle took pinpoint aim, and Breana's purple eyeshadow mixed with the red liquid.

"Oh, you're going to regret this!" wailed Breana.

This time, she grabbed a big spoon and catapulted a huge load onto Danielle's apron. I tried to come to Danielle's rescue but slipped on the floor over the dripping mess and landed with a loud thud. I lay on my back and laughed at the top of my lungs, full throat, until I felt my muscles throbbing in my stomach. Danielle leaned down to help me, but my legs were so wobbly with laughter that she crashed onto the floor next to me. Again, we laughed, holding our bellies.

"What in the world is going on?!" Chef Sayle looked down at us from above. Immediately, we all fell silent.

Our counselors warned us that we would get detention until Christmas break if we misbehaved again. It was my first strike, and at first, I thought I was going to freak out, but for some reason, I was calm. I needed that laugh more than anything, but I felt sorry for Chef Sayle. He looked seriously concerned about our mental laughing fit. Breana and Danielle were a touch more stressed than I was, but only because it wasn't their first time misbehaving. I had taken the blame so they didn't end up in detention.

They tried to fight it, but I was convincing enough that I had started the food fight. Breana hugged Danielle and me goodbye when we stepped out of the office as if we wouldn't see each other for days.

"I love you guys." Breana showed her usual affection.

"Yeah, yeah, you two aren't bad." Danielle grinned but tried pulling out of her arms.

"I'm so glad I met you!" I concluded as we all went our separate ways to head to our next class. I was grinning like crazy; I finally had real girlfriends. Not ones that tried forming me into what they wanted, but ones that accepted me the way I was. I missed most of the break, but I made it to Paul's locker in time to tell him about our food fight and the red streak in my hair. My leather boots squeaked when I abruptly took a step back after turning the corner—*strawberry blonde hair.* My grin went quicker than a fly you can't seem to catch. I leaned against the wall and took a few deep breaths before peeking around again. Paul was talking to Jamie, her body leaning against his locker, her hand playing with his arm. His eyes were fixed on her as she leaned forward, her lips touching his ear as she whispered something to him. *Come on, push her away, Paul . . .* I clenched my lips together, but instead, he leaned forward as well, his lips now dangerously close to her neck. She bit her lip lustfully, her eyes widening at what he said, and mine welled up with tears. I ran in the opposite direction, regretting giving free rein to hope last night. Paul had jumped into bed with Jamie at the first opportunity he got. *Who said he wouldn't do it again?*

"Oh, hey, Emily!" Madison tried to grab my arm, but I backed away.

"I can't talk right now, Madison!" I pressed out without slowing down, looking directly at the exit door. All guys were the same. Some were just better at hiding it than others.

Chapter 8

Within Seconds

Jon

"You free to go to Marna's later?" I asked Paul as I rested my hefty body against my locker. I'd never used this sucker before. I wasn't even sure what my combination was. The school hallway was packed with people eagerly heading to their last class. I, however, was less keen. The drugs had worn off, and I had slept through chemistry. Not that my teacher minded—he didn't bother trying to wake me up anymore. Paul rummaged through his locker.

"I asked if you're free to go to Marna's later." I didn't like how he pretended I wasn't there.

"I can't," he finally mumbled as he stuffed crumpled paper, worn gym clothes, and empty plastic bottles into his backpack. The annoying crackling of the bottles forced me to close my eyes. I leaned against the wall; the usual headache had set in.

"Okay." My eyelids fluttered through the darkness as people walked by. I could hear them discussing the latest football game, the missing homework, or the art project they had been working on all night. Such trivial topics, as if their lives didn't hold something more interesting. I reached for the headphones in my jeans pocket and twirled them apart.

"Hey, Paul." A flirtatious, far-too-shrill voice caused a heavy stab in my head. I pressed my fist against the locker and opened my eyes to give Jamie my nastiest glare. But she had no eyes for me at all. She was busy playing with the drawstring on Paul's way-too-bright orange sweater. He kinda looked like an oversized pumpkin in that crap.

"What do you want, Jamie?" Paul hissed as he slammed his locker shut.

"I couldn't help but notice what you're wearing today." She bit her lip, removing some of her red lipstick with her teeth while letting her fingers run over Paul's chest.

"A piece of shit?" I threw in, amused at how far Jamie was willing to go to get Paul back.

"It was either that or freezing to death." Paul pushed her hand away. What he had with Jamie wasn't love. It was more like an obligation—football and cheerleader captain, fulfilling a perfect image for a perfect life.

"Trust me. I considered freezing to death for longer than a second." A waggish smirk crossed his lips, and I laughed out loud. Paul rarely expressed his dislike, and I felt a bit proud that he did.

"Funny." Jamie glared at me as if I was the problem. Nothing new to me. She stepped between Paul and me, and I leaned back to enjoy this show. This girl, no matter how annoying, could be helpful. Little German had gone pale when I told her they had slept together on Halloween. It must be lingering in her brain like too much salt in an otherwise good dish.

"I wonder what Emily would say if she knew who gave you that sweater." Jamie's eyebrows jerked up on her forehead as she thrust her hands onto her hips. Paul's mouth fell open. Knowing him, he wouldn't dare cross Jamie now. He was the good guy or some shit.

"Fuck off, Jamie," he said expressionlessly, as expected, with an anxious undertone.

"What if I won't?" she said with triumph. Paul snorted, his eyes twitching with panic over to me. I would usually come to his rescue, but I knew better than to get in his way when it came to Little German. In the end, he would blame me if it went wrong. I plugged in my headphones, pulled up the hood of my sweater, and pretended to be busy on my phone. It was his business and might provide a loophole for me to crawl into. I held my phone at the right angle to watch the scenario on the cracked black screen and pricked up my ears.

"I know you miss me, Paul. All the things you could do to me . . . Emily could never give you that. She's too innocent, and I know you like it wilder. So do I."

I peered over and saw her hand travel up his stomach. Her long, manicured nails dug into his skin.

"Don't you remember how you grabbed my breasts, how my wet pussy dripped for you as you slid in and out of me?" I noticed Paul's muscles tensing under that much-too-tight sweater. "How I was riding you for hours, screaming your name in sheer pleasure?"

My urge to laugh disappeared, and my jaw clenched. Jamie was good at this shit. Even though I had never fucked her before, I immediately got a boner in my pants. I rolled my eyes and glanced down the hall to see if there was a girl who wouldn't mind disappearing with me for a while. My dick was begging me to either make up with Kiki—after all, the sex was damn good—or go back to one of my superficial, no-attachment relationships. I was sure Molly over there would—

I saw golden, wavy hair and a much-too-fragile figure in the range of my eyes. Little German. She peeked around the corner, her eyes fixed only on Jamie pressing against Paul as if he were a stripper pole. Paul put his arm around Jamie's lower back and pulled her toward him with a yank so he could whisper into her ear. I lost my spit when I saw Little German's panicked eyes. This was too easy. One dirty line from a bitch like Jamie, and all he could think with was his cock. My fist balled. I thought he would treat her better than me.

"The only reason I lasted for hours was that I didn't feel a thing. Whereas Emily . . . gosh, she feels so fucking good, I had to restrain myself from coming within seconds."

My eyes shot away from Emily to Paul's backbone. My fist opened again. After such humiliation, even a stubborn donkey like Jamie should know that the game was over. A proud grin spread across my face, but it quickly faded as his words sank in. I didn't expect them to have done it already. I would've bet Emily was a girl waiting for Valentine's Day or that kind of corny crap. His words about her tight pussy made my cock pulsate. *Fuck.* I looked back to the corner, but her golden hair was gone. Good for me because if she thought Jamie and Paul were still secretly dating, I might get a taste of her sooner than expected. I didn't have to go back to Kiki or an old fling. I sprinted to the bathroom, locked myself in a stall, and gave myself a quick handjob while thinking about Emily's body. She would be mine—just like she was supposed to be mine in the first place. I just needed a bit more patience until she realized that Paul was too boring for her. He couldn't take her on this wild ride she'd been searching for. Because I knew that's what she truly craved, not someone who made her happy but someone who made her rage. She wasn't that innocent—and shit, Paul was right. I came within seconds.

After taking the pressure off, I went outside to have a smoke. My headache still plagued me, and my skin itched. I felt completely sober now, and my mind roared as my body shook from withdrawal. The school bell had already rung for the next class, but I didn't care. I went to the usual spot behind the garbage containers. Jeffrey, a dude I occasionally had a smoke with, was sucking at a blunt on the ground. He greeted me with a wordless nod. I pulled on my square until the ash grew long enough to fall off. I exhaled, not knowing what the smoke was and what my hot breath fizzled out in the cold air.

"Can I get a hit?" I asked Jeffrey, and he handed me the blunt with a blank face. The guy was way too high on it anyway. Wordlessly, I took a few drags and felt my body finally relax. When the blunt burned down, I tumbled through the empty corridors to US History without encountering a single soul. I yanked open the door, which opened faster than I had expected, and I nearly fell into the room. The entire class raised their heads, looking up from the weekly test.

"Fuck," I muttered, struck by my far-too-obvious appearance. I looked at the seat in front of mine, expecting to see the only eyes that differed from the judgmental ones. Typically, Little German looked at me with care and concern whenever I was late for US History. She didn't see the fuck-up in me but the sorrow. *Fuck, I took too many drags.* But this time, her gentle figure was missing from the chair. I searched every seat, every row, but nowhere did her pale gray eyes meet mine. *Where the hell is she?*

"Mr. Denson!" Mr. Harrison stood before me, shaking his hands in the air.

"Yeah, um . . . sorry I'm late. I had to go to the bathroom, and there was a line." I walked past him and grabbed a test sheet from his desk. The subject was Pearl Harbor. I hadn't read anything about it lately, but I would know every answer anyway. History was my thing.

"You won't need this." Mr. Harrison snatched the sheet of paper out of my hand.

"Shit, why?" I growled, hoping to intimidate him enough to let me write this test.

"You're expected in the principal's office, Jon."

I expelled my breath sharply. "Fine."

In the office, I listened to the same spiel as always.

"Mr. Denson, I have reports that you completely slept through your first two classes. Once again, you didn't do your homework and disrespected my teachers."

I nodded slightly with my eyes half closed as Mrs. Smith continued to list my misbehaviors. My coming to her office had become somewhat of a routine.

"Young man, your future is at stake here. You're a junior now. College isn't far away." She spoke loudly as if I had trouble understanding her.

"I don't want to go to college." I shrugged, stoking the fire inside her.

"Mr. De—Jon." She was already far too familiar with me. "Mr. Harrison told me how good you are at history. You always get full points on his tests, and he told me your way of thinking and reflecting on events is unique. You're gifted."

"Yeah, right. Gifted." I looked at the floor and huffed. As if Mr. Harrison cared enough about me to worry more outside of class.

"You're lucky I'm friends with your stepfather, Humphrey."

"Don't call him my stepfather." My hand clenched into a fist, and my teeth gritted as I ground them together. She sighed loudly and gave me the same judgmental look I was already used to. *Where the hell is Little German?*

"You have detention until Christmas break. I hope the time you spend there will make you realize the consequences of your actions." She handed me the typical detention sheet on which I had to collect signatures from the counselors. I stood up and crumpled it before stuffing it in my back pocket. There was no way I would sit there for an hour every afternoon listening to the clock tick. I shuffled toward the exit, but her words interrupted my walk of annoyance.

"Oh, and Jon? Next time, I'd appreciate it if you didn't show up to school high. I won't tell Humphrey for now, but I will if you end up in my office in such a state again."

I snorted and left the office without responding to her blackmail. My mother had a similar history with drugs as I did. She breathed them in during her youth. When she met my father, they almost destroyed each other. It wasn't until she was pregnant with me that she found the strength to beat them. At least, that was what she told me, unlike Dad, who still reached for the bottle when she wasn't looking. She turned into an innocent angel, went to church and weekly meetings, and prayed before meals. My dad refused to believe in God; they fought, and she left, placing the blame for their failed marriage on him. I stayed with my father. Even though my little sister, Lauren, begged me to move with her to Mom's, I couldn't leave Dad alone.

I was all he had left. One day, Lauren wanted to surprise Dad with a painting she had done for him in art class. She was only ten, and Tim was drunk as a skunk. He tore it up as it showed him and me on one side and Mom, her, and Humphrey on the other. The tears in her eyes almost killed me, and I beat my father down in my basement, locking him up like the animal he had become and opening the door for a few days only to give him food and water. After those days, he had sobered up and had been a good father to Lauren. Sometimes I wished someone would do the same for me, but I had nothing to fight for . . .

"Little German!" I shook my head as I saw her slumped shoulders. I'd been standing in the hall, leaning against a locker, not moving, and judging by my dizziness, apparently barely breathing. A glance at the clock told me I must've been in this state for several minutes. Shit, weed had this weird effect on me lately that I didn't appreciate at all.

"Jon . . .?" She remained frozen in her spot. I quickly strode towards her, but she bolted away as if I were the evil wolf about to rip a sheep. Yet it took me only two steps to grab her by the arm. Then, she dropped against the locker with a loud bang to dodge me.

"Shit, you okay?" I backed away, seeing the horror written all over her face. I didn't mean to hurt her. Red and puffy eyes, blue lips, as if she had been outside for a long time, hair ruffled by the wind.

"Just leave me alone!" She tried shoving me away, but her arms were too weak, and her lower lip was trembling.

"Fuck, no." I placed my palms gently on her shoulders, my brows knitting together. "Look at me."

Of course, she didn't. Her eyes never lingered for more than a sec.

"Emily," I said, knowing her real name had this magical effect on her. She stretched out her neck and looked up. My muscles tightened as I reached for her cheeks to dab the tears away. Softly, I wiped over her skin, and her lips parted. I stared down at them, remembering how they tasted.

"I can't do the same as him," she suddenly whispered and forced my gaze away from her lips.

"Why not?"

She bent her head. She was crying because she'd seen Jamie all over Paul. It seemed forever ago, or perhaps that was my weird sense of time. I sighed, knowing I had the power to put her out of her misery.

"Please, Jon . . ." She winced again as my hand was still resting on her cheek.

Damn, I felt so weak when she gave me that puppy dog look. She was so frantic, so meek and vulnerable. I somewhat admired how bravely she showed her emotions, but even more how she kept handing me the power to hurt her. Even after everything, I could feel her trust. I backed away, and she gasped for air. I didn't want to see her like that. I prefer the boiling-with-rage Emily. The one who thought she could make me feel insecure by talking to me in German. The one who made me bleed in the water for my best friend. Everything was better than this empty shell.

"Listen, Paul didn't—"

"What are you two doing out here and not in class?!"

Damn it. My chemistry teacher looked at us with his finger raised. When he recognized me, his nostrils flared even more in anger. Little German took a hasty step away from me.

"Jon, I've already been to the principal's office today! I'll get detention!" She covered her mouth though she whispered. *It looks like I'll go to detention after all.*

Chapter 9

Joining the Game

Emily

"LOOK WHAT WE HAVE HERE. A LITTLE GERMAN IN detention." Jon's breath tickled the nape of my neck. He was so close from behind that the table he was leaning against creaked. I held my breath as my nails dug themselves into my knees. About a dozen other students slumped in their chairs, building card houses, scribbling on their notepads, or sleeping with their faces on their lower arms, their clothes reeking of smoke. They frowned and grunted when I walked in. I had brushed my hair, so it covered my face just like I always wore it when I was *Puppe*. But as an arm draped protectively over my shoulders, I looked up self-consciously to see Jon scowling at them. Their bodies tensed, and they focused back on the scribblings on their tables. Although I appreciated the gesture, just like the coffee this morning, it was done by the wrong person. It was supposed to be Paul, not Jon, protecting me like that. I quickly extricated myself from his embrace and sat down in the front row, knowing that there was no way Jon was going to sit there too. But I hadn't considered that he was in a different mood than usual. *But why was he nice to me today?* He didn't care about anything. I knew, after everything I'd heard from Paul, Kiki, Danielle—the list went on and on—I couldn't trust his words. But it wasn't the words I was struggling with. Gosh, I wish they would be because they were way easier to understand. It was his actions, this hot and cold behavior. The way he was alone with me compared to how he was when other people were around. How we sang "Fix You" together, how he noticed me every time I walked into a room as if he could feel my presence in his core, or how he was always there when I needed someone the most. Thinking about these little aspects made my cheeks warm and my stomach turn.

"Little German. If you ignore me, I'll speak louder."

"I'm only here because of you, so be quiet," I said back, hushed, looking at Mr. Stacey, who was counting the smartphones. Mr. Stacey, or as I called him in my head, *Mr. Yellowtooth*, had collected them all when we entered the room 15 minutes and 33 seconds ago, saying the worst punishment was boredom. *How do I know the exact time?* Behind him, he projected a massive clock that seemed to tick half as fast as a normal clock. Time didn't pass in this dreadful room with only two windows barely letting in any light. Mr. Yellowtooth returned to his chess game when the number of smartphones matched the number of students. He was playing chess . . . with himself. *So sad.*

"Fuck no. You skipped class and threw food around. I just held you up."

I tilted my head to give him a bitter look, surprised by his face so close to mine. My eyes fell on his lips, which were only a short move away from mine. His gaze lingered on me, and I felt my wall melt like butter in his hands. Immediately, I traveled back to my dream, and my breathing deepened. *He kissed my collarbone, parted my legs, let his fingers slide over—*

"I like this bad side of you. You should let it out more often." Jon pulled back, knowing he had successfully planted another seed in my brain. I gasped and swallowed, trying to get rid of this memory, um, dream.

"Be quiet, Jon. I don't want to get in any more trouble," I mewled, leaning my torso forward and folding my hands on my desk. *But is he right? Do I have a bad side?*

"You think he could bring us in trouble?" Jon laughed loudly, and I turned my head to glare at him.

"Sei ruhig! Er kann uns hören!" *Be quiet! He can hear us!* I hissed, knowing that he would still get what I was trying to say even though I spoke to him in German. But instead of leaving me alone, Jon stood up, jumped across the table, and sat next to me. My pulse quickened. Mr. Stacey looked up curiously but did not comment on Jon's seat change. Jon was right; he didn't mind or had already learned that Jon didn't respond to back talk. I rolled my eyes. Great. My plan to keep Jon at a distance by sitting in the front row didn't work, and now we were also prime entertainment for Mr. Yellowtooth.

"Talking German again, hm?" Jon let his eyebrows dance and gave me a smile that even carried a bit of cuteness. I concentrated on my fingernails and bit down my lower lip to suppress the smile that wanted to grow on my heated face.

"Yes, and if you don't shut up, I'll do so for the entire next week."

"Oh, you plan to talk to me again every day?" Jon grinned, his dark chocolate hiding behind his puffy eyelids. I had no idea what he was high on, but whatever it was, it showed his sweet side. *He must be on something, right? I mean, he's never that playful.*

"Maybe," I pressed out, hopeful that he'd be like that more often but also worried he would be. He leaned over and brushed a strand of hair behind my ears as he wetted his lips with his tongue. We held intense eye contact for a moment as if playing a game of who could last longer without looking away. I wasn't sure if the recent events with Paul and Jamie made me linger longer than usual, but I couldn't tear myself away. I wanted to win this time. To prove to him that he couldn't play games with me.

"I missed talking to you." He spoke softly, making it even harder for me to triumph. My blood was throbbing harshly through my veins, and I bit on the flesh on my cheek. With each second that passed, I realized more and more that he would have no limits . . . while I did. I had accepted a game against a cheater. He let his thumb brush over my chin and leaned in further. He would do anything to win this round, even kissing me in a freaking detention room filled with an audience. My heart shuddered, and I promptly backed away, flew to my feet, and stumbled two steps away from him.

"Mr. Stacey!" I almost shouted as I stepped toward his table. Everyone turned to me with tired but surprised eyes.

"Um, yes . . . Ms. Um. You're new. What's your name?" Mr. Stacey shook his head.

"Ms. Klein . . . I need to use the bathroom."

"Sure." He sounded slightly disappointed, as if he hoped I would have asked him to play chess together. I quickly left the room without daring to look at Jon again. I couldn't because right now, he meant danger, and I could only deal with one grenade about to go off at once.

In the bathroom, I closed the stall behind me in sheer silence—the one in the back. I leaned against the blue wall covered with sentences, names, dick drawings, and other slang stuff I had never heard about. I closed my heavy eyes for a moment, going through my options, my breath finally calming.

After I had seen Paul and Jamie . . .

"Ah. . ." A whimper struggled up my throat. I had no idea why they whispered so intensely in each other's ears. I should've walked right up to them, but I'd decided to assume instead of ascertaining and ended up on Boonville's streets. Before I knew it, my legs had carried me to the Shield house, a freaking twenty-minute walk I made in fifteen minutes because I was running. I had no idea if Paul's phone was still in the jeans pocket, but I had to take my chances. My entire body was shaking out of madness when I finally held it.

Before leaving, I quickly washed the sauce out of my hair. On my way back, I debated whether or not to check his messages. I craved the answers, and I knew if he gave them to me personally, I wouldn't be sure if I could trust his words anymore. They didn't add up with what I'd witnessed. When I decided to check, I stumbled into a deep puddle. My whole shoe was soaked, and I was freezing. I moved my toes, but my sock still hadn't dried. With nothing to distract me in the last few minutes, plus Jon's smell and attention taunting me, I wasn't so sure about my decision anymore. If something was going on, I deserved to know; if not, at least I could sleep more calmly. I was sure Paul would understand why I did this. I pulled his phone out of my bra, where I'd hidden it from Mr. Stacey. There was plenty of room there anyway. I slid the screen open, ready to break his trust, hoping it wouldn't be worth it. I opened his messages without letting our image distract me again, and Jamie's name was on the top line. I pressed on it, holding my breath. It was a picture of Jamie wearing Paul's orange sweater from this morning. Sensually, she cuddled with the fabric on her arm. My heartbeat escalated. I wasn't making it up. Below the picture was one message.

Jamie: I've missed your smell

"Oh my gosh!" I covered my mouth with my palms and accidentally dropped the phone into the toilet. *Shoot!* I fell to my knees as I watched it swimming in the dirty water, the screen flickering and then turning black. And together with it . . . my heart.

I walked back into detention feeling sick to my stomach. My entire face was numb, and everything turned blurry around me. I dropped onto my seat, Jon's hands immediately on my shoulder.

"You okay?" he asked, his irises pulsing with worry.

"Can we go to Marna's after this?" was all I could press out of my dry lips.

Chapter 10

Trust and Parenting

Paul

I SPRINTED UP THE PORCH WITH FROZEN SKIN AND A BURNING IN my chest. I turned the doorknob and gulped for air when it opened without me having to insert a key. *Fuck, I'm gonna blow this place up if Emily's not here!* Questions about why she didn't come to the car and if she had gotten sick or held up at school ran through my head. I waited almost an hour in my car, regretting that I had never memorized any number to reach her.

"Hey, Paul!" My mother welcomed me from the couch with a taco from last night in her hand. The sounds from the TV revealed that she was watching her weird housewife show. Ignoring her, I rushed past her to Emily's room. Everything was in place, organized, and clean. But not a single sight of my beautiful girl and her adorable smile. I leaped back, landing on my healed foot, and bolted to the living room.

"What's wrong, honey?" Mom stood at the now closed door. She wiped her mouth with a tissue and lifted her eyebrows.

I clasped my hands together pleadingly. "Mom, I can't talk now!"

Without slowing my steps, I flew down the stairs. But there was no sign of Emily in my room either. I dropped to the ground and threw my clothes up with fidgeting hands and an ever-shortening breath. I had to find my freaking phone.

"She's doing fine." My mother's sweet voice, the one she always used for distraught kids, filtered through to me. I whirled up and took a step toward her.

"Where is she?" I almost barked at her.

"She's fine, Paul." My mother glared and waved her hand to follow her. "Let's talk upstairs. I can't stand the mess you live in."

"But—"

But she left me in the mess I had created myself. I took a breath so deep my lungs hurt and rubbed my face. I needed to calm the hell down. It wasn't normal to freak out like this just because I didn't know where she was for an hour. But this little voice told me that she would be with Jon. Just like the last time, she didn't reply to me and worked with him on a project. When I got upstairs, I gulped, and my mother patted the space next to her on the couch. I wanted nothing more than to be able to put that night in late November behind me. I thought I could, but that sickening aftertaste that history would repeat itself wouldn't leave my tongue. I sat down on the couch without a word, dreading the answer I had eagerly wished for just a few seconds ago. If she was really with him . . . I wouldn't know how to deal with it. I assumed I had forgiven her for kissing my best friend, but I hadn't. Not entirely, anyway. Because it was about much more than a simple kiss—I'd seen it in her eyes when she had a panic attack in Jon's room when she caught sight of him with Kiki. I noticed how important it was for her to prove to him that she belonged to America while playing beer pong. She liked Jon . . . but not on a friendship level.

"Paul?" My mother waved her hand in front of my face. I sat on the couch with a pillow in my arms, crushing it harshly.

"Yes." I exhaled and slowly loosened my grip.

"Are you okay?" Mom leaned toward me and rested her hand on mine. "I noticed you weren't home last night."

I squeezed her hand in return and managed a smile. In the past, I had never had to explain myself to my parents. Still, the mere fact that she and my father were doing me the favor of taking in a girl I had only known for a few weeks . . . she deserved honesty.

"I was out for a run and ended up at Jon's place. He needed my help."

Mom nodded understandingly and didn't ask further. Sometimes I wondered how much she knew. Probably more than I thought, considering how often she'd seen Jon or me on drugs. One day, my weed stash was suddenly completely empty. Zack swore that he hadn't taken anything, and my mom gave me a scowl that afternoon, one I didn't often get to see on her. Still, we never talked about it. In general, we never really talked about our emotions. Our relationship was based on trust. And that's something I always admired about my parents, their unconditional trust in me and each other. All my other friends wished they had parents like mine. Especially Jon—he'd told me a few times.

"Wait a minute, how did you even know I was gone?"

Mom looked at our hands and took a second before answering. "I went to your room last night because I heard unusual noises."

"Unusual noises?"

Mom tucked at her earlobe, "Emily was screaming."

"Why was she screaming?" My mind was suddenly sharp again.

"I'm not sure. Emily said something about a nightmare."

"Oh . . ." I pressed my palms onto my neck.

"Do you have any idea what's going on with her? She looks like she's barely sleeping lately." Mom's voice sounded hesitant, and she looked to the ground, deep in thought. I wish I knew the answer to that question myself, but I hadn't asked her about her feelings lately.

"She misses her family a lot," I explained hastily. I didn't want her to worry or suspect anything worse.

"Oh, that would make sense." Her face lit up.

"So, where is she?" I interrogated again, feeling calm enough now to know the truth.

My mother sighed and looked at me. "The school called. Emily skipped her last class."

"Emily?! Impossible!" I took my hand from Mom's and held up my palms. Emily wanted to be liked by everyone, even by her teachers. There was no way she would skip!

"That's what they said." Mom shrugged, almost as incredulous as I was. "I'll talk to her later when she gets home."

"I'll pick her up." I jumped up and looked for my keys in my jeans. Detention should be over soon.

"You won't."

"Shit, I will."

"No, you won't." Mom's voice got harsher. "And watch your language!"

I hunched my shoulders. Just like Emily, my mother had a gift for making me beg for answers. Mom grabbed the pillow I'd thrown on the couch and smoothed the fabric on it.

"She texted me to apologize and asked if she could go to Breana's. I said it was okay."

"She just ended up in detention. Why are you letting her hang out with a friend?" I yelled while angrily slapping my hands to my head.

"How often have you been hanging out with Jon after detention?" She pointed her finger at me.

Jon . . . the likelihood that he was there too burned in my mind, and my palms formed into fists. "But—"

"I think talking to a friend is what she needs right now, Paul." Mom scowled at me for questioning her parenting skills. I gave her a confused look. It didn't make sense to me that she would let Emily get away with this behavior.

"Look, I don't know what's going on between you two, and I don't need to know, but—" Mom stood up and planted her warm hands on my shoulders. "If you want this to work, you must give her room to breathe."

"I need to be there for her!" I put my hands on her wrists, pulling them away to stop her motherly gesture.

"Geez, you're just like Henry." She blinked and walked back to the couch. "When we had our first fight, he wanted to pretend it didn't happen. He didn't understand that it was important to give me space to process it," she explained as she sat back down and gazed wistfully out the window into the cloudy day.

"Well, you two are married. So I'd say Dad did the right thing," I countered, crossing my arms.

"Actually . . ." Mom glanced at the front door and paused for a moment. Then her eyes wandered back and met mine. "It almost destroyed us."

My mouth dropped open. I'd never talked to my mother about how she'd gotten together with my father.

"What do you mean?" I sat back down next to her on the couch.

A sparkle crossed her eyes as she got pulled back into her past. "Well ... his behavior made me run to someone else instead, honey. Someone who gave me the space I needed. Who was easier to be around, with no pressure."

I couldn't believe her words. *Did I know my parents so little?*

"Who?"

"That doesn't matter, honey."

"Then how come you guys got back together?" I held my breath.

"Your father and I went our separate ways for a while. Then, in college, we met again and fell in love. We were fortunate to get that second chance."

I nodded. My parents did get that second shot, but I knew I couldn't rely on faith when Emily and I lived on different continents. I rubbed the back of my head.

"Promise me to give Emily time and a chance to make her own decision. Don't pressure her to give you something she may not feel ready for." My mother threw me a raised eyebrow, and blood rushed to my head.

Did she think I was trying to pressure Emily into sleeping with me?!

"Mom, we are not having you know what ..." Geez, I couldn't believe I was talking about this with my mother.

Her eyes widened, and she giggled. "Oh ... that's not what I was talking about, honey. Although it's nice to hear that you haven't done it yet."

"Mom!" I tossed her the pillow, and she caught it mid-air, laughing out loud with her face to the sky. I couldn't help but smile as well.

"Well, I don't want to sound like an annoying mom, but what in the world are you thinking walking around in just a T-shirt? It's freezing outside!" She raised her eyebrows and fiddled with her fingers on my goose-bump-covered arms.

"It's a long story ..." I sighed and slid deeper into the couch.

"Well. Emily won't be back for a while, and my show was boring today. I need some gossip," Mom joked, settling down on the couch with the rest of her taco. I considered telling her the story because her revealing some of her emotional worlds to me made me want to do the same.

"You remember Jamie, right?"

"Oh, that bitch. I never liked her." My mom spoke with a full mouth.

"*Mom!*" I sputtered, surprised to hear swear words coming out of her mouth.

She swallowed. "I'm sorry, but I always wondered what you wanted from that girl. She was awful!"

"Yeah, I don't get it either."

We both burst out laughing.

"Anyway, I put on her sweatshirt today because everything else was dirty. She noticed and read into it that I wanted her back. Which I don't!" I shook my head as hard as possible. "But she insisted, so I took it off in the middle of the hallway and threw it at her. I only had this old shirt left in my locker, but I preferred to freeze than give her the wrong impression."

Mom gave me an affirming thumbs-up. "I couldn't be prouder of you, honey."

"Thanks." I grinned back. "But have you seen my phone? I can't find it."

Mom raised her brows and sighed. "Please don't tell me that you lost your phone again."

After chatting a little longer on the couch, I went to my room with a much lighter heart. Talking to mom about my business was a way more considerable help than I could've ever imagined—even more than running. Emily always told me how her mom was not only her mother but also her best friend. I couldn't relate to the fact that you could talk casually with your parents until today. It was refreshing, and I felt calmer dealing with this entire situation. I picked up clothing after clothing and threw them into a basket. I cleaned this shit hole for hours and finally washed my clothes. But even when this room was more organized than ever, I couldn't find my phone. I lay down and stared at the ceiling, satisfied with my change in attitude. Because being good can win. My father was living proof of that.

Chapter 11

New Rules

Jon

THIS SHIT PLACE WAS DIM, THE LAMP ON THE CEILING WITHOUT a bulb. The only light came from a window half covered by the yellowed, nicotine-stained blanket, falling directly on Little German. I put the blunt between my lips, watching her. Her eyes examined the table littered with black burns from cigarettes, bongs, tobacco, and other substances swimming in a pool of dirt. Judging by her curious face, I could tell that this world was still intriguing to her. I remembered how I felt back then. It was pure madness, an adrenaline rush. Not anymore. Now it was my fucking everyday life, and I was ashamed of that.

"Why are you grinning like that?" Little German raised her brows at me. I then noticed I was full-blown smiling. I didn't understand why. Dragging her into this world wasn't the plan. The last thing I wanted was for her to think that doing this shit was cool . . . it was the opposite of that. It was a cry for help. People in this world weren't here by choice. They were here because they were fucked-up, unable to find a way to deal with their lives otherwise. Yet having her here, by her choice, I felt intrigued for the first time in years.

"Seeing you in this scenario is odd, I guess." I inhaled the herbal taste of the blunt until I felt the smoke burst into my lungs. The way she frowned at me made me want to provoke her. Every reaction, whether good or bad, was something I wanted. So I blew all the smoke in her direction.

"Really?" She gave me an annoyed face, making my dopey grin widen even more. I bet she was tidy and hygienic with her neat appearance and fresh scent. I'd never seen a shirt on her twice in a row. It sucked that I'd never been in her room. I intended to change that. Maybe I could put something of mine in her backpack under the pretext of picking it up. Today I was lucky, but I had to manipulate more meetings like this.

Marna came into the room with a stupid smile. "I hope you didn't smoke too much without me."

"Just started," I growled. I forgot that Marna had gone to the bathroom after we'd woken her up from her afternoon nap. I couldn't care less if she was here or not, but Ted wasn't around, and she was the one who took it upon herself to sell dope in his absence. I think they were siblings or something.

"Looking good, Jon." Marna winked at me with freshly applied purple lipstick and a way-too-sweet scent of peach perfume, yet my sight returned to Little German, who rubbed her nose. She had a natural smell, shiny hair, and no lipstick sticking to her teeth. I liked that she didn't put on a mask like other girls.

Marna turned away from me, walking up to Emily and poking her nose like she was a toy. "I gotta say, I'm surprised to see you again, Eva."

My jaw tensed. "Yo, Ma—"

"My name is Emily," Little German interrupted and slapped Marna's hand away. My muscle cheeks pounded. I was kind of amazed that Emily didn't even hesitate to make that clear. A few weeks ago, she grabbed my hand out of fear of Marna, and now she was giving her a superior face. That was pretty badass.

"Whatever." Marna bent down so I could see her plump breasts, barely hanging in her bra. Her tongue wetted her lips, and her other hand rested on my knee. My cock didn't twitch from Marna's obvious flirtation. She had been bothering me with naked pictures of her body lately, but I had a rule. I wouldn't fuck with those I did business with, plus she wasn't even my type. A gulp came from Little German. I looked over, seeing her cleaning her fingernails, which were not even remotely dirty.

Marna grabbed the blunt out of my mouth. "Thanks, babe. I hope we will get some time alone after." Marna slid her finger over my cheek, but I backed off. She walked to the couch, and my eyes narrowed when she crashed her shoulder against Little German. I bared my teeth, but Emily scooted away from her with a disgusted face. Damn, I had no idea Emily could look at someone like that. *Let's test something . . .*

"You know I will always have time for you," I commented on Marna's statement far too late, and both girls tilted their necks at me in surprise.

Marna put the blunt to her voluminous lips and shot Emily a glance. "Oh, I know, Jon. We got something special."

I analyzed Emily as if she were a painting in a museum, her sagging shoulders rolled up, and she stared blankly at me for a moment before crossing her arms in front of her chest. *Is she pouting?* Damn, I couldn't tell if she was jealous or snapping at me for being blunt about being a flirt. I relaxed in my chair, my arms and legs super soft and supple from the venom.

"I believe it's my turn." Emily rose to her feet when Marna handed the blunt to me. Her chest rose with small gasps, her eyes covered with the glittering nervousness she usually had. My cock twitched. There was the Emily I had missed. The one who was scared but still managed to overcome her fears.

"Oh, is it?" Marna looked at me.

"Don't look at me. She wants that shit," I snapped at Marna.

"Watch out, or you'll ruin her," Marna challenged me. My muscles flinched—I wouldn't ruin her!

"I don't need your opinion, thanks." Emily glared at Marna, her index and middle fingers splayed, ready to receive the blunt. She'd barely said a word on the bus, only stared out the window and watched the damn lame streets of Boonville. Marna gave her the blunt before sitting back on the couch, mumbling, "Freaking bitch."

"You got a problem, Marna?" I spat at her. Emily quietly sat down in a chair next to me instead.

"Nope." Marna rolled her eyes, but her shoulders sagged. I glanced at Emily self-consciously taking a drag far too long for her small person. I itched to grab the nub from her mouth. The last thing I needed was to bring her back to Paul all drugged up. I would never hear the end of it. When she exhaled, she leaned back and closed her eyes. Her tense muscles eased, and her face softened as she let the aftereffect soak in. Shit, this was a cry for help.

"You okay?" The question crossed my lips quickly. I could've asked her earlier, but I didn't want her to change her mind about coming here with me.

Without opening her eyes, Emily replied, "I . . ."

She hacked into her fist and handed the stub back to me. A wide grin spread across her round cheeks. "I'm more than okay now."

It's crazy how fast and intense this stuff affected her. If I'd taken one puff as she did, I wouldn't have noticed anything while her eyes were already hazy.

"If you're such a little bad girl now, you should try these instead." Marna pointed to a bottle of pink pills. Not Xanax, but something that had already given me far too many blackouts. I'd just filled my stash with it.

"Don't," I growled at Marna, who pushed her lower lip forward, suppressing one of her ugly laughs.

"This is not your decision, Jon!" Emily rose from her chair in one swift movement, her chest heaving, and I knew I was in for another argument.

I looked at her, rolling my eyes. "This shit is not for you. Trust me."

I brought the blunt back to my dry lips as I blinked at it. There were only two puffs left. Suddenly, my eyes landed on Emily's purple sweater, then wandered up her body.

"I. Don't. Care." Her lower lip trembled, and her eyes pleaded, but her voice shot arrows. With a growl, she snatched the stub from my hand, inhaled the last of it provocatively, smashed it into an overflowing ashtray, and stormed out of the room without acknowledging Marna. This shit was unlike her.

"Wait a minute!" I yelled after her, but the door had already slammed shut.

"You've upset your girl." Marna giggled as she put her legs up on the couch to enjoy her high and that I had screwed up . . . fuck, I didn't even know what I did wrong this time.

"She's not my girl," I snapped as I slowly picked myself up. My legs wobbled a little as I fought my daze.

"Then why are you running after her? Did you turn into one of those soft boys like Paul?" Marna cackled loudly, and I felt a solid urge to silence her.

My teeth clenched. "Get laid, Marna. That desperation doesn't suit you!"

"Piss off!" She threw an empty pill box after me. *Fuck, I hope she'll continue to sell my shit.*

I expected Little German to be in the backyard, but she was gone. I kicked against the gate. *Why does she have to be so fucking dramatic?!*

With anger welling in my chest, I tumbled down the path through the open gate. I let out a shaky breath when I found her on the sidewalk at the bus stop. Her hands were over her face. I clamped my lips. This girl always had to cry when I was around, and it got on my nerves that I triggered that in her. When I reached her, she took her hands away, but it wasn't tears I was met with but a burning face, out of anger.

"You can't decide what's good for me and what's not, Jon!" she screamed, and I had enough. Anger flowed through me like lava. I hadn't done shit!

"Just because you know how to hit a blunt doesn't mean you're ready for everything else!" I barked back, thinking this would settle it.

"You don't get it!" She straightened up. "I didn't even say I wanted those pills!" Her temper flared, and my head throbbed. Flustered, I pinched the bridge of my nose and waited for the surge to subside.

She didn't notice my headache. "You're trying to manipulate me, but you know what? I'm not your fucking doll! You can't put words in my mouth!"

I staggered back a bit. "I'm not manipulating you."

I tried to convince her by giving her my scowl, but damn, it didn't terrify her anymore.

"Bullshit. You do it every second I'm around you!" Her little fist flew through the air as she stomped on the ground. *Hell, that's kinda cute.*

"Then give me a damn example." I stared at her.

"At the lake." Her breath shortened, and her voice lowered even though we were the only people there. I swallowed hard. I had thought we would pretend it never happened. But then again, I couldn't recall manipulating her.

"I didn't manipulate you at the lake."

"Seriously, Jon? You tried to decide for me!" She ran her fingers through her hair, looking up at the sky.

"And which decision are we talking about?" If I had decided, she wouldn't have chosen Paul. A gross feeling spread in my stomach. At the lake, I spoke my fucking truth . . . and I wished I hadn't.

"You seriously need me to tell you? Were you so high that you don't even remember what happened?!" The tears I had expected showed. Still, I wished they didn't.

"Shit, I remember." I sucked in as much air as possible before I said something that could worsen things. I tried harder than anything to forget how she had chosen him over me, unsuccessfully. She whirled back to face me, took a step closer, and stared at me with a fire in her eyes I had never seen before. Carefully, I tried to brush the strand of hair covering her birthmark from her face—touches like that always worked on her—but my mouth fell open as she slapped my hand away.

"You had no fucking right to tell him I liked you first!"

Her audacity surprised me. The smoke gave her way too much confidence.

"But you did. You said it yourself." I reminded her.

"I didn't!" She scoffed back, and my pulse quickened. "We only saw each other a few times. I barely knew you enough to decide whether I liked you."

My mouth went dry. *She didn't like me first? Heck, no, she did!*

"Don't tell me shit. You asked me to kiss you and make your stupid #3 reason come true."

"My stupid three reasons?!"

Shit, I shouldn't have said that. "I'm just saying you were all over me . . ."

"I was drunk, Jon. And you were not the only one I flirted with." Her voice didn't carry a hint of a shake anymore. She was pure madness, and I loved it. I held her stare, sucking my lip. That disgusting play fight she had with Paul in the shower crossed my mind. *Fuck, did she like him first?* I had justified all my actions with the argument that Paul stole her from me. If it wasn't true . . .

"Fuck!" I growled loudly and turned away from her, losing the battle of looks for the first time.

"Don't you dare turn away from me now!" Emily tugged on my shoulder rudely, not even realizing that she had won. I couldn't think straight—my body was tired from smoking weed, but my mind was reeling from her obnoxious behavior. She shouldn't have started this shit.

"What do you expect me to say now!" I shouted, to which she froze.

She took a deep breath with her eyes fixed on me like a laser pointer. "I expect you to stop destroying my relationship with Paul. I expect you to let me decide not to put words into my mouth. Because if you continue doing this, I don't know if I can be friends with you."

How the actual fuck did this turn from an argument about those stupid pills to a fight about me destroying her fucked-up relationship?!

"Friends, huh?" I huffed, and she looked down at the ground.

"Yes . . . friends." Her voice trembled as she breathed in and out slowly. Then she dropped back to the sidewalk. "And if that's not enough for you, then we can't hang out anymore."

Not hang out? Hell no. I sat beside her on the sidewalk and stared at my black sneakers. The winter wind was the only sound, along with my screaming thoughts. I spat on the ground as we kept silent. Part of me wanted to walk away. If that was what she wanted, fuck it, why should I care. But my feet weren't moving one bit.

"Fine, I've been manipulating you," I admitted, and her head jerked over to me.

"You're admitting it?"

"Yeah. You were easy to play with . . . at least I thought so." I gave her a tired smile.

"That's not true."

"As I said . . . that's what I thought." I raised my brows gently, not wanting another argument. Instead, I reached into my bag and pulled out a plastic bag filled with those pink pills.

"Here," I said with an expressionless face as I took a pill out. "Take it or leave it."

Her eyes widened. "Are you serious?"

I had to grin. Emily looked damn cute being stoked. Although I didn't like that she had unraveled me, it was about time I surprised her with more sides of me.

"Yes. It's your choice."

She inhaled deeply and stared at the pill in my hand. I bet she was making a pro-and-con list. Then she took it. Part of me was disappointed, but I didn't dare comment.

"Thanks."

"The effect isn't strong, except combined with alcohol. Then it's a killer and will make you forget everything." I took a deep breath and looked at the first pale stars in the sky.

"Oh," she said, still staring at the pill in her hand.

"Also, there's something you should know." There were new rules, but they made this game become even more interesting.

Chapter 12

Friends with Complications

Emily

"So yeah, Paul told Jamie to piss off." Jon finished his story about what I'd seen Paul do with Jamie. I was confused, the weed in my veins clouding any judgment. I wanted to believe his words, but it didn't make sense to me . . .

"Why had Paul given her the hoodie he had worn this morning, then?"

"Shit, how should I know?" Jon snorted. "But I know Paul wouldn't cheat on you, especially not with Jamie."

"He already did," I reminded him.

"And why did he do it?" Jon gave me a *you're not stupid* look. I smiled against my will—due to the weed, not him. Paul had seen Jon and me kissing. *Jealousy.* That was our biggest issue at the moment. Paul didn't trust me, and judging by me going to get high with Jon after seeing him talking with Jamie, stealing his phone, checking his messages, and dropping it in the toilet . . . *ugh, yeah,* I didn't trust him either. I wiped my fingers over my face and rubbed on the pimple that had grown over the day.

"What did I do . . ." I mumbled to myself. I repeated the story all over again. Paul would have every reason to mistrust me . . . if he found out. I sat back down on the pathway, resting my head on my palms. I felt slightly dizzy. My heart was pounding, and my fist was balling from my stupidity. It wasn't like I'd wanted to betray Paul at Halloween. He had asked for too much too soon . . . I had panicked, unsure if I could be this girl he wished for, this perfectly innocent person that couldn't even hurt a fly. I bit my lip, which was hurting from the cold. I was far from perfect, and Paul deserved perfect. Goosebumps traveled over my skin, and I shivered, my arms around my shoulders. *How on earth am I supposed to fix this?*

"Come here." Jon raised his arm for me to get warmed by him. I shook my head till my sight turned black for a moment.

"Friends aren't allowed to keep each other warm?" he asked.

I trembled at how he said *friends*; it left a bitter aftertaste in my mouth. But I knew friends were all we could ever be.

"Then take this. I don't want you to freeze to death." Jon handed me his jacket.

"Thanks." I quietly accepted it, too tired to go in for another argument. I put it on, placing my hair behind my shoulders.

"So if you were me, would you trust Paul?" I asked, hoping for the answer that would take all of my worries away.

"Fuck yeah. Look at all the shit I've done and how Paul's still by my side. He's the most loyal bastard there is." Jon rolled his eyes. He took out a cigarette and lit it. My chest suddenly felt lighter, and I inhaled the air filled with fresh smoke. It didn't gross me out anymore, and for some weird reason, I trusted Jon's words. I was used to him messing up and hurting me, and it was easy to forgive when you become used to something from a person. You had no expectations, meaning you couldn't be hurt. But with Paul . . . he had always given me the impression I could trust him with my most precious property—my heart. I created such high expectations for him that when he broke them, everything felt shattered.

I sighed loudly when the bus pulled up. I went ahead as Jon took one last drag before throwing the stub onto the path. A few people were on the bus, either looking at their phones or with headphones plugged in, watching the streets. Jon slumped next to me, closing his eyes immediately and resting his head on the seat. I bit my lip, a bit disappointed by our abruptly ended conversation. But then again, if we were *friends,* I should be able to say whatever was on my mind.

My voice was raspy when I spoke. "Why didn't you tell me about Jamie and Paul right away?"

"Little German . . . I beg you, just let me be," Jon pleaded, not opening his eyes one bit, his voice a slow, loud grumble.

"This one last question, and then I'll be quiet. I promise." I squeezed his shoulders, and he opened his left eye to peek at me.

"I'll first believe it when you prove it." Jon slowly straightened up and looked at me with only halfway opened eyes.

"Try me." I threw him a smirk.

"Okay, Mrs. I Have to Know It All." Jon raised his brows, and his view fell onto my lip. I was still biting on it. Quickly, I stopped and darted my eyes straight ahead.

He leaned into my ear. "Because earlier, I had still planned to fuck the world out of you."

Jon's hot breath crashed against my skin. My thighs clenched, and I had to swallow harshly at the feel of this pulsing in my stomach, which usually only Paul could awaken.

"What?" I gulped, turning my head to look at Jon. But, again, our lips were too close, our gaze too intense, and my heart beating too heavily.

"Yeah. But now you've made it clear we are and only *ever* will be friends. I've nothing to hide anymore." He leaned back again, closing his eyes, but plastered on his face was a smirk.

"I thought Paul was your best friend. Why would you—"

"Shhhh. You said one more question, Little German," Jon interrupted, his breathing slowing down. I pouted and squeezed my legs together, feeling my underwear turning wet. No matter how much my brain screamed not to want Jon, one dirty line from him was enough to make my body betray me. I closed my eyes too. The effect from the blunt, joint, whatever it's called, was barely present anymore. I'd only taken a few drags. I didn't want Gena to catch me high. I told her I would hang with Breana, and I didn't want to give her any further reason to mistrust me after I ended up in detention today. *Gosh, what happened to me that I abused her trust like this?* Maybe Mrs. Stone had a good reason to keep me on such a tight leash. I was a hormone-controlled teenager, high on a bus, horny from a boy who wasn't my boyfriend, with a toxic pill tightly pressed together in my fist. But I liked not being the naive little girl anymore.

By the time we came to Paul's street, my body had recovered, and I had made up my mind. I took off Jon's jacket when the bus doors closed behind us.

"Thanks."

Jon took it and pointed down the street. "Should I—"

"I can walk up to the house myself, thanks."

"Okay, then." He shrugged.

I bit on the inside of my cheek. I was dreading to say the following, but I had to make sure he wouldn't mess this up. "Could today, um . . . remain between us?"

"You want to lie to Paul?" Jon pointed out bluntly.

I swallowed. "Just this one last time. Then never again."

I couldn't tell Paul the truth, not after finding out I had acted out of impulsiveness. I would be the perfect girlfriend, rebuild our trust, and live happily ever after.

"Okay, but you better never lie to me," Jon said and then went in the opposite direction.

"I won't."

But I did. I lied when I told Jon I didn't like him first.

Chapter 13

Playing It Cool

Paul

VOICES. I PRICKED UP MY EARS WHEN I HEARD THE FRONT DOOR close quietly. Only one person in this family would turn the doorknob so gently. My chest lifted and lowered faster, and I groped for the blanket. I snatched the remote and shut off the TV. I'd been watching a silent documentary about last year's tornadoes with subtitles so I could hear when Emily would return. Hell, I hoped she wouldn't catch a whiff of how desperate I was when she came down—if she was even coming down at all. I gulped hard as Emily's footsteps wandered into the living room. My mind begged to hear what she would say to Mom. I hopped up, crept to the door, and slowly opened it. Their voices were soft but loud enough for me to understand.

"I'm glad you had a great time with Breana," Mom said.

"Yeah, it was nice."

My neck hair stood up at Emily's voice. It was raspy and shaky, like this talk would feed from her very last energy.

"Honey, you know that I trust you, right?" My mother's voice turned sugary. By the silence, I assumed that Emily nodded. I squeezed the doorframe.

"But I got to ask why you ended up in detention. Are you in trouble? Is someone at school bothering you?"

I let out a soundless laugh. Mom didn't believe either that Emily could ever misbehave. She was too perfect.

After a long pause, Emily finally replied. "I've been missing home lately."

A harsh stab rushed into my chest. I doubted Emily was telling the truth.

"Breana and Danielle tried to cheer me up, and we had a food fight. My clothes were dirty, so I went home the next hour to shower. I felt uncomfortable walking around covered in tomato sauce . . ."

That was a reasonable explanation, but something in her voice was off . . .

"A food fight?!" My mother laughed out loud. "Gosh, that's daily business for me."

Emily let out a brittle laugh. "I'm sorry if I worried you."

"Oh, honey." My mother sighed. "I'm 45 years old, and sometimes I miss my mother so much that I get crazy ideas myself."

I let out a breath. I was 99 percent certain they were hugging now. I returned to the bed and lay down. I would follow my mother's advice. Give her space and let her breathe. But heck, all I wanted was to run up there and ask her where the fuck she really was.

When my mind was about to drift to sleep, the basement door creaked open. My eyelids fluttered, but I kept them closed. A little wind wandered around my legs when Emily lifted the blanket before her ice-cold body cuddled up on my chest.

"Babycakes . . ." I opened my eyes slowly. *Fuck, why is her skin like an ice sculpture?* I wrapped my arms around her and pulled her onto my chest. Her hair was damp. Her apple shampoo hid any traces of her stopover.

"Hey . . ." she whispered back, molding herself closer to my body.

My jaw clenched, and I tried to get my breathing under control. *Please don't ask her where she was!*

She remained quiet, the silence nearly killing me, but I fought through it.

"Paul . . ." Her hug around my body loosened, and she ran her fingers through her hair. "Is everything okay, um, between us?"

"Of course!" I pulled her close again so she wouldn't see my face. "Why wouldn't everything be okay?"

Let's ignore that I turned into a jealous control freak.

"I feel like after what happened at the lake . . ." Emily stammered but stopped mid-sentence. "Never mind."

I set my hand on her throat and elevated her head. Her eyes met mine while she blinked to hold back tears. I loved looking into her eyes. They reminded me of a summer thunderstorm before the rainbow appeared. But lately, the clouds had gotten out of hand.

"Sorry if you texted me and I didn't reply. I've lost my phone."

Her head shot up, and she lifted herself on her elbow. She looked at me with her mouth slightly parted. Her sight twitched to my lips as she pulled in her own, biting onto it. Shit, I instantly felt my blood shooting into my dick.

"About that . . ." She sucked at her lip now. Gosh, how much I wanted to suck it myself. She wore a plain T-shirt, and her nipples pointed through it from the cold. My fingers reached for them, and—

"Paul, did you hear me?"

I swallowed. I didn't. All I heard was the blood pulsing through my veins.

"I'm sorry, I just . . . I missed this. I missed us." I pulled my sight away from her lips and returned to her eyes. "And all I can think about is kissing you right now."

The rainbow appeared. "Then why don't you?"

Instinctively, I cupped her cheeks, and while pulling her in, she grabbed hold of my wrist to join me halfway. Our lips aimed at the other, desperate to reduce the tension built up over the last few weeks. My entire body relaxed the second her pouty mouth plastered onto mine. Eagerly, she explored my tongue, and I met her with even more desire back. At our first kiss, she barely opened her mouth, only dipping in carefully with her tongue, following my lead. This time, it was her crashing ahead, and fuck, my cock pulsed like crazy with her confidence. This girl kept surprising me, escalating this hurricane in my chest. I would love to bury my dick inside her. Her innocence was compelling, and it turned me on, knowing she trusted me to introduce her to an unknown world. But I had to be patient and do it right.

Emily climbed on top of me, curling her hip against mine. Her lips traveled down my neck, and her warm tongue glided over my skin. I grabbed her by the waist, threw her around, and pressed her into the sheets. I ran my tongue from her chin to her neck, sucking and biting her skin until she was marked as mine. She moaned from my not-so-soft touch, my dick now as hard as a rock, when her hips glided up. I smiled into her neck. She enjoyed me being rough. So far, I had been soft, ensuring she felt safe and protected. But right now, she was asking for the opposite, and I wouldn't question why. I enjoyed being dominant in the bed, the one in charge, prioritizing the other person to get to the highest of highs. My left hand pressed her hips into the mattress until she couldn't move. I licked over the freshly bruised skin at her neck and clasped my right hand below her shirt, massaging her breast and squeezing her nipples.

"Ohhh!" Her eyes shot open, and she let out a loud squeak.

"Did I hurt you?" I immediately pulled away. I had gotten lost in the moment. The last thing I wanted was to hurt her. So I turned the reins over to her.

"Um, it's a new feeling. But a good one." She bit her lip again, throwing them back at me.

"Great," I smirked, and I pulled her shirt over her head, throwing it onto the ground. She immediately covered her boobs with her palms.

"Hey, don't hide. Everything about you is beautiful to me."

I gave her a soft kiss on the lips. I should pedal back. She still needed more time to explore this world further with me. And I was even glad she did because the suspense rising in me, the honor to be the one giving her her firsts, thrilled me. She gave me a slight nod, breathed in, and took her arms away. Her breasts were beautiful to me. They were tiny but well shaped, her nipples pointing up from the cold. I lowered my head to reach them with my mouth. Slowly, I teased them with my tongue, continuing the massage with both hands. She tasted like heaven. Her fingernails dug into my back, and she let out the loudest moan I'd ever heard from her. I sucked at her nipples more harshly, making her moan even louder.

Fuck, she's so sexy. I lowered my right hand, and my fingertips traveled softly over her skin to her sex. Lifting her pantie with a bow, I realized she hadn't planned this. I grew even more impatient, knowing she trusted me enough to feel attracted to her no matter what she wore. Because I did—seriously, she could be dressed in a potato sack, and I would still get horny for her. My fingers lifted up her panties, and I was met with a pool of wetness in them. I let out a loud growl through my teeth and rolled my eyes into my head.

"I want to have sex with you." She breathed heavily as her hip rocked impatiently against my fingertips. Hearing her say this let some drops of pleasure escape my cock. Shit, I wanted to have sex with her too, but not like this. Not with her being high, having hung out with Jon, and many not-outspoken things between us. She felt my hesitation and immediately backed off.

"You don't want to!" she squealed, and tears built in the corner of her eyes.

I grabbed her hand against her, trying to pull it away. "Not like this. I want it to be special."

"Oh . . ." she mewled when I caressed her hand. If I were Jon, I would've followed her request. Fucked her roughly, caring only about my needs being fulfilled. But I wasn't him. I was me. And I didn't want her for one night. *I wanted her for forever.*

"But that doesn't mean that we can't do anything." I parted her legs and let my fingers dive over her inner thighs, dipping my head between them. She slid down the bed with a grin. Her legs shook, her hands wrapped into my hair, and she muffled the orgasm that crashed around her with a pillow.

"Paul!" she gasped. *A lovely sound I would gladly get used to.*

Chapter 14

Winter Wonderland

Emily

Ten days till Christmas Eve . . .

THE SNOW FELL AND COATED THE DARK ASPHALT WITH AN eye-numbing white. Each day, the snow grew higher, the snowflakes thicker, and my shoes more slippery. Wrapped in a light blue parker, the only warm jacket I had gotten from Target, I waited for Jon to finish his cigarette so we could head to detention.

"You should quit smoking," I commented as I rubbed my earlobes, nearly numb from the cold.

"Or you could get a beanie." Jon puffed and took a slow-motion drag. Then, with his eyes closed, he inhaled for as long as I wouldn't have thought his lungs could handle.

"Okay, that's it! I'm going to go inside and talk to Mr. Yellowtooth. He's better company than you anyway." I gave him a cheeky smile.

"He's creepy. Please do me a favor and don't play chess with him again."

"He's not bad. I'll even miss him a little when detention is over." I shrugged as I walked backward, feeling the snow crunch under my leather boots.

"You're weird, and you're going to lose again," Jon called after me.

"It's not all about winning," I said, my middle finger flying bashfully. It was such an unfamiliar movement, and I struggled to extend it.

"You're probably the only person who looks cute flipping someone off." Jon snorted, now tossing his stub away and loping after me. I stuck out my tongue instead.

"Emily! What do you say, another round today? I promise I'll go easy on you." Mr. Stacey waved and moved his arm to a chair the second I walked into the classroom. Jon sneaked up behind me.

"Not creepy at all, hm?"

"Shh!" I shushed him before turning back to Mr. Yellowtooth. "I would love to, Mr. Stacey. Give me a moment to take off my jacket."

He nodded hurriedly, and I heard whispers from the other students. But I didn't care—not anymore. Playing chess with him was better than staring at this big clock or fighting Jon's flirtation. Even though it had lessened since we'd agreed on our *friendship*, I still felt this burn in my chest every time we touched, and he couldn't touch me when I sat by Mr. Stacey's table. Jon waited in the front row, next to my usual seat. I took off my jacket and my scarf. The heater was strong in the building. All I had on was a plain Boonville High T-shirt with the winking pirate mascot. I felt American wearing a school shirt as if I would finally fit in. Jon gave me an odd stare.

"What?" I sighed, prepared to initiate another argument with him. It took me a while to admit it, but I appreciated our bickering. Raising my voice at him, forming out loud my opinions, yet always making up afterward . . . it was a thrill for my recently blossomed confidence.

"Um, nothing." He swallowed and let himself drop onto the chair. "Mr. Stacey is waiting for you."

I shifted my head; his pencil tapped impatiently on the chess game. I gave a sign I would be there in a few.

I turned back to Jon, sitting down. "You think I look foolish in this shirt, don't you?"

Jon's eyes twitch to the side, looking at my shirt. "No, the color suits you."

My brows curved. This was a bright blue—I doubted it could suit anyone.

"Then what is it that bothers you?"

Jon snorted with crossed arms. "I'm not bothered."

"Right. You give me your bothered face for no reason." I shot him a glare.

"Go play chess, and stop annoying me," he mumbled, taking out his little black book.

"Ugh, fine!" I grizzled, shoving my jacket on the table. *Hot and cold, cold and hot.*

"Wait. . ."

I smiled broadly. "Yes?"

"You got a pen?"

I screeched but fiddled in my bag for a pen anyway. That evening, I guessed at what Jon could've felt aggravated with: my neck spotlighted hickeys, marking me like a dog who peed on his territory. The next day, I covered them with makeup.

Eight days till Christmas Eve. . .

"Do you think Leni would like this?" Breana asked, holding up a set of brushes and acrylic paints.

"If you want to use those to paint something for him, sure," Danielle said before shuffling through different Christmas cards.

"I was thinking we could paint on each other!" Breana swept her wild curls out of her face.

"Body painting?" I gagged.

"It's fun! Gets you all hot inside for what will follow after. You should try it with Paul!"

"Maybe one day . . ." I turned back to the shelf, biting my tongue.

"You still haven't?" Breana squealed too loud, leaving this pinching noise in my ears. I pressed my teeth together. Since he said he wanted it special, I'd waited for him to make a move.

"Emily—"

"Breana, leave it." Danielle glared at Breana.

"I didn't say it was negative! It's cute how you're taking your time." Breana kissed me on the cheek.

"Him . . . you mean," I mumbled under my breath, but she didn't hear me because she was leaning over to Danielle to kiss her on the cheek as well.

"Don't." Danielle pushed her away.

"Ugh, fine." Breana gave me a *she's so uptight* look. "I will search for a present for you two now!" And gone she was.

Danielle didn't show her affection a lot; a simple hug meant the world coming from her. I appreciated their differences. Danielle was the best regarding relationship advice and how to stand your ground. She already had a few years on Timo's and her watch. And Breana was like me in the honeymoon stage. We could giggle about our loved ones in hourly conversations. She was as clueless as I, except for the sex part.

"So he's the one wanting to wait?" Danielle picked up the topic.

I sighed. "Yeah, I tried it a while ago, but he rejected me because we weren't in the best place. I've been waiting for him to make a move since."

"Why are you waiting for him?" She shrugged with a straight face.

I leaned against a shopping cart and fiddled with the ends of my hair. "I don't know . . . I'm worried he will reject me again."

"Pfft, you're a strong, beautiful woman, Emily." Danielle shuffled the Christmas cards as if we were discussing our latest homework. "You want to have sex with him, then take matters into your hands."

She pulled out a card and dropped it into her cart.

"I guess I should . . ." If I had confidence, maybe, yet her words stuck with me. I walked over to the notebook section. There was this little black book, which I slowly let my fingers graze over. I had seen it before. It was always wrapped between Jon's fingers, but I couldn't get a peek inside. I pulled it off the shelf, twirled the leather band around it to the side, and flipped it open. The leather was soft, snuggling itself against my fingers. The paper was slightly yellow, with no lines or check patterns. I bit my lip as I still couldn't take my eyes off this notebook. It wasn't the prettiest, the biggest, or the most expensive. It simply felt good in the hands. Danielle grabbed the notebook from me. "I know how much you enjoy writing your lists of goals and to-do's, but I doubt Paul would be happy about this."

"I didn't want to get this for Paul," I explained and snatched it from her hands again.

"Oh . . ." Danielle narrowed her eyes at me, then back at the book. "No!"

"What?" I bit my cheek and looked down at my basket filled with a key chain pen and the notebook.

"I know Jon has this notebook too." Danielle stepped right in front of me, looking over her shoulder, probably ensuring Breana wasn't close. "Are you planning to give Jon a Christmas gift?"

"No, I—" *Ugh, Danielle has this magical gift of reading my thoughts.* "I wanted this for myself."

And this wasn't a lie. I hadn't brought my notebook from Germany because I barely had space in my suitcase. I used to write a diary almost every day. It used to help me understand my emotions better. Especially back then, when—

"Hm, you have a similar taste, then," Danielle pulled me out of my thoughts. "So what will you get for Paul?" She smiled, her mood back to normal.

"I was thinking . . ." I waved my hand for her to follow me.

Seven days till Christmas Eve. . .

"The reindeer belongs on the front lawn, not in the tree!" Henry groaned toward Zack, who had hung the giant reindeer in the crown of the oak tree. Zack curled up in the middle of a branch, laughing.

"But it looks much more impressive up here! I mean, a deer in a tree? That's freaky!"

"Jesus . . ." Henry wiped his face. "Come down and help me get the rest of the lights out of the house!"

Zack nodded and jumped out of the tree with a loud bang, catching up with Henry before he got to the door. It was almost Christmas break, so Zack was enjoying a hiatus from his ADHD medication. He was much more lively right away. I genuinely enjoyed it when he was full of positive energy. I rubbed my earlobes again. Paul and I were busy untangling some of the strings of lights. My phone buzzed. I took it out and pulled off my right glove to unlock the screen. It was a message from Madison.

> **Madison:** Hey, Em! I wanted to ask again if you're available to hang out soon. Maybe right after school? Miss talking to you.

"Who's texting?" Paul asked, his focus lingering on his lights.

"It's Madison. She's been asking a few times now if we can hang."

"You're kidding, right?"

"You can't blame Madison for having an evil mother," I defended her, but Paul only blew out some air. I knew he disliked Madison after her not having my back for the first months I'd been in America. Yet, what mattered to me were the sister vibes we created by sticking together against her mother . . . ugh, thinking about Mrs. Stone made me shiver. I was lucky I hadn't run into her again since she'd dropped me off at the Shields' place.

> **Me:** I've detention till Thursday. Let's meet on the last day of school for coffee!

> **Madison:** You got detention? Already can't wait to hear that story.

I placed my phone back into my jacket.

"Hell, no matter how long I try to untie this knot, I only make it worse. It's impossible!" Paul pulled at multiple strings, making them wind up even more.

"Here." I tossed Paul the lights I had already untangled and took his from his hands.

"Thanks, Babycakes!" He plastered a kiss on my cheek, then continued to hang the fairy lights on the window frames. My body heated up. In the last few days, more and more houses had put up their Christmas lights, and the whole city was aglow with green and red. Some places kept it classic and to a minimum. A fir tree, a bright star, and that was it. But there was one street where I felt a great need to wear sunglasses. Their electric bill had to be gigantic that month. Gena and Henry kept it at a higher average. A reindeer, a few Christmas lights, and a sprig of mistletoe by the door. In Germany, we hardly decorated houses with much light, more so the interiors. I knew I would miss this next year when I returned to Germany. I shook my head to get rid of those negative thoughts.

"Done!" I walked over to Paul, who was standing on a ladder.

With a tight grip, he swirled around. "How did you manage to do this?!"

"I have a good knack for that kind of stuff."

"Sheesh, you truly know what strings to pull."

After some nervous breakdowns from Henry, we finished decorating. It looked odd with the deer parked in the tree, a scary-looking snowman decorated with fake blood, and a knife plunged into its belly. Zack wanted to add his touch, and there was no way to stop him. Gena stepped outside, excited to see the results.

"Ohh, this looks—*Ew! Zack!*" she squealed, and we all had to laugh. Zack and Gena ended up in a long discussion about why a murdered snowman wasn't something people would like to see looking out of the window.

"Emily, please back me up. This isn't scary, right?" Zack begged me for support.

"Actually . . ." I threw Gena an apologetic smile. "I'm sorry, Gena, but I kinda like the reindeer in the tree."

"*What?!*" Both Paul and Gena shouted, and Henry cackled out loud. His laugh echoed through the entire street.

"It's like there's a story here. People won't drive by thinking, 'Oh, that house looks nicely decorated.' They'll be like—" I jumped and waved my arms around. "I saw this house today with a reindeer in the tree! That looked cool!" *It's perfect because it's imperfect.*

Paul looked at me, confused, and I let my arms drop. Zack gave me a thumbs-up.

"And what about the snowman with blood? Is that also cool?" Gena pointed at it, eyebrows pressed together in disgust.

"Well, um . . ." I looked at the snowman, debating if I could find something to make Zack get away with it. "Sorry, Zacky, but he's disturbing."

"Ugh. I almost wanted to ask you if you want to play Zombieland with me again." Zack pouted and walked away with a dramatic cold shoulder.

"Off the knife goes!" Gena ordered.

Paul hugged me from behind, and I snuggled my head into his neck.

"I already can't wait to spend this first of many Christmas celebrations with you."

Paul kept saying stuff about the future as if picturing it made him happy. But for me, the future was a reminder spending another Christmas together while living on different continents could feel lonely . . . but I didn't mention it. Instead, I said, "Me neither."

Five days till Christmas Eve. . .

"Emily, I asked her out!" Mr. Stacey smiled widely till his one yellow tooth got a tad too prominent.

"How great!" I tried my best not to look at it.

He'd begun telling me about his personal life in our daily chess games. He just wanted someone to talk to. I could understand.

"I didn't go great. She said no." His shoulders plunged.

"Oh . . ." I pretended to debate my next move to give myself a few seconds to find something positive to add. Then I moved my queen away from my king. "Well, you learned from it. Asking someone else will be easier next time."

"You're right! I could ask everyone now!"

I pressed my lips together; I didn't mean that. Yet I liked his growing confidence. "Yes, you can, Mr. Stacey."

Then I turned around, seeing Jon fighting his hardest to hold in his laughter. I widened my eyes at him, clasping my lips tightly together. His laugh was infectious, and I could feel mine crawl up my throat.

"Checkmate!" Mr. Stacey almost shouted when he defeated me again. "You should've kept the queen with the king. He was nothing without her."

After winning, Mr. Stacey was in such a good mood he let us out thirty minutes earlier. People suddenly said goodbye and thanked me, proving my point that doing whatever the heck you want is the go-to for life.

"You got to watch out, or Mr. Stacey will ask you out next time!" Jon burst into laughter when we were alone in the parking lot.

"He wouldn't do so! I'm his student!"

"You told him he could ask anyone!"

I covered my mouth, screeching, "I flirted with my teacher?"

"I'm afraid you did!" Jon laughed even louder.

"Oh my gosh, I should go back and explain! I never meant to—"

I turned around, ready to sprint back inside. Jon caught me on my elbow, pulling me back, and I tumbled over the slippery ground, falling right into his arms. Our looks connected. My skin tingled again where his hands held me. I was in the danger zone.

"I was kidding, Little German," Jon corrected calmly, never pulling his gaze away.

I quickly stepped away, my voice raspy. "Sorry."

"It's nothing." Jon shrugged, but my mind was spinning.

"Um, see you tomorrow." I waved, walking in the opposite direction.

"Hold on, isn't Paul picking you up here?" Jon shouted after me. But I pretended I hadn't heard him. *I can't let it come to moments like this anymore.*

"How was detention today?" Paul asked as he gently ran his fingers through my hair. We were lying in bed, watching an episode of *Grey's Anatomy*.

"Boring," I lied, hiding my face in his chest, feeling my cheeks warm by thinking about today.

"Hm . . ."

I placed my fingertips on his chest, feeling his heart thumping. Suddenly, it went faster. "Have you seen Jon lately? I haven't talked to him in a few days, which is odd."

My entire body tensed, and I pulled my hand away. I'd been with Jon in detention for almost two weeks now. If I mentioned it now, it would surely get him worried.

"Not really." I bleeped and pretended I was focusing on the dialogue on the TV. Watching it in English made the show even better. The emotions were rawer, more intense. Even though the German speakers did a great job, it made a difference when someone acted with their entire body or only their voice. I could barely believe I couldn't even form a proper sentence a few months ago.

"Oh, I hate Alex!" Paul complained when this character did something insulting to Meredith.

"You will soon love him." I spoiled a bit.

"But he's an ass!" Paul shook my body slightly. "How can you like him?!"

"He's just insecure, you will see—" I turned around until my chin rested on his chest. "He isn't as bad, trust me." I kissed his lips.

"So you're into the baddies?" Paul talked during our kiss.

"Maybe," I teased and turned back around. It was cute how Paul pretended to like the show, constantly asking questions about the characters, keeping quiet when tears welled in my eyes, and laughing out loud when I made a remark that was funny to me but not funny overall. *A perfect boyfriend.* I nestled my head deeper against his chest, closed my eyes, and breathed in his fresh ocean—wait a minute. He was wearing a new scent. One that matched his natural scent even better. It was no longer so oceanic and salty, more alluring with a hint of lavender.

"Are you using a new perfume?" I sniffed his chest like a detective finding a clue.

Paul let out a short cackle. "I use deodorant. But yeah, I picked up a new one the other day when you got lost in the clothing department trying to find your parka."

My head shot up, and I propped my chin on his chest to look at him. "You're kidding, right?"

My face was all serious, eyebrows straight, not a muscle twitching.

"Um . . . no?" Paul drew in his lips and tapped his finger briefly against my nose.

"You smell amazing!" I leaned down again and inhaled his natural scent mixed with nothing but deodorant.

"What does it smell like?" Paul probed, continuing to brush my hair with his fingers.

"Like home." I immediately breathed a sigh of happiness, closed my eyes, and enjoyed this ordinary moment.

Paul pressed a kiss to my forehead. "Just the way it feels to hold you in my arms."

I bit my lip and smiled across both cheeks. Things were going well. My gray world was shrouded in white, like the outside. But the snow would melt eventually. It was only a matter of time. Nothing stayed this perfect forever. Paul grabbed his phone, focusing on it.

"Hey, you're missing an epic line from Meredith!" I slapped him against his arm.

He laughed. "Check your phone."

I pressed Pause on the remote and leaned over to my nightstand, where my phone was on the charger. Lately, the battery was dying after a few hours. I swiped the screen, seeing a notification from my social media.

Paul Shields has tagged you in a picture.

I hadn't been active on social media since I got here. Where I lived in Germany, people took it seriously and posted on it daily. I felt pressured to constantly put pictures out of there for people to analyze and judge. Mainly because I barely even knew those who followed me, acquaintances from here and there I had only exchanged a few words with. Paul's social media, on the other hand, was only his friends. No more than 200 followers, all people's faces I either knew from school or his stories. And he shared . . . a picture of me resting on his chest with closed eyes. In the caption, it said:

Never seen something cuter before. Love u @emilyy_97

A face-numbing grin spread over my face. Maybe the snow would stay thick longer than expected.

Chapter 15

Cookies & Connections

Emily

Two days till Christmas Eve. . .

"Hey, Mom!" I stretched my legs out on the couch in the living room. I was just about to doze off.

"Yes, tomorrow is the last school day before Christmas break," I explained to her, wiggling my toes to sense them again. We'd been missing our calls a lot lately, and I even declined her call on purpose once. Not because I didn't want to talk to her, but to hear her voice made me miss her even more, and hearing his voice in the background . . . it made me not want to go back forever. "Uh-huh. I miss you, Lucas, Kelly . . . Pani! How's Pani doing? Is he still purring like ever?"

I could barely remember what it felt like to cuddle that big, fluffy orange cat. My mother sniffled into the phone that he was still sleeping in my bed every night. My eyes lowered, and I bit the inside of my cheeks, immediately knowing something was up. But I knew asking wouldn't help, but that didn't stop the guilt from building in my chest. I had left everyone behind for selfish reasons, but even now, I would do it all over again. My completed list was like an approved certificate.

"I think about you all the time, Mom. We'll celebrate together next year. I promise."

A promise as if made for another lifetime. The front door closed, and I straightened up and saw Henry coming in with many grocery bags.

"Mom, I have to help Henry with the groceries. I love you!"

While listening to her goodbye, I hurried over.

"I'm ready to learn more dishes, Em." Henry smiled broadly as I helped him with all the little bags.

In Germany, we always put everything in one big bag because, unlike here, we didn't have anyone packing for us at the checkout, which is a great side job for students, by the way.

"You will love today's one." I placed the bags on the counter in the kitchen. Henry was fascinated by me taking Culinary Arts. He rushed to the store to get all the ingredients when I told him about the soups we had learned. Since then, we'd been cooking together almost every night, and in just a few weeks, I'd spent more time with him than with my father in an entire year.

"Is Gena still at work?" I asked, putting a can of tomatoes in the kitchen cabinet.

"Yeah, a kid didn't get picked up today. Gena found her behind a bush."

My chest tightened, and the front door slammed shut again.

"Let's make Gena a nice meal then."

"Can I help?" Paul asked as he took off his scarf. It was Wednesday, which meant he had just returned from his college course in environmental science.

"Only if you tell us what you learned today." Henry grinned proudly, and Paul nodded.

"So—"

The door flew shut again. Loud footsteps came up the stairs, which meant—

"Hey, Zack, buddy!" Henry exclaimed, overjoyed all his kids were home.

"What's up?" Zack yawned loudly, flopped his bag on the couch, and entered the kitchen. "Hell yeah, is Emily cooking today?"

"We both are," I corrected him, looking down to see a puddle of water on the floor from the snow.

"Zack!" I screeched, pointing at it.

"What?" He shrugged, unaware of what a mess he'd made. I blew out my lip; Paul placed an arm around me, kissing my hairline.

"You're going to clean this up before your mother gets home." Henry put on a serious tone. But as hard as he tried, there was still a lot of kindness in his voice. Zack noticed, reached into a grocery bag, and pulled out the cookie dough ice cream—my favorite dessert ever.

"Hey! I asked Dad to buy this for Emily!" Paul tried to grab it, but Zack sprinted out of the kitchen, Paul right behind. "Give it to me!"

Henry and I looked at each other and burst out laughing.

"What you're cooking better be good, or I'll eat the ice cream!" Zack warned as Paul triumphantly returned to the kitchen with the bucket in his hand.

"Since it's the last school day before the winter break, let's bake!" Chef Sayle was in more of a sugary mood than a salty one, and this time, he initiated a little playfight with flour. With white eyelashes, we ate peanut butter cookies shaped like stars and Christmas trees.

"So yummy." Breana chewed, overly expressive. She had been in a good mood for all of December.

"I am soo stuffed!" Danielle held her stomach, some cookie crumbs still stuck to her lips.

"I told you not to eat too many." Chef Sayle winked, not taking his advice, and slipped another cookie into his mouth. We all laughed. Everyone was in a good mood, looking forward to the Christmas break. But I wasn't . . . the Christmas break meant detention was over, and with that, the time I spent alone with Jon.

"I won't eat until tomorrow night! Even though we're only five, my grandmother cooks for ten people." Danielle rubbed her belly. I giggled. My mother was the same. She cooked so much last year it didn't fit on the table, and we ate the leftovers for days after. "Will you be here for

Christmas break?" I asked Danielle, remembering how she was gone for Thanksgiving.

"No. First, I will be with my grandparents in Chicago, and . . ." She looked around at who was listening. Chef Sayle was busy talking to some other students. "I got in," she then whispered.

"Oh. My. Gosh!" Breana squealed, jumping up and down, pulling at Danielle's arm, but she remained stiff.

"Got in where?" I asked, not remembering her mentioning anything to me.

"Oh right, I told Bre when we hung out after school when you had detention."

I swiped the curtain bangs out of my face. *Ugh, I hate missing out.*

"I applied to a one-week course at a cosmetology school. Each year, they handpick a few high school students, and the ones with the best results get a scholarship after graduation."

"That's a huge chance!" I beamed at her, aware of how expensive it was to attend college in America.

"Yeah . . . I'm quite nervous."

"Being nervous isn't bad, Danielle," I reminded her. "When someone believes they are perfect, there won't be any growth. You can be confident, but nervousness will bring out your best."

Danielle smiled, grabbing my hand. "Thank you, Em."

I squeezed her hand back. Breana looked away with widened eyes, her jumping coming to a way-too-abrupt stop. I quickly focused on her, knowing she was like a sharpened bomb waiting for a reason to explode.

"What about you, Bre? Will you be here for the Christmas break?"

Her eyes sparkled up again. "I'm sorry, babe, but I'm going to be out of town for the break. You have no idea how much I begged my mom to let me stay, but no, we're going to Minnesota to visit my uncle."

"Don't be dramatic, Bre," Danielle pitched in. "Spending time with family isn't something that horrible!"

"I can second that." I sighed, wishing I could see my family for Christmas.

"You don't understand!" Breana defended herself. "Things with Leni are going amazing. What if he forgets about me while I'm gone?" She grabbed another cookie and stuffed it in her mouth.

"He won't forget you that quickly!" I tried talking some sense into her. Danielle leaned back in her chair.

"*How do you know!* It's like ten days. So much can happen!" She walked up to me and shook my body with her hands. "336 hours, Emily! That's over two months in male-hormone-driven days!"

I almost slipped on the muddy floor of the school hallway and bounced into someone's shoulder.

"Watch where you're going!" hissed a voice I hadn't heard in a while. Jamie glared at me from above. I quickly took a step back and refound my balance.

"Sorry, I didn't see you." I clutched my box of cookies tightly. I had been really thankful for the school being so big, but now I had to face her for the first time since that bonfire. My grip around the box relaxed. She looked different than usual. Her flawless makeup was reduced to a base, the natural look suiting her better. She looked to the ground, playing with a broken nail. She could've walked away at least twice by now, but it was like she was contemplating telling me something.

"Are you okay?" I finally asked when I couldn't bear the silence anymore. But again, I struggled to interpret her face because she shot me a death glare instead.

"You have some nerve asking me that!"

"I'm sorry." I opened the tin and pulled out an extra-giant cookie. "Want a cookie?"

I tried to be nice to her, even though every vein in my body bristled against it. But after all, she was struggling with heartbreak, and the last thing I wanted was to add salt to the wound. This could've easily been me.

"Do you know how many calories this thing has? I have enough problems because of you!" She shrieked and deliberately bumped her shoulder against mine. I sighed and put the cookie back. At least I tried.

I strolled to my locker to empty it for the holidays. Fourth period,

US History, was free for everyone. When I arrived, Jon slumped against it. I couldn't help but smile.

"You know we don't have detention today, right?" I handed him my box to hold.

"I know." He opened the lid and grabbed the cookie I'd offered Jamie. He took a careful bite. "Ugh. Yours are better than mine."

He chewed as I opened my locker like a pro. I had finally gotten used to American locks.

"Than yours?"

"I have culinary in 2nd period." Jon continued chewing.

I gulped. "You are into cooking?"

"I wouldn't say I'm into it, but Chef Sayle isn't too bad," Jon said while munching.

"He's the best!" I corrected him before looking around, searching if Paul was close. Jon reached for another cookie.

"Hey, don't eat all those! They're for the Shields." I snatched the box out of his hand. Jon chuckled and let his tongue slide across his lips to consume the last crumbs. I focused back on packing my things but felt Jon's gaze like a dagger on me.

"Okay, what do you want?" I put my head back and gave him an impatient sigh. I needed him gone before Paul showed.

"Can I not stand here waiting for my friend to finish whatever the hell she's doing there?" Jon leaned against the lockers, crossing his legs. I focused on getting out my books, even though my body flinched at the word *friend*. "The lockers don't get robbed over the holidays, you know?"

"I want it empty so I can start fresh next year."

"Oh, don't tell me you're one of those chicks with New Year's resolutions?" Jon complained, and even though I didn't see him, I knew he was rolling his eyes.

"And what if I am?" I teased back, stuffing some books into my backpack. Then I turned to him again.

"Okay, this friendship can't work. I've tried. I really did." Jon sounded serious, but his flickering eyes betrayed his playfulness. We both chuckled, and I couldn't help but notice that Jon had been pointing out our friendship a lot . . .

"Seriously, Jon." I closed my locker and tugged my bag back on my shoulders. "I know you well enough to know that you want something."

Jon raked his fingers through his hair, and I gave him my big-eyes look in return. The one my mom always said was impossible to resist when I wanted something.

"Man, it's annoying when you're right." Jon peered in all directions before leaning in. "The pill, did you, um . . . take it?"

My eyes narrowed. "Why do you ask?"

"I just want to know." Jon shrugged, his eyes twitching around like a ping-pong ball.

"It doesn't make any difference." I winced, feeling the playful energy between us slip away.

"It does." Jon's tone turned serious. We would fight again in a matter of seconds. Usually, it was something I wouldn't try to avoid, but I knew Paul could be here any second now.

"Fine." I pulled in my bottom lip and sucked on it vigorously. "I haven't taken it yet."

"Okay." Jon smiled, suddenly glancing behind me.

"Why do you—"

He interrupted me. "Watch out, a jealous Paul is approaching in three, two—"

I whirled around with a nervous smile. "Paul!"

Chapter 16

Below the Belt

Paul

LEFT AND RIGHT, I BID ACQUAINTANCES GOODBYE WITH A handshake, brief hugs, or polite nods.

"Have a nice Christmas break!" Leni waved as I passed him with Breana tucked around his neck, on my way to one particular locker. I grinned wide because I had two weeks to get cozy with my girl. Two weeks in which we would have time for ourselves to connect and have that special night I'd been looking forward to ever since we were close to doing it.

"You too, man." I stepped around the corner backward. While turning, my wide grin faded as I saw Jon standing next to Emily. I recognized her from behind in her light blue parka and leather boots. Her hair was pulled up into a messy bun, some loose strands falling onto her neck. Jon leaned in, inches from her face. I held my breath, and my jaw cramped. I couldn't see Emily's face, but Jon's eyes were tender. His typically stiffened lips stretched into a pleasant smile. I'd seen this look on him only when we left Marna's with a new stash.

"Emily isn't your drug, you bastard!"

A girl sneaked past me in a large circle, giving me a frightened look.

Shit, I didn't want to say that out loud. Jon's eyes shot up, and he jerked away from Emily. She turned around far too hastily.

"Paul!" She smiled, flustered, and rubbed the palm of her hand with her thumb. I eased the painful tension in my jaw as I walked in her direction, trying to put on a cheerful face.

You didn't see anything. There's no reason to be jealous. They're just friends.

But my heart was still hammering when I arrived next to my girl.

"Hey." The corners of my mouth twitched up, but Emily's brows arched in concern. I put an arm around her, planting a kiss on her hairline. My eyes didn't wander away from Jon. His poker face had become impossible to interpret again.

"We were just, um—"

"I was searching for you. I know wherever she is, you're not far away," Jon interrupted, and though it was brief, I could hear Emily gasp. Her eyes found Jon's, and he gave her a smile I would have loved to punch off his face. But my mind was still resisting it. I had to pull myself together ... *for Emily.*

"That's right." My grip around Emily's shoulder tightened slightly. "What's up?"

Jon's phone rang. He pulled it out of his pocket and held it up to signal our conversation was over.

"Kiki, what's up?" he rasped and wandered down the hall. That fucking bastard got saved by his phone.

"Kiki?!" Emily wheezed. But I was relaxed. If Kiki and Jon were talking, it meant he was distracted with getting back her forgiveness. "Why is she talking to him again?" Emily's eyes narrowed after Jon in the hall.

"I don't know. Why are you talking to him?" Emily twirled to me while taking a step back. My heart jumped, and I brushed my fingers through my slowly growing stubbles. "Sorry, I—"

"No." She lifted her chin, laser staring at me. "You were the one talking to him first. You can't expect me to not talk to him when he's always around you!"

Blood rushed into her cheeks, and her nostrils flared. I expected her to react emotionally, but anger wasn't on my list. She tapped her left foot on the floor with crossed arms.

"You're right. That wasn't fair." I inhaled deeply until no oxygen floated into my lungs anymore. *Keep yourself calm, Paul.*

"You're not gonna argue with me about this?" Her mouth fell open slightly.

"There's no need to." *I'm not like Jon, after all.*

I smiled and pulled her into my embrace. Her little arms wrapped around me hesitantly.

With her cheek pressed onto my chest, she mumbled, "Okay . . ." Almost as if she was disappointed. I didn't fight her back.

"Give me a kiss, please." I tried lightening the mood. She lifted her chin for a quick peck, but her attention quickly disappeared as she glanced over my shoulder.

"Emily!" Madison, Emily's former host sister, waved for her to come across the hall.

"Madison and I are going to get coffee. See you later at home?"

She looked over her shoulder at me one last time, her eyes falling to the floor as I let her hand slip out of mine. I remained watching her while Madison pulled her into an overly affectionate hug. I still couldn't understand why she was friends with this girl who was closely related to the dragon. I saw the evilness in her eyes. It was slim, but it was there, eager to get Emily back to her. I scratched my face and rested my back against the wall. I barely recognized myself anymore—as this jealous control freak. I hadn't cared much about Jamie when she hung out with male friends. But with Emily and Jon . . . they made my heartbeat escalate up to my throat. This gut feeling screamed at me to make sure they were never alone. My balled fist landed on the locker with a hard thud as I pressed my forehead to the cold metal. *I need to go for a run.*

A hand suddenly rested on my shoulder, and I turned around. It was a guy I'd never talked to before, but I knew he was a stoner. Dark circles, greasy hair, and a red shimmer in his eyes.

"Dude, you've got a lot of nerve." The guy smirked as if I had made a joke.

"Why do you care? My punch wasn't hard against the locker." I gave him a confused shake of my head. *Why would a guy like him even bother that I was destroying school property?*

"Not that." The guy snickered. He glanced around and leaned closer to my left ear.

"You kissed Jon Densen's girlfriend!"

Sweat built on my forehead. This was the last push, making me lose control. I grabbed the boy by his sweatshirt and dragged him close to me.

"What did you say?!" I roared, feeling evil spread through every vein in my body. His eyes widened in fear. "Talk!"

"If one of us even looked at her funny in detention, we got his death stare. He was all over her. Sorry, man, I assumed they were together!"

I pushed him away from me. The guy stumbled backward and grimaced. "Shit, you got some serious issues!"

I turned around, fighting for air. I was afraid my veins would explode. This dude gave me the final stroke, hitting me below the belt without knowing it. I straightened my shoulders, walking toward the exit. *Emily wants bad? I can give her bad.*

Chapter 17

A New Record

Jon

I SWIFTLY MOVED THROUGH THE CROWDS OF PEOPLE. THE LOOK Paul had given me was unlike any other. Darker, more serious. Shit, it didn't scare me, but it made me think. I was out of the game. I'd sworn to myself when I'd given Little German the pill. I stumbled out the side exit to avoid anyone trying to make small talk, my phone attached to my ear. My skin chilled as I kicked outside, but I'd rather walk than sit in a car with her and Paul. Even after all this crap, I made her nervous. I could tell by how she bit her inner cheeks and kept looking at her fingertips. I took in a cold breath as I held my face into the slowly setting rays of the sun. It was kinda cute how much influence I had on her, but I wasn't the only one who noticed. Paul did, and it was an issue. *She liked him first . . . not me.* I should save enough money to buy a car to cut down on the threesome meetings. I snorted loudly as the snow crunched under my black sneakers. Me and saving money—everything I got would go straight into Ted's or Marna's pockets . . . I should replenish my supply soon.

"Jon? Are you listening to me?" Kiki's voice on the phone startled me. *Shit.* I had totally forgotten I was on the phone with her.

"Um, sorry. The connection was off." I pinched the bridge of my nose, my eyes squinting.

"Listen, if you don't want to talk to me—"

"Fuck off. Of course I want to talk to you," I dropped with my usual harshness. I softened my voice when I heard her gasp. I had sent this girl through hell. I should try to be a little nicer.

"Sorry, um—you're important to me, you know."

My chest tightened. *Why on earth am I nice?* It was like I'd been caught in a fucking pink-tinted movie lately.

"Oh, Jon . . ." she breathed into the phone. "Need a ride?"

I told her where to pick me up and searched my wallet for my emergency pill, preparing myself for the emotional talk Kiki would for sure want to have. Kiki had a really fucked-up place in my heart. She was an A-grade student, with doctors as parents, who she wanted to make proud by taking the same route. Her parents forbade her from seeing me because I kept her from studying whenever I was around, which made me want her even more back then. The forbidden thrill was a kick I'd chased for way too long. For years, she always found her way back to me . . . or in my bed. No matter how much I fucked up. It was nice to have this familiar person who knew exactly how I liked it. But over time, she grew more important to me than she should have, only increasing my self-hatred whenever I hurt her again.

We drove silently as I sucked at a square, leaning out of the window. Kiki's fingers were shaking a bit as she clutched the steering wheel. She parked her car on the path next to my house. Wordlessly, we walked through the entrance. It looked like Tim was still busy at work or shit because there wasn't any sign of him being home. Down in my room, Kiki jumped into my arms.

"I missed you, Jon!" she whined and snuggled her nose into my neck. I shuffled my shoulders to get some distance between us.

"What about what I did to you? I cheated on you, and not for the first time," I told her bluntly, her grip around my neck loosening. My mouth pressed in a straight line. I was positive I'd overdone it this time. Taking her back now would mean I disrespected her—I felt sick.

She sighed and let herself drop onto her back on my unmade bed. "Of course you had to destroy it."

I also sat down on the bed but remained in a straight position. "Yeah, that's how I am, remember?"

"I know." Kiki sat back up, her eyes glistening. She placed one palm on my face and ran her fingers through my hair. "But like you said earlier, no matter how fucked-up we are, we'll always be important to another."

That's it? She uses the only nice line I'd told her in weeks to justify my actions?

I placed my hand on her wrist and slowly moved her hand from my body. She gasped, and I looked to the side, resting my head on my shoulder. I couldn't stand seeing her upset. People kept saying I didn't care if I hurt Kiki. But heck, those nights seeing her pain when I woke up with no memory after. The nights I let fate decide if I would even wake up the next day.

"You do care about me, right? You just said so on the phone!" She tugged at my arm. Her eyebrows tried to dance the tango together.

"You want to repeat the story all over again? How long has this been going on? Years? It might look like I don't mind, but I fucking hate to hurt you." The words blurted out of me. I almost sounded like Emily when she was raging about something. Kiki's mouth dropped open, and I slowly stood up and slinked to the door. *I need to sleep.*

"Then stop hurting me," she begged with the corners of her eyes hanging down, holding out her heart to me.

I rubbed my face, standing in the middle of the room. "Fuck, Kiki . . ."

When I removed my hands from my face, she stood right in front of me.

"It's not hard." Kiki surprised me by pressing her lips to mine. Her cherry gloss was my favorite flavor. It made me fucking weak, my cock pulsing. Unfortunately, ever since Thanksgiving, I hadn't gotten into the pleasure of soft lips around my dick.

"Kiki . . ." I snarled, but the boner in my pants tried moving closer to her hip.

"Yes, baby?" she whispered into my ear sensually. I let her take my hand to bring it into her denim jeans below her panties. The slick liquid instantly pooled over my fingers. *Fuck, she's so juicy.*

"We're on fire for each other. We belong together. You just gotta accept it," she breathed out loud and nibbled my earlobe.

"Hmm . . ." I moaned, frustrated. There was no need to convince me we were good together physically. She rocked her hip against my hand and bit into my shoulder. *Fuck, I'm too underfucked.*

I closed my eyes as I let my finger slide over her wetness, picturing everything I had already done to her sultry body.

"You don't want to hurt me . . ." She rocked even harder against my hand, but I pulled it out—this was wrong. Immediately, she dropped onto her knees, pulling down my pants.

"Kiki, hold on—" But her mouth was already swallowing my cock.

"I missed tasting you!" she gushed, and I could feel her fucking throat at the tip, taking it in as deeply as possible.

"Fuck!" I cursed as she moved her head back and forth. I wrapped my fingers into her long hair and tugged it at the roots for support. Eyes falling close.

This is wrong, Jon. You'll hurt her again . . .

That voice . . . Little German? I let out a loud groan as the hallucination kicked in. I was unsure if it was from the pill or if I was simply turning crazy when I saw pale eyes. Kiki pulled away a bit. She didn't just want to taste me. She wanted to feel me inside of her. But I wouldn't be able to last long, not with this girl staring at me from inside of me.

"Don't stop!" I squinted my eyes.

"But—"

"I will take care of you right after, I swear," I promised, holding her head gently in place. A broad grin formed on Kiki's face as she realized my pleasure and eagerly took my cock back into her mouth.

You did so well, Jon, but the game will be over as soon as I find out you're with Kiki again. You know that, right? I'm not like her forgiving you for everything. Emily's voice grew even louder.

"I'm not playing the game anymore . . ." I grumbled between my teeth as Kiki's tongue swirled around me as if I was a scoop of ice cream.

She stopped. "What?"

My eyes shot open. *Ugh, Jon, just shut up!*

"Nothing. Please continue. I'm almost there."

I smiled, hopeful this would be enough for her to pretend I hadn't said something odd. I fisted her hair, and she dived back around me. Then, as she licked and sucked me with such eagerness, my knees shook.

You don't want to know how I taste? How you feel inside of me? How I scream your name?

Emily giggled, my cock pulsing even harder. I pictured grabbing her apple butt, squeezing the nipples of her small tits, and feeling her tightness around me. My sight turned into a thousand fireworks as I came unexpectantly fast.

"Oh, Emily!" I moaned as I released the almost painful pleasure.

"*What?!*" Kiki fell back onto her butt, ending with me splashing my sperm onto the carpet instead of her mouth. *Fuck, did I say Emily?!* I was still on that high of coming, trying to understand what the hell happened, but I couldn't. This wasn't Little German in front of me . . . it was Kiki. I created a new record of hurting her in no time.

"Um, I—" I could barely form any words. Then, stumbling a bit, I pulled up my pants.

"You gotta be kidding me! She's the reason for you rejecting me at first, isn't she? It's not because you're trying to be a better person!" Kiki's face was getting red stains from her anger, and her lip gloss was all smudged around her swollen lips.

"Fuck no!" I stumbled, still collecting my ability to speak. My basement door flew open, and footsteps crashed down the stairs as Paul came at me like a bull, letting his angry face speak for himself. His eyes were dark, narrowed, with no sign of care or worry. I laughed as his balled fist landed on my face with such force I immediately crashed to the floor. The light around me turned darker and darker. But my smile was not vanishing. *I deserve this.*

Chapter 18

Special Stupid Gift

Emily

A small bell rang as Madison opened the door of the little diner. I had seen it on my school bus rides. The Crispy Biscuit was decorated in reds and browns, with a rustic interior and a menu that blinded me on the wall. Different age groups sat together, chatting or watching the snow through the windows as it quietly drifted onto the street. The calm and smell of hot coffee left a warm, fuzzy feeling in my belly. Madison didn't wait for the waitress to seat us but went to the table on the far left. She took me by the hand, but her touch irritated me, like she thought I couldn't walk alone. I didn't push her away because she was still used to the old Emily. The one who barely opened her mouth and was afraid to enter the kitchen.

The red leather seats in the booth groaned a little as I put down my bag with all my books.

"Gosh, it's freezing outside!" Madison said while taking off her purple wool scarf. I remembered Mrs. Stone sat on the couch, knitting with wool in the same color. My muscles tensed as I took off my parker.

"Yeah, but the wintertime is perfect for cuddling." I replaced those dark memories with how Paul and I had put on his fireplace last night.

One of my favorite memories, even though it was such a simple moment. Just us, watching the flickering flames, holding each other tightly. Paul gave me many little moments that screamed perfection. He was the boy in the movie, and I was his main character. Something I still struggled to understand.

"Hmm . . . Jackson prefers something else than cuddling." Madison giggled into her sleeve. But her mouth fell flat when the waitress came over and poured us some coffee. The second she was gone, Madison leaned in and whispered, "You know what I mean, right?"

She gave me flashbacks about how she made fun of me whenever I didn't understand her back then, but I swallowed it down. Overall, I felt sorry for her. She couldn't escape from her mother as I did.

"I know you're having plenty of sex, Madison," I said and took a sip of my black coffee.

"Shhhh!" Madison looked around frantically. "Lots of friends from church go to this diner!"

She poured too much sugar into her coffee. Then, she mouthed with her cup right in front of her lips, "So, did you and Paul do it by now?"

I sighed and clamped my fingers around the cup. I wanted to know what it was like. Finally, be experienced and up to date with everyone else. Because no matter how much I tried, I still felt like the clueless little girl.

"Not yet, sadly." My smile was forced and twitchy. Madison tasted her coffee with an approving nod.

"You're saying this like it would be something bad. I wished I would've waited longer."

I groaned. "Everyone says that, but it sucks not knowing what it's like. I want to get it over with."

"Get it over with? When?"

"Let's just say I bought something the other day, and he will be able to wrap up for Christmas." I rubbed my palms, thinking about the revealing underwear I had chosen.

"You're giving him your V-card for Christmas?!" Madison covered her mouth.

"That's the plan." I smiled, anticipating this moment and having a thousand questions about it. "Does it, um . . . hurt badly?"

I clenched my hands around the hot cup again, the blue from the cold slowly fading away. Madison smiled and leaned forward yet again.

"It always depends. For some, it hurts, but others don't feel much. I was lucky. It wasn't painful for me," Madison explained calmly, with no judgment left in her voice. "Sometimes it can even take a few tries until it works."

"Oh, okay." I chewed on my dry lips. I never considered this. All the books and movies I'd watched always portrayed it as beautiful after the first pain faded.

"Don't worry about it. Paul is one of the good guys. He'll for sure do it gently and at your pace." Madison placed her hand on mine and squeezed it. I nodded, pulling my hand away this time. I didn't need any reassurance about Paul being the right choice. I knew he was the *right* choice.

"You should come by my place sometime. I could give you a lesson on you know what."

"Thanks, but I still don't feel comfortable seeing your mother." I drew the line and gave myself an imagined tap on the shoulder.

Madison's smile dropped. "Do you think you will ever be able to forgive her?"

Forgive how she abused me? How she should've given me a safe home but almost got me to collapse again? "Probably not."

"More coffee?" trilled a waitress with shining silver hair. Without waiting for my reply, she poured in the coffee. It would probably take a while until I got used to the free refills, something Germany didn't have. We even had to pay for water.

Paul's car wasn't in the driveway when I hopped out of Madison's passenger seat. She didn't mention her mother again for the rest of our coffee, but she asked many questions about me, and I was sure she knew more about me after one hour compared to the three months I'd lived with her. I took off my boots in front of the door and walked up the stairs into the living room, carrying them in my hands.

"Hello?" I called, but no one answered me. I peeked into the kitchen and found a sheet of paper.

Hey kids! We're out on a date tonight. There's pizza in the fridge. P.S.: Emily, eat early before the boys destroy it!

I walked past my room to Zack's.

"Zack?" I knocked at the door, pushing my ear against it. No reply. I was all by myself. I dropped my shoes and sprinted. This was my chance to prepare for the special moment Paul needed. I grabbed the blue lace underwear and the scented rose candles I'd bought with Breana and Danielle from my room. Moving at full speed, I showered. While shaving my legs, I cut myself accidentally, leaving me with a long scratch.

"Ah!" I cursed, but the pain was clouded by the excitement I felt. Thirty minutes later, I was showered, shaved, my hair blow-dried, and my body creamed. In Paul's room, I put on the push-up bra. I admired my chest from above when suddenly they looked like B-cups. The dark blue fabric of the bra was covered with silk and black lace. The thong was so thin that my butt cheeks were not covered. I'd hesitated when I bought them, but then I remembered the first time Paul saw me in my underwear. It was on Black Friday in Macy's dressing rooms, and I suddenly felt overly confident to wear something this revealing. After much debating, I even bought garters I put on while praying to not cause a hole in the tights with my fingernails. I made the bed, grabbed a lighter out of the drawer, lit up the candles, only burning myself twice, and finally placed myself on the bed with a racing heart. And then, I heard keys and a door smashing open.

"Please let it be Paul . . ." I whispered into the lit-up candle room. I had thrown a blanket over the window to ensure our privacy. I pointed my ears, hearing footsteps rush down the stairs. I gasped for breath, but Paul didn't look around the corner; he dashed straight into the bathroom.

Great, ten minutes of overthinking and finding the best position.

"C'mon . . . heart, calm down. It's just sex."

But it didn't. Because no matter how often I tried telling myself that losing my virginity wasn't a big deal—it was more than important to me. That's why I wanted it to be Paul so badly. A person I knew for sure wasn't playing any games with me. Once given, there was no return.

Chapter 19

Bad Timing

Paul

I PUT THE SHOWER ON ICE COLD. MY SKIN SHIVERED, BUT I DIDN'T care. My mind was on fire, destroying my senses. Blood dripped from my knuckles, coloring the water a light red. I held my fist to my face as I realized what I had done. *I punched my best friend.* I flattened my hand and pressed it onto the wall.

"Fuck . . ." I turned off the water, grabbed a towel, and wrapped it around my waist. I was glad Emily was hanging out with Madison right now. *I'm not in the mood to see her . . .* to listen to more and more lies. I pushed open my door with my fist and walked into my room. Flickers of candle shadows danced, making me freeze.

"Hey." I heard her soft voice, shaking like the flames on the wall. I swirled around, seeing Emily in sexy underwear, standing right in front of the bed. Her arm was awkwardly shoved into her hip, her cheeks flushed. Even though she looked helpless, she was a work of art. The most beautiful girl I had ever seen. My lips curved into a broad smirk—she wanted me. Even if she had hidden her friendship with Jon, she was trying to seduce me, not him. The bleeding in my heart stopped, fixed by her bandaging it with her actions.

"I had bought these candles with Breana and Danielle the other day, and um, this thing. . ." She tucked at the fabric of her little panties. "You said you wanted it to be special, and no one is home right now."

She bit her lip. My grip loosened off my towel, causing it to fall to the floor. I tried to catch it in the free fall but stumbled ahead instead. She giggled a little at my gawkiness, the tension dropping with the beautiful sound of her smile. I waved at the towel, laughing about myself. She looked down at my naked body, and her eyes widened when she saw my penis. She had seen it countless times, yet she still made that curious face at it. We were supposed to talk about what happened, but I only desired to touch her skin, feel her pulse, and shower her with kisses. My cock twitched almost painfully.

"I interpret this as special enough," she said while walking toward me on her tiptoes. I looked to the ceiling, taking a controlled breath. I had too many negative emotions. I didn't want our first time to be tainted by them.

"I wanted to be the one to surprise you," I said, hoping this could delay us.

"I know." She grazed my skin from my cheek to my cock until her little hand wrapped around it. Softly, she stroked me. Not too much and not too soft either. "But I beat you to it." Her eyes had turned twice as big as the reflection of the candles flickered in them. Screw those thoughts. She wanted me; I was here and wouldn't let anyone ruin this moment. Especially not him.

Emily leaned in closer to my ear, her voice only a whisper. "I want this. Not tomorrow, not in a week, a month. Now."

I grabbed her waist and pulled her close, lingering a second in front of her lips before savoring them. She followed my lead with a gasp, and our tongues swirled, heating up the cold room. I grabbed her buttcheeks, squeezed them hard, and pulled her up to me by her ass. She wrapped her legs around my stomach and clamped her arms around my neck. While kissing her harder, I walked until my knuckles smashed against the wall. The ripped-open skin burned like hell as they collided with the wood.

"Oh, Paul . . ." she breathed into my mouth. My favorite sound. I rubbed my cock against her underwear, the ultra-soft silk against my tip.

This was for sure the best Christmas present ever. I pushed harder with my hardness against her panties.

"Ouuu . . ." she whimpered, and I threw her onto the bed. She giggled, but her smile faded when she locked eyes with mine. There wasn't much light here, only what the candles gave off, but I noticed how her eyebrows curved tensely. I brought my head between her legs to reassure her she had nothing to fear. I would first dive in when she was ready for me, with no further doubt on her face. Pulling off her panties slowly, I could feel her body shivering from my touch against her thighs. I pressed my thumb onto her, the wetness spreading onto it. I let my tongue glide around her inner thigh. Reaching her clit, I gleefully sailed my fingers over it. Her panting for air increased. I lowered my head, softly kissing her sex. Peeking up, I could see her reaching for a pillow to muffle her noises. I threw the pillow away from her.

"No one is here. I want to hear how much you like it." I licked my thumb to taste her—*fuck*, she tasted incredible.

"Okay!" She gasped so loud I was even a bit surprised. Not letting her wait longer, I pressed my tongue into her, licking her with all I had. She tucked her fingers into my hair as her moans turned wild and out of control. Her legs tensed, and another puddle of wetness surprised me as she came, that I could even taste it on my tongue. With a grin, I slowed my pace as her orgasm receded, her muscles relaxing.

"Wow, that was . . . better than in my dream," she panted, a grin plastered onto her face. She was ready. I lifted myself to her, my body resting slightly above hers.

"You already dreamed about this?"

She turned silent, and her eyes twitched to the side. I let out a brief chuckle. It was cute how she felt ashamed for having a sex dream.

"Well, this was just the beginning."

I reached for a condom in the drawer and lifted myself up on my knees to put it on. Emily watched me from below, still smiling and calm about what would happen next. I ripped open the plastic, pulled out the condom, and glided it over my hard cock.

"What happened to your hand?" Emily pointed at my ripped-open knuckles, the smile I had worked hard to get there gone. *Shit.* My jaw clenched, and I hid my hands by cupping her cheeks. "It's nothing."

"It's not nothing!" She pushed me, repulsed, grabbed my hands by the wrists, and sat up. "Did you punch someone?"

"Let's not talk about this now."

"Did you punch Jon?" she cried out loud, scooting her body away from mine. My cock lowered as if someone had let the air go out. I backed off and slumped my back against the wall side of the bed.

"Why do you immediately think I punched him?"

"So you didn't punch him?" Her voice was scattered with hope. I sighed and pulled the condom off, throwing it on the ground in frustration.

"Nope, I did."

"Why?" She looked at me with obliviousness. Fuck, I was tired of people always expecting only the best from me.

"I think you know," I fired back, trying to keep my emotions at bay.

"I only hung out with him, Paul." She swallowed, her eyes growing pleading. "There's no reason for you to punch him!"

My lips turned into a line. *So she hung out with Jon too? Seriously?!*

I stood up from the bed and faced her, almost laughing because I couldn't believe what was happening. "You're really defending Jon? After everything he did, you're still on his side and not mine?!"

My mouth became entirely dry, and my chest felt tight as if tons of cement were lifted onto it.

"We're just friends . . ." Emily repeated, tears dwelling in her eyes before she covered her face. I grabbed some boxer shorts and glided into them.

"Then why did you feel this urge to hide this friendship from me?" I pushed, removing any filters I had left. I wanted the truth, even if that meant we had to fight.

"I . . ." She sobbed into her hands. "I don't know. I was afraid you would disapprove."

"I'm not someone who tells you who you can or can't be friends with. All I wanted was honesty."

I walked to the closet and took out a shirt and running pants, but even after putting them on, I hadn't gotten a reply to my question. She still cowered at the wall in the corner of the bed, whimpering. *Fuck, I can't stand to see her like that.* I sat on the edge and leaned over to place my hand on her knee. She looked at me with an ocean pooling out of her eyes. I sighed, gathering everything I had left in me.

"You're still not sure who you want . . . right?" My voice was exhausted, but there was no regret. I had spoken out the truth, which was overdue for too long. She picked at her fingertips, biting her inner cheek. No reply needed.

"I will go for a run." I got up, but Emily grabbed me by the wrist.

"Please don't leave now," she begged, her fingers clamping onto my wrist.

"If I stay, I might say things I will regret."

And with those words, I shook her hand off and walked up the stairs out of the basement. My eyes burned like hell, but I had made my turn. Now it was her time to react. And I could only hope I didn't put myself into a checkmate.

Chapter 20

Sixty Thousand Thoughts

Jon

I AMBLED THROUGH THE SNOWY STREETS OF BOONVILLE WITH NO destination. My nose was swollen, and my eye pounded with every blink. Paul had hit me good, but still . . . I felt nothing. Even in such physical pain, I laughed. How fucked-up was I to say the name of my best friend's girlfriend while my ex was sucking my dick?! *I'm a fucking joke.*

"Ahhh!" I kicked an empty beer can over the street and ran after it to kick it again, again, and again.

"Why!" I screamed into the dark, my sight in the air as if I was talking to some shit god. When I regained consciousness, they were gone. No sign of my loyal best friend or my helping elf. They didn't even let me explain. They usually always let me explain. *I fucked up? No problem.* I had the right words to make them forgive me for anything. Most people were easy to read, their goals and beliefs. After seeing Emily for the first time, I had her figured out. Shy girl, naive, ready to do anything to prove you wrong. And I was right about that . . . but that didn't help me understand her better. No words that worked for others worked with her. In the beginning, it was a game, then it was a test to see if she was worthy of Paul, and now. . .

"Fuck, I don't know!" I looked around me as snow prickled onto my forehead. The last thing I needed was someone calling the cops because I looked like a crazy homeless dude. I forced myself up and stumbled over the fresh snow in a park until I reached a bench. Dropping my body onto it, I cleaned my nose with my sleeve and took out my black book. Drugs weren't helping. I needed something better, so I began scribbling.

My world was grim
Lifeless, empty of meaning, an end product of the mistakes from my youth
I did not care
I had come to peace with it, embraced being a failure, and even enjoyed it.
Playing with people's feelings, having no worries.
I felt free
But you wrecked that.
You injected me with something I wasn't familiar with.
A serum spreading and consuming me gradually from the inside.
I hate it
But I can't help but not hate you for making me feel again.
Even though this feeling is painful, I feel more alive than ever.
I do care
Even though it can only end one way: with me buried beneath the soil.

I shut my book, feeling much calmer. Writing was always a way for me to understand my head. An average person had over 60,000 thoughts per day, and fuck, I bet half of mine were about Little German and the other half about how I could stop them. My phone vibrating on my thigh, and I reached for it with a slightly dizzy head. But my body froze, seeing the one name that made me lose control. If there were an award for bad timing, it would definitely belong to her. I placed the phone on my knee and watched the screen as it didn't stop ringing. But I couldn't pick up. If I did, I had to tell her we couldn't talk anymore. The second I got the notification of a voice message, I dialed my mailbox.

"J-Jon?"

Her voice was shaky, and I could literally hear the tears falling from her eyelashes. I clenched my fingers on the bench.

"Paul, h-he. . ."

Another pause filled with sobbing. I jumped up. "Ugh, talk faster! Paul, what?!"

"He found out about us being. . ." A harsh swallow. *"Friends."*

And I swallowed twice as hard.

"Sorry, forget I called. I shouldn't have."

I spat out, hating that calling me felt wrong to her. I was standing in the way of their happiness? Fine, I would vanish. I searched for her number, my thumb hovering an endless second over the delete button.

Are you sure you want to delete *"Little German"* from your contacts? *Yes.*

And preferably out of my life as well. My skin shivered as I saw her recent call turning into a random number. I also pressed it—delete, delete, delete. I didn't trust my high brain anymore. I got up with a loud sigh, my body feeling heavier than average. It was time to search for new people to hang with because I respected Paul too much to expect him to forgive me for this. I walked again with no destination. I thought I did the worst when I ruined his football career, but I've done even worse by chasing after his girl. He was better off without me, as well as Little German. Everyone, basically.

My phone rang again, and I picked it up without looking at the screen. I had to scare her away.

"I can't help you!" I barfed into the speakers.

"Wow, this is how you're greeting your sister? Really charming, Jon," my little sister fired back. My steps grew calmer.

"Oh, Lauren. Sorry, I expected someone else."

"Who would've thought."

My sister and I were alike regarding one thing: our unfiltered attitude. Except for that, she was the entire opposite of me. I made sure she was.

"So, what do you want?" I asked with a much softer tone.

"It's Christmas in two days."

"Yes, so?"

"I have presents for Humphrey and Mom, and I was wondering if you want me to write your name on the cards and—"

"Just Mom's," I interrupted her. "I'm covering whatever you paid on it."

"I can cover my half myself."

I smiled at the phone. "Lauren, let me do this. You don't get much pocket money, and—"

"And you don't have a Christmas present for me yet." She laughed into the phone. Fuck, I totally forgot about that. I would need to get something tomorrow morning.

"Of course I have a present. Can't I do something nice for you?"

"You never do something nice."

Her statement made me tremble. Something that usually only got an eye roll of my attention suddenly caused a heave in my chest.

"Well, I'm trying to be better," I said more bluntly.

"Mh-hm . . . sure you are," Lauren commented, and I could hear her fingers typing and a dog barking in the background. I was on speaker and only left with half of her attention. "However, you're coming for Christmas dinner, right?"

"Didn't plan to."

Lauren always tried to feed the connection between Mom and me. But ever since she married that dickhead and replaced me with his perfect son, I didn't have much interest in spending more time than necessary at their place.

"I already covered for you at Thanksgiving. You said you owe me, and I'm demanding the favor."

I missed those times when I could bribe her with Barbie dolls.

"Fine, I could come by for a couple of minutes."

"You're the best. Love you!" She made some kissing sounds and hung up. I didn't only lose three of the most influential people in my life, but I was forced to go to a stupid Christmas dinner.

If I had known this day would turn out like this, I would've stayed home. I came to a complete standstill and looked up.

"You got to be kidding me . . ." I groaned into the cold air. I was standing in front of Paul's house. It was silent, but Emily's breaking voice lit loud in my head. I stood there for at least twenty minutes, waiting for a movement. The bloody snowman made me feel like I was at the twisted beginning of a horror movie—just that I was the creepy guy stalking the innocent girl. Eventually, I walked toward the door. I pulled out my phone and typed out a message.

Me: I'm outside.

I'd deleted her number, but that didn't mean it was deleted from my brain. A few minutes later, the door opened a crack. Emily's eyes widened as she saw me standing there. She quickly squeezed out the door, closing it with no other sound behind her.

"You came . . ." she whispered, hugging herself with her fingers tucked below her arms.

"Yeah, um . . ." I pulled in my lip and lifted my phone. "You called."

Emily peeked at me with the most giant eyes I had ever seen, and then she stepped ahead and . . . she hugged me. I could barely gasp at how fast she snuggled into my embrace and how my arms wrapped around her body in double time. My heart throbbed in my throat. Was this a hallucination again? I looked up, seeing a mistletoe right above us. What the actual fuck was happening. I heard whimpers from Emily, and I softly stroked her head with my fingers. She was in pain, a pain I had caused her. I clenched my teeth, resting my forehead on her head. Her smell of apple and scented candles . . . it was tantalizing. We stood like this for a few minutes, and heck, I wouldn't have minded standing here holding her for hours. But eventually, Little German pulled away, wiping her face. Then, without looking at me, she rushed back inside, leaving me with a warm chest. I finally felt . . . and it wasn't pain.

Chapter 21

The German Way

Emily

Christmas Eve . . .

"EMILY?" PAUL SAID MY NAME FOR THE FIRST TIME SINCE last night, and my grip on my fork tightened. "Yes?"

"Can you pass the chicken, please?" he asked, focusing on his peas.

"Sure," I squeaked, handing him the stupid chicken without looking at him. I slept in my room last night, and we avoided each other all day. When Jon sent me a message saying he was out last night, I thought he was messing with me, and when I saw him . . . I was being controlled from the outside, like those characters in Zack's video games. My brain ordered me to stand still, but my legs headed straight for him. His touch was tender and unexpected, revealing a side of him I had never even in my wildest dreams believed existed. My heart stung when I broke away from him, but if I wanted Paul to forgive me, I couldn't be friends with him any longer.

"How do you like the tomato soup? I tried to do it like you taught me," Henry asked proudly, not even noticing the tension at the dinner table.

I swallowed a spoonful, feeling it burn down my throat. "It's good. Just add a pinch more salt next time."

"Even more? Wouldn't that be too much?"

"Referring to Chef Sayle, there's never enough salt." I forced a smile, and Henry did his usual loud cackle. Paul cut the chicken so forcibly that his cutlery scratched the plate. When he asked me if I hadn't decided who I wanted, I wanted to scream no. But my lips trembled, wanting to make sure I wouldn't lie to him again. A frog built in my throat, and I quickly took a sip of water. I didn't want to like Jon. He was obnoxious and drove me crazy with one breath. There was only yelling and pain with him, not how I envisioned a healthy relationship. Heck, I doubted this boy could even be in a committed relationship. Kiki proved he couldn't. I shook my head—it shouldn't matter. Zack munched on one of the cookies I had baked in Culinary Arts.

"Damn, those are hella good!" he said with crumbs flying out of his mouth.

"Don't talk with your mouth open!" Gena warned and poured herself and Henry some wine. "You want some too, Emily?"

I opened my mouth to say yes, but a shy "No, thank you." escaped my lips. I doubt I could keep my composure if alcohol was involved. Seeing Paul sitting right across from me made it hard to avoid not begging those ocean eyes for another chance. It was quiet for a moment, my toes curling up.

"In Germany, we open presents on Christmas Eve," I shared, feeling still irritated about Americans opening presents on Christmas morning.

Zack made a weird freezing move. "Let's celebrate Christmas the German way! Please, Mom, that would be soo cool! Emily deserves her culture on Christmas, don't you think?" Zack spoke so fast I could feel my pulse rushing up. Henry and Gena looked at each other.

"Yeah, right, because you care about culture now, Zack," Paul mumbled.

"I do!" Zack scratched his neck. "So?"

I shot Gena an I'm-so-sorry-look, but she smiled instead. "I like the idea."

"Let's celebrate the German way!" Henry agreed and jumped up from his seat, closely followed by Zack.

"After dinner." Gena raised a finger with glowing cheeks, either heated up from the soup or wine.

"Oh, man." They both slumped back down on their chairs. I giggled, seeing the same impatient expression in Zack's and Henry's eyes. The apple didn't fall far from the tree. *Does this German saying make sense in English?*

"Then eat faster, especially you, Emily!" Zack glared at me.

"Why, especially me?"

"You're the slowest eater in existence." Zack waved his hand through the air and drew a big circle.

"I hate to say it, but I must agree." Paul chuckled, and my heart skipped a beat when he finally looked at me.

I let out a soft laugh myself. "Okay, okay!"

Paul's eyes were sparkling, the anger from yesterday barely present anymore. I reached for the bottle of wine. "I changed my mind. Can I have some?"

"Of course, honey! It's Christmas!" Gena sang and rushed into the kitchen to return with another glass.

I focused on eating fast to make Zack happy, and about half an hour later, we were all gathered on the couch, handing each other presents. I held my third glass of wine, already feeling it burning my cheeks. I should slow down, but I was enjoying the easiness it handed me. I gave Henry a CD with some German songs. As he had a collection of jazz music, I figured he wouldn't mind another addition. He immediately put it in his old-fashioned CD player, and we spent Christmas Eve listening to NENA and Rammstein. Kinda odd, but hearing those songs made me feel closer to home.

For Gena, I got her a ghost detector. I knew it wouldn't actually work, but considering how many TV shows with ghost hunting she watched, I figured this would make her smile, and it did.

"I'll search through the house with it later!" she squealed. For Zack, I had some paint for his haunted house next year. He took it wordlessly, but I noticed by the sparkle in his eyes—he loved it. Then, he threw me a piece of paper saying, *Three times the zombie slaughtering*. I laughed out loud at this gift but thanked him. Lastly, I reached for the present for Paul. Biting down on my lip, I handed him the neatly wrapped package.

"Thank you, Babycakes." Paul smiled, and I let go of the breath I wasn't aware I was holding. First, he tried to peel off the plastic, but impatiently, like his father and brother, he ripped it off in one move. It was a book about renewable energy systems, focusing on wind turbines. I hadn't seen them in America, and it was a way to produce sustainable energy. In Germany, we had plenty of them. Next to it, I put a little notebook, but not the one that looked like Jon's. That one was sitting in my drawer, already filled with many thoughts. Paul opened it and read what I'd written on the first page.

Never apologize for trying to make this earth a better place.
—Your Babycakes

"Wow ... thank you." He stumbled, his cheeks flushed. I rubbed my cheeks with my sweatshirt sleeves.

"You're into renewable energy?" Gena asked, taking the book out of Paul's hand to look.

"Heck yeah. We only have this one world to live on."

Paul handed me a little box, and I thanked him with a smile. His eyes twitched nervously to the side when I carefully tucked the paper away. I opened it, and my mouth got parched. It was a golden necklace with a pendant in the shape of a heart. I flipped it around, seeing the date we'd met engraved on it. *October 3rd.* Tears gathered in my eyes—I'd never received something this precious from someone before.

"Oh ... Paul, this is too much." I thought he had given up on us, but this was not a gift out of defeat.

"It's not." He shrugged and shot me a smile that made my legs as soft as butter. I handed him the necklace and turned around, and he gently locked it around my neck. I grinned and plastered a big kiss onto his cheek. *We could get through this!*

"Our present is something for you and Paul." Gena gestured at Henry, who got up to get something out of his jacket. Two envelopes, and he gave one to me and one to Paul.

"You already do enough for me. You didn't have to get me a present!" I said, holding the envelope to the side of my head.

"Of course we wanted to get you a present, Emily! You're our daughter." Gena waved me off, and my tears doubled. Paul had already ripped the envelope open and stared at its insides blankly. Henry and Gena looked at me expectantly to do the same. I carefully opened it, ensuring I didn't rip whatever was in it.

"Plane tickets . . ." I swallowed down all the air around me, holding a plane ticket to Germany in my hand. Confused, I looked at them. "You want to get rid of me?"

"Of course not, honey!" Gena startled. "It's just for a week. You'll travel with Paul and Henry to visit your family."

"I-I'm visiting my family . . .?" I stuttered, still looking at the ticket like it was written in another language.

"Yes." Gena looked with worried eyes toward her husband, who just shrugged. Then she turned back to me and grabbed my other hand. "We noticed that you were sad lately, and we can't even imagine how hard it must be for you to not be able to see your family, especially over Christmas, so—"

This is good! I woke up from the shock, jumped up screaming, and stopped her words by pulling her into a tight hug. She pulled me even tighter into her embrace, sighing happily.

"I always meant to travel to Europe. I was all in on that idea," Henry added when we pulled apart again and grinned at me widely. I ran into his arms next. "Thank you, thank you, thank you!" Seeing my family again was exactly what I needed right now. Plus, introduce Paul to my world, like he'd showed me his. He would meet my mom, Pani, my brother! Even finally understand why American beer tasted like pee. I could show him the wind turbines, ask my brother to drive fast with us on the Autobahn, and show him my favorite sunset spot up the hill.

"I got to call my mother!" I sprinted into the hall to get my phone from my room. I went to my recent calls and pressed my mother's number.

"Oh Emily! Frohe Weihnachten!"

"Mama! You won't believe it, but Gena and Henry got me plane tickets to visit you and Lucas over the winter break!" I looked at the tickets again, confirming the dates I had told her. But after looking up, I still hadn't gotten a response from her, except for a gasp.

"Mama?"

"Oh, Emily ..." she then finally said, but not in a happy tone.

"Why are you not screaming out of excitement about this?" My entire body stiffened.

"Lovely, if you leave the United States in your exchange year, your visa will be invalid, and you can't return."

"*What?!*"

I lowered the tickets. I tried to convince my mother for another minute that there must be a way. But she checked the documents, confirming it. If I left now, this would be the end of my exchange year, but I still had six months left.

"If Henry and Paul still want to come, tell them to stay with us! I'm so thankful for them taking you in, and I want to give something back."

My skin shivered ... Paul in Germany without me? And on top of that in my place? That was too absurd.

"I doubt they will still go, but I'll offer it to them."

With hanging shoulders, I returned to the living room, searching for Paul and his comfort, but he wasn't there anymore.

"I've got bad news." I explained to Gena and Henry that I couldn't go. They apologized a trillion times that they should've done their research and were incredibly sorry. I told them it was not their fault, and them wanting to make this come true for me counted. I found Paul sitting on the bed in the basement, still peeking at his ticket.

"I have bad news."

"Already heard. You can't go ..." he mumbled, not looking up.

I sat beside him, placing my head on his shoulder. "Words can't even describe how disappointed I am."

I expected him to wrap me in his embrace, but he remained tense.

I pulled away from him. "Paul?"

He tilted his head. "Ever since I met you, I've wanted to visit Germany."

"I know." My disappointment doubled.

"I think I would still like to go." His voice was hesitant but decided.

I swallowed my spit and coughed. I hadn't expected him to want to do this without me, but then again, this was an opportunity I wouldn't want him to miss because of me. He deserved it.

"I will miss you . . ." I sighed, knowing I couldn't be selfish right now. "But yeah, you should go. It's only a week, I'll be fine."

He didn't say anything and stared at me gently.

"Please give Pani many cuddles from me!" I tried lightening the mood, but Paul lifted his hand and softly stroked my chin. I smiled at him, but it vanished when I noticed the glistening in his eyes. "Paul, is everything okay?"

He remained stoic, with his look magnetized to mine.

"I want you to try and understand, okay?" he whispered, a sickening feeling spreading in my stomach.

"Understand what?"

He got up and took the fireplace equipment to peek into the ashes from last night. "I think having this time apart will be good."

"What are you talking about?" My heart was beating so fast I feared it could crash out of my chest.

"You and me . . ." He sighed, stabbing harsher into the leftover wood. It tore into pieces. "I think it's best if we take a break."

A break . . .?

"I thought we were fine . . . you gave me this necklace!" I fumbled with the necklace around my neck.

"Emily." Paul put down the equipment and blanketed his hands over mine. "I think there are some things we should both figure out for ourselves. Take some time to think, some distance." He swallowed, now looking away again. "And that only works if we're not together."

"You're breaking up with me . . .?" I whispered. Paul bit his lip, his eyes focusing on the plane ticket still on his sheets.

"Just taking a break."

"It's because of Jon, isn't it?" I pulled my hands away from him with a trembling heart, flying to my feet. I ran my fingers through my hair, feeling hot tears burning away my mascara. I couldn't lose him.

"How often do I have to tell you I made a choice!" I grabbed his hands, begging him to believe me. He looked down at our locked hands and furrowed his brows. "You never told me, Emily."

I pulled my hands away and pressed them onto my mouth to swallow my gasps. I really didn't.

"I . . . I want you. I really do . . ." I pressed out between my fingers, but my heart made a double beat.

"You don't know how much I want to believe you . . . but your mouth is saying one thing while your eyes are telling a whole other story."

Paul planted a soft kiss on my forehead and left the room. I cowered on the ground, feeling like screaming, crying, and laughing simultaneously.

I sprinted upstairs into my room, ripped open the nightstand drawer with trembling hands, and pulled out a little plastic bag that carried one pill.

"The effect isn't strong, except combined with alcohol. Then it's a killer and will make you forget everything."

And without further thought, I swallowed it down, relieved I'd had three glasses of wine.

Chapter 22

Ugly Truth

Paul
Christmas. . .

I GRABBED MY BIG SUITCASE OUT OF THE ATTIC. IT WAS ALL DUSTY; the last time I used it was . . . heck, about three years ago when my family went on a trip to California? My chest thudded when I pulled the plane ticket out of the envelope. The idea of crossing that damn ocean made me lose it. And not because I would see the world; I was electrified to discover where Emily was from. To find out what she had secreted there. I dropped the suitcase on my bed. When I heard her telling my parents she couldn't go . . . damn, I wanted to yell at the American border rules. I wanted to meet her parents with her by my side. To become a part of her family, like I made her a piece of mine. To experience all of this while taking time out from what troubled us the most.

I threw sweatshirts, jeans, underwear, and socks into my suitcase. I debated on holding off until we could visit Germany in the summer together, but when I saw her enter the basement, I realized we'd be going in circles if I stayed. Last night, it repeated again. After finding it too slippery for a run, I cruised around in my car. When I came back soothed, I spotted Jon staring at the house. I parked at enough distance so he wouldn't notice me and waited. Shit, he stood there for such a long time, and I was about to go to him because my body was turning into an ice sculpture. Then he headed for the door, and when Emily stepped out and ran into his embrace like he was her savior or some shit, it hit me. I was far from being the only one in her heart. I grabbed the book Emily had given me last night and placed it above my clothes. Last night, I had distracted myself with it, and I only had a few chapters left. I would give them until the end of this year, during which I wouldn't stand in their way. When I returned, if she still wanted to be with me . . . Heck, I would gladly let go of all my grudges and drive into the sunset with her. But if she wanted to be with him . . . no, he would fuck up again. No way she would want to be with him after getting to know how he truly was. I harshly pulled the stuck zipper, almost breaking this old thing. I slumped on the bed, my stomach turning at the possibility of him doing something right for a change.

"Paul?"

Emily peeked around the corner like a scared mouse, but I didn't feel like the cat with the upper hand . . . I felt like the cheese.

"Yeah?" My muscles stiffened. *Please don't come closer. . .*

Her perfume wafted up my nose as I breathed in to gather my strength. I just had to get through today, into the car, to the airport, onto the plane. A week was nothing compared to the life after. Slowly, I allowed myself to look at her, and my breath shook. She looked terrible. Her skin was greasy and her eyes bright red, surrounded by a dark shadow. She was still in her pajamas, even though it was 2 pm. I jumped up.

"What happened to you?"

"You happened." She sucked in her lower lip, chewing on it while her eyes focused on my packed suitcase. I breathed in deeply and took a step back.

"This doesn't mean I don't love you, Emily. I'm hurting as much as you are." *Probably even more.*

"Oh really?!" She shot me a glare, her arms shooting down into fists. "Have you cried your eyes out all night?! No! It was me! I was willing to fight through this because I believe in us, while you—" She paced around the room, searching for the words. "While all you do is run away!"

She slapped me with those words. *Doesn't she understand at all why we have to do this?*

"I'm not running away."

"Then why do you want to take this break?! You're meeting my family now! That's not something to do when you're on a break or whatever this is!"

"We need this." I cursed through gritted teeth.

"I don't! It's you! You're being selfish!" She stomped on the ground with her left foot, fists flying through the air.

"Me being selfish?!" I raised my voice as well. I was anything but selfish. I was giving her this chance to figure out her fucking feelings, no matter how much I disliked her getting closer to him.

"Yes! Otherwise, you wouldn't want this for whatever reason!"

My chest flared with heat. "I can't believe how naive you're being right now!"

"Naive?!"

It was like a mirror had crashed into a million pieces as she looked at me with an evilness I didn't even think was possible.

"Sorry, you're not being naive . . . You're just. . . not getting it." I quickly tried to take it back, but it was too late.

"And you know why I don't?! Because you never talk to me about how you feel!" Emily poked her finger into my chest. "You always run or pretend like nothing happened. My mother always kept quiet instead of confronting my father. I won't make the same mistake as her!"

I caught my breath. This was the first time she'd ever mentioned her father. Countless times I wanted to ask, but I never did because I didn't want to push her into talking about something she might not be ready to. I didn't like talking about negative feelings, but that didn't mean I didn't care about them.

"I don't want you to make that mistake either."

"I . . ." She stumbled, suddenly lost for words herself. "Thank you."

We both turned quiet, and I sat back down on the bed, my shoulders turned in.

"Can I be entirely honest with you? No matter how ugly the truth is?"

She nodded quickly, sitting down on the bed next to me. "That's all I ever wanted."

I took a minute to think about how to rip off the bandage without sabotaging myself. I steeled my voice and turned toward her.

"I need this time off for myself, and I don't even care if this makes me selfish. I feel like I can't trust you anymore. I'm constantly wondering when you're not with me if you're with him. And knowing you were . . . it makes me hate you a little. I need to know I'm the person you truly want."

I said it. A part of me was filled with hate toward her and Jon . . . and especially toward myself. I didn't want to feel like this anymore. I needed a break.

"I understand." She gulped but didn't say anything more, which I appreciated.

"Now you," I instructed her. She stared at the ceiling for a few minutes.

"The other night . . ." She wiped her eyes. "When we almost did, you know what . . . I said I'd had a dream about this before."

I focused hard on keeping my face stoic.

"But the truth is . . . it wasn't with you. It was with Jon."

My chest tightened, and my hearing faded to a muffled sound. When I thought I couldn't feel worse, *fuck,* I was wrong. I tried gasping for air, but my throat was blocked.

"Everyone kept telling me to stay away from him. I even told myself, but he . . ." Emily whined, looking at me with puffy eyes. "He drives me mad. I can't stand him."

Air floated back into my lungs. "If you can't stand him, why do you care about him?"

She pressed her palms onto her face. "I don't know. I somehow like how he annoys me."

"You like that he pisses you off?" I tried my best to keep calm, while inside a war tortured my head.

She shook her head. "I can't explain it."

I flared my nostrils. I'd tried everything in my power to build her up. Heck, I even invited her to live with my family. *But now it's him who she dreamed about?*

I stood up, ready to escape this situation, but she grabbed me. "But with you, I feel safe, appreciated, happy. That's why I chose you. You're good for me."

I swallowed down the urge to grab and kiss her. All she saw was herself right now. I didn't just want to be the one she wanted. I wanted to be the *only* one she wanted.

"But you aren't good for me, Emily." I pulled my hand away from hers and gave her one last look. "At least, not right now . . ."

I picked up my suitcase and walked out of the room. That wasn't the Christmas I expected to have, but we would make up for it next year. I was sure of that.

Chapter 23

Who Knocks Out First?

Jon
Christmas. . .

I WAS RUNNING LATE, AS USUAL. I ROLLED MY EYES, PULLED DOWN my beanie, and swiped the frozen snow off my leather jacket. I should switch to my winter jacket; it was getting colder with each day. I inhaled my square sharply, sucking at it until I was almost at the filter. I flipped it away on the street as I heard a man's rasp. Yet I didn't flinch. "Jon, we've been waiting for you."

Humphrey smiled at me with his icy eyes, and I immediately got chills. He put me off more than I liked with his full white hair and the perfect toothpaste smile. He looked at where I threw the stub onto the street and wrinkled his nose. "You should stop smoking."

I ground my teeth. Humphrey threw the first punch. He reminded me on every occasion that I wasn't a good son. I wanted to fire back, saying at least I didn't show up high, but for some reason, I didn't. For my sister's sake and my mother's . . . and I was simply not in the fucking mood for a fight.

"Merry Christmas," I grumbled instead.

"Right . . ." He sucked in some air. "Merry Christmas, Jon."

One point for me. Maybe there did lie some truth in the stupid saying to kill people with kindness.

I strolled through the hall until I heard him rasp again. With my fingers pressed into my wrist, I turned around. "What now?"

"Please take your shoes off, Jon."

I looked down at my shoes. They were covered in mud and melted snow. I took them off wordlessly, and he pointed to slippers. "Those are my extra pair of house shoes. You can—"

"No." I tried to contain a laugh. Me wearing those ugly-looking shoes wouldn't even happen on my worst day.

"The floor is cold."

"I don't care." I glared this time. This man was never used to hearing no. I assumed it was one of the countless reasons I didn't get along with him. This time, I was getting my way, but I didn't feel I had made a point. It was still even.

After walking wordlessly through this big-ass house, we finally arrived in the dining room. My mother and sister were already seated, and I had to smile when Lauren jumped up, squealing to welcome me. Her dress slipped to the side, revealing the top of a pink bra. My brows furrowed. Why was she showing her cleavage!

"You're late, Jon." My mother looked up from her plate, her overdrawn eyebrows pinched together. She had put in the extra effort today. Her hair was tightly arranged into a low bun. None of her black hair stuck out anywhere. She wore glittering diamonds around her neck as if they had been her best friends for her entire life.

I let out a sharp breath through my nose. "I can leave again."

I hated her pretending she didn't use to be the same fuck-up as I was. Sure, she'd pulled herself out of it—I gave her credit for that—but it had taken her years, decades even. She should cut me some slack.

"You made it!" Lauren swung her arms around me and placed her head on my chest like she always did when we were younger. I would definitely have to talk with her about her outfit choice and warn her not to trust older boys.

"Hey, Jon. It's good to see you again."

I look to the side. Frederick—or as I liked to call him,

Fuckerick—gave me the same toothpaste smile as his father. With his dimples and shiny red hair, I wondered how his father changed his type to the darker look of my mother.

"You too," I lied, aware if I said one bad word to him, he would have me in handcuffs again for police assault like the first time we met. You can imagine how he looked at me when I got introduced as his stepbrother. I didn't start this shit, though. He'd pushed me onto the car's hood out of nowhere.

Steve walked back in with a giant goose on a silver platter. "Let's eat!"

We ate in peace at the huge table for a few minutes, talking about my sister's latest art project and her teacher's praise for it. About Fuckerick's latest case, in which he rescued an old lady from a robbery, leaving out asking me how school was going because they knew I barely made it to junior year. I would give this about 45 minutes before I could make a run for it.

"Jon, why don't you take off your beanie? It's impolite to keep it on," my mom tried whispering—impossible as she sat on the other side of the table. Everyone stared directly at me.

I scrunched the meat between my teeth. "Sure."

I took it off, wiping one long curl off my forehead.

"What happened to your eye?!" Lauren screeched and instantly covered her mouth. Humphrey and Jackson wrinkled their noses as they looked at me with disgust. Fuck, I had forgotten my eye was still swollen and shining in a bright purple. My mom looked straight at her plate.

"Hit a pole," I mumbled and swiped my curl above it again.

"Jon, if you're in trouble with some people . . . You know I can help as I'm the police commissioner in this town." Humphrey gave me a too-kind nod.

I balled my fist around my silverware. Not only was his son a policeman, but he was the one running this town's circus. It had brought me many issues when Marna and Ted discovered my new stepfather was the police chief.

"I don't think you can arrest a pole," I growled. He hit me close to a knockout.

"Jon—"

"I said I'm fine!" I shot up my feet, my silverware clattering on my plate. My mother clutched her hands against her chest and took a sharp breath, and my sister bit nervously on her lip. Frederick let his eyes wander all over me, as if he was preparing to tackle me if I made one false move.

"Jon, sit down," Humphrey commanded, and a bitter taste spread in my mouth. I looked at my sister, who mouthed *please* to me. If it weren't for her, I wouldn't have come tonight. I drew a deep breath while slowly lowering myself down again. I should've taken something. I could even feel the blood pulsing through my veins.

Humphrey darted at me, "It's clear this wasn't a pole. We know you've been going through a phase, and we wanted to use tonight to—"

I was on my feet again, throwing my napkin onto my plate. They couldn't even wait till dessert. "Sorry, Lauren, but I can't do this."

"Please listen to us. We all care about you and want the best for you," Lauren pleaded. I stumbled back. Lauren knew about this attack? *You've got to be fucking kidding me!* I reached into my back pocket, pulling out the envelope with her Christmas gift and the money for our mother's present. I had gotten her two tickets for the St. Louis Art Museum. It would've been nice to drive there with her for some quality sibling time, but screw this.

"Ask Frederick if he'll go there with you instead." I threw the envelope at her and dashed out of the room.

"Jon, wait!" I could hear her chair pull back.

"Let him go, honey. This is not the right time."

But my mother's gentle voice stopped her from following me. I was glad she did. I was willing to hurt anyone who came too close to me in this mood. Outside, I immediately lit up a square and sucked at it multiple times as snow poured on me at full speed. I kicked the garbage can until the trash scattered over the ground.

"Fuuuck!" I screamed, having only the echo of the night answering me.

I reached into my pocket. My stash was empty, and I didn't even get any Christmas money. Quickly, I searched my contacts for Marna.

"You up?"

"For you? Always," she exhaled heavily into the speaker.

"I'll be at your place in ten. I need a refill. But I don't have any money at the moment."

"I know plenty of other ways for you to pay." Marna giggled into the phone and hung up. I had reached a new low point.

Chapter 24

Christmas Miracle

Emily

Christmas . . .

"See you in a week," Paul said with his puppy eyes look that used to make me smile but now made me shiver. When the door shut, I wanted to run after him and scream again that we didn't need this break, but I watched the car pull out of the driveway instead. My nails dug into my palms to not break down on the spot. Paul had been a gentleman. From holding open doors, walking outside the pathway so I could be secure on the inside, showering me with kisses, backrubs . . . or watching hours of a show he didn't genuinely enjoy. He had placed me on the highest pedestal, putting my needs before his while I . . . I swallowed so hard that this pressure built in my throat, and I pulled the blanket over my head. While I kept thinking about his best friend.

It had been five hours since he hugged me goodbye to leave with Henry for the airport. Gena had driven with Zack to her mother's for a few days. She asked me if I wanted to come along, but I told her I wasn't feeling well. That wasn't a lie because I felt sick all day and was sleepy. Tied-to-the-bed sleepy. But I definitely had other reasons than me being under the weather. She was close to canceling, but I stopped her because

I knew how much she missed her mother. They left after she brought me soup, tea, and her friend's contact to call if I needed anything. But now I was alone . . . the voices grew louder, and when I did manage to drift off to sleep, I dreamed about the last few months and every mistake I made, each time waking up covered in sweat and sobs coming out of my personal hell. A sob tore from my throat—I didn't want to feel like this anymore. I sat up and dialed the only number I knew had the power to make this stop.

I let it ring about ten times before jumping out of my bed. *I won't let him ban me out of his life as well!* He was the person who'd brought me into this mess—the least he could do now was to help me deal with it. I grabbed a grey sweatshirt and fluffy socks. Keys. Parka. Boots. A special key chain. When I stepped outside, I didn't even care that the snow crashed onto my forehead. It was a ten-minute walk until I could finally feel nothing again. I knew he had more of these pink devil pills.

A ten-minute walk turned into twenty because the wind was whipping my face, and I took a wrong turn a couple of times—I had relied too much on Paul when it came to orientation. I finally found myself in Jon's front yard with blue lips and numb fingers. My socks were soaked from the snow seeping into my boots. I rang the doorbell, but no one opened up. My shoulders slumped. The storm had increased. Frustrated, I pushed down the handle, experiencing my little Christmas miracle. The door opened silently, and I slipped inside. The trust Americans had in their neighbors still astonished me—Germans always locked their doors. My boots were dirty, so I took them and my soaked socks off. Tim wasn't involved in this mess, and I wouldn't let him be the one who had to clean it up. I made my way to Jon's basement door, but then I heard Christmas music from the kitchen.

"Jon?" I shrieked. Motivated by the craving thumping through my veins, I rushed to the kitchen. But my motivation crumbled the second I saw Tim standing at the stove, cooking and singing into a spoon.

"Laaaast Christmas, I gave you my heart!"

It smelled like I had walked into a Christmas factory. Even though the kitchen was small, it was decorated with a Christmas wreath on the table, topped with cinnamon sticks and red candy apples. The candles were almost burned to the end, giving off a sweet scent. Above me was a mistletoe branch, and a whimper escaped my throat, thinking about how Paul and I hung one up together. I covered my mouth with my hands to not let out more sobs, but Tim had already swirled around.

"Holy crap, *Little German*?!"

I swallowed harshly. "Hi . . ."

He dropped the spoon and turned down the speakers. "What are you doing here?"

"I, um . . . I'm so sorry. I, um, I will . . ." I pointed down the hall, going backward.

"Hold on. You aren't looking well." He pulled a chair away from the table. "C'mon, have a seat."

I debated on what to do for a second. The storm had worsened. If I went back out there, I could already picture the headline. *German exchange student found frozen to death due to lack of orientation.* Sitting down sounded like the better option. Carefully, I placed myself on the wooden chair.

"It's Emily, right? Sorry for calling you Little German, but that's what Jon always calls you." He shot me a smile, and I accidentally bit my tongue. *Jon talks about me with his father?*

"Both names are fine." I tried to smile back, but my cheeks were still frozen, and it hurt.

"Then I will call you Little German as well," he said, letting out a soft laugh. "You want some tea? You look like you almost froze to death out there."

I nodded quickly, and he got out a teakettle and poured in some water.

"Why were you out in the cold? Aren't you celebrating Christmas with the Shields?" he asked while turning on the stove.

"I did last night. They left today."

"They left you alone on Christmas?" He sat down, pressing his chin back. "I don't understand . . . the Gena and Henry I know are caring people."

"They are!" I quickly added. "Henry flew with Paul to Germany. They had gotten me a ticket to come with them, but my visa would expire if I left, so I didn't. Gena drove down to her mother with Zack. I could've gone with them, but I—"

"But you were too sad because you missed home," Tim interrupted.

"Yes." I studied my red hands, trying to understand how I'd ended up talking to the father of my boy—*ex-boyfriend? Break boyfriend? Ugh, I don't know*—Paul's best friend.

"Well, Jon isn't here at the moment. He's at his mother's house." Tim got up to put the by-now boiling water into a cup.

"Oh . . ." I fiddled with my hands. I couldn't sneak down in the basement searching for pills . . . *or maybe I could?*

"Looks like dinner is almost ready." Tim beamed, taking out plates.

"I'm sorry for bothering you. I'll go so you can enjoy your Christmas." I stumbled up again, intending to get to Jon's room, but Tim crossed his arms.

"Gena would make me a head shorter if I let you go out there again. Plus, I made food for three anyway, and I don't mind company."

"You were about to eat alone?" I gave in, sitting back down.

"Yes. Though I expect Jon to be back soon."

He pointed at the cup, and I quickly clasped my fingers around it. The burn from the heat hurt a bit, but it was comforting. Tim got up again to stir some pots, drawing a little spoon through the sauce for a taste check.

"Perfect. It has a slight touch of cinnamon, just how I like it for Christmas." He turned to me again. "I hope you like cinnamon?"

I nodded, but a wave of sadness overcame me, picturing Tim eating this love-made food by himself. A picture I was kinda used to from my father though . . .

My parents divorced when I was twelve. My father's and my relationship wasn't the best. I only spent the second Christmas day with him, Christmas Eve, and the first day with my mother, brother, and . . . her boyfriend, Richard. I shuddered, even though hot tea flushed down my throat.

"So you said Jon's coming back soon? Is it because he knows you're cooking as well?" I tried to distract myself from the fact that Paul would meet him.

"You're curious. Exactly like Jon has told me," Tim said, and I sank a bit in my chair. *Gosh, I have to stop being nosy.*

"I'm sorry, this is not my business."

"I don't mind, but my cooking isn't the reason," Tim reassured me and filled the plates with potatoes, beef, veggies, and a brown sauce. He sighed as he placed the dishes on the table.

"It looks delicious!" I told him, deciding not to dig further into his family life.

"Thank you, Little German." Tim grinned proudly and handed me some silverware. "There's nothing more comforting than home-cooked food."

"Definitely." My stomach growled. I hadn't eaten anything all day.

"Guten Appetit," I said in an instant. It's something we said each time before we ate in Germany. I had taught it the Shields when I'd moved in with them. Tim gave me a confused look. "Um, eat well, I meant!"

"No, please repeat it so I can learn it. I always wanted to learn some German." Tim took his first bite.

"Alright, so basically, before dinner, we say Guten Appetit. It's an unspoken rule."

"Guuuutn Appiti?" Tim imitated me with a heavy accent that made me laugh out loud.

"Almost!" I giggled and cut the potato on my plate to fit my mouth, but I struggled to swallow it as if my body was still resisting food. Tim continued asking me word after word. He reminded me a lot about Gena, wanting me to teach her the most random words.

"Okay, so those ööö's and äää's are impossible to say!" Tim defended, slumped back in his chair, rubbing his full belly.

"Yeah, they're the elite regarding German pronunciation," I joked, my plate still more than half filled.

"Öööööööö!" Tim almost sang, and I nearly choked on my beef because I had to laugh.

"What the fuck is going on here?!" Jon's voice surprised me; this time, I literally choked. Trying to suppress the coughs, I turned on my chair. Jon stood there, all wet, like a tortured dog. Tim hopped up and handed me a cup of water when my coughing worsened. I sipped on it consciously, feeling Jon's stare at me.

"Little German was teaching me some German words," Tim announced to his son proudly.

"I could hear," Jon remarked, but I still didn't dare to look at him. I put down the glass with shaking hands.

"You want some food? We still have some left," Tim offered and gestured at the empty chair next to me. My eyes traveled to Jon, who flinched when our looks connected.

"Actually, some food sounds good." He hesitantly pulled the chair next to me and sat down. Tim cocked his head at me but smiled even brighter. "A Christmas miracle."

"Oh, shut up." Jon rolled his eyes at him, his palm pressed flatly onto the table.

"Gutin Apppetit." Tim handed him a plate.

"You're trying to make my father annoy me with German as well?" Jon cringed, being his typical grumpy self, but I could see how a genuine grin fought itself to the cold surface.

"Little German told me about Culinary Arts and your chef!" Tim pitched in.

"He wants me to make everything way too fucking salty," Jon replied with a full mouth. He ate so fast I was afraid he didn't even chew.

"Hm." I shrugged.

"What, hm?" Jon paused, his fork in the air, typical glare on.

"Nothing. I just didn't expect you to have any issues with salt." I shrugged again, and Tim coughed out the sip he was about to swallow.

Jon eyes me for a second. "So do you pour sugar in whatever you cook?"

My cheeks grew warm, and not because of the candlelight. Tim didn't notice and got up to refill his plate. When water from Jon's hair dropped onto his plate, he rubbed it out of his face. I accidentally dropped the fork I had still held even though I had stopped eating. His eye had gotten bad, shining in purple, green, and yellow. My toes curled. Jon noticed my reaction and quickly placed his hair over his eye again, and then he gave me a warning look before he looked at his father. I nodded and bit my lower lip.

"That was one of the happiest Christmas dinners I've had in a long time," Jon said as we walked down the steps into his basement. I wasn't sure if he was serious or being sarcastic.

"Oh really?" I said, but Jon didn't reply. He fell onto one of the couches. I carefully sat down on the armchair as far away as possible. *We're just friends.*

"I don't get why you're here." Jon shook his head. But I noticed his hazed look—Jon was high, and high Jon was usually more kind than sober Jon. I sighed, resting my body on the chair.

"I don't know how this happened either," I whispered into the cold basement.

"You fucking confuse me."

"Ditto," I admitted, and my skin shivered, seeing his bruised skin again. "I'm sorry about your eye . . ." I forced myself to look at it, but my eyes squeezed oddly.

"I deserved it, didn't I?"

I shook my head so fast that my view got blurry. "No, you didn't."

Jon rolled his eyes and changed the topic. "So you wanna tell me why I walked in on you and my father having a Christmas dinner? You secretly dating or some shit?"

I fiddled with the ends of my hair. I couldn't be up-front and ask about pills. Instead, I reached into my parka and pulled out the gift I had bought for Jon. It was a key chain with a pen and a flame thingy dangling on it.

"I know it's nothing special. I saw it at Target, and I thought of you."

"It's not from the Dollar Tree?" Jon muttered.

"No," I pouted. "But if you don't want it—"

"No, please give it to me."

We both leaned forward, and Jon took it into his hand, analyzing it.

"I don't understand why this reminded you of me?" he asked.

"I noticed you're always scribbling in that black book and asking others for a pen. Now there's one you will always have with you," I explained, feeling stupid to think he would appreciate something like this. His eyes shot up to me, his mouth parting. And then he smiled from one ear to the other. He looked so cute—*No, he can't be cute!*

"Thank you, Little German." Jon got out his keys to put the chain onto it. My chest relaxed.

After smiling at it for another second, he headed to a drawer and pulled out something wrapped up in newspaper. My heart did a double flip.

"Sorry, I didn't have anything else to wrap it in." He handed me the bundle, and I hesitated to take it.

"You got me a present?" I gaped.

He shrugged one shoulder. "I didn't exactly search for it." He rubbed his arm, his eyes twitching to the side. Jon Henry fucking Denson got me a present. I carefully unstuck the tape and pulled out something red and fluffy.

"A beanie!" I held it up in the air with a grin. "Thank you, Jon."

I immediately put it on and rushed to the mirror in his bathroom. I couldn't believe Jon had remembered how much my ears always froze. This wasn't just any gift . . . it was a precisely considered one.

"It suits you." Jon smiled when I returned, and my entire chest burst into flames. I cleared my throat and took it off, returning back to the armchair. I had to remember what I'd come here for. But Jon looked so happy. I couldn't. . .

"I should go!" I squealed and rushed up the stairs without a reply. I had done it again, found a reason to see him, but forgot my reason while with him. I couldn't let Paul be right. I had to find another way to stop this trembling in my chest.

"Little German, wait!"

I heard him coming after me, but he took twice as long as I did. He was full-blown high right now—a state I craved myself.

He tried grabbing my shoulder, but I shuffled away. "Don't touch me!"

He backed off, confused, for a good reason. Now it was me who was acting hot and cold.

"What's going on, Emily?" He said my name, and the air pulled out of my lungs again.

"Nothing," I stammered, my eyes twitching to the kitchen door to make sure Tim wouldn't walk in on us.

"It's not nothing. You're at my place at freaking Christmas. What about Paul? His parents? Shouldn't you be singing Christmas songs while baking cookies or some shit?" He lifted my chin with his thumb. "Hey, you can talk to me."

My lips trembled hard, and my throat turned entirely dry. His thumb made small movements over my chin, and I had to fight to not close my eyes. *It's now or never.*

"C-can you give me more pills?" My fingers clutched the beanie, and Jon took away his hand.

"*What?*" He spoke so loudly that Tim could've heard it anywhere in this house. I covered my face with my hands, embarrassed I had asked him that question.

"You took the pill!" Jon paced back and forth. "You're here because you want more! Not because you wanted to see me!"

I bit my lip; seeing him was an extra, but it wasn't what made me wander through a snowstorm. I tried opening my mouth, but no words came out.

Jon stopped his pacing in front of me again. "Why?"

I swallowed even more harshly, and the words fell out of my mouth before I could catch them. "Paul broke up with me."

Jon's face froze, and he stared at me.

"Hello?" I waved my hand in front of him.

"Please tell me I had nothing to do with it," he blurted out, and I turned around to grab my parka.

"You know the answer to that question," I breathed, feeling my eyes burning as fresh tears built in them. I had to get away from him.

"Fuck!" He slammed his fist against the wall.

I twirled back around. "Sh! Your father!"

"Fuck, fuck, fuck . . ." But Jon kept cursing, walking in circles.

I drew in a breath, motivated by last night's feelings. "So, can you help me out with some pills?"

"I don't have any," he growled and came to a halt.

"Of course you do! You're always high. There's no way you would run out of anything." I stomped on the ground.

"Shit, I'm not your drug supply, Little German!" He pointed a daring finger at me. "Plus, this shit won't help you. It will only make it worse!"

"Then why are you depending on it like oxygen if it's so bad, huh?!" I provoked, not breaking his stare.

"It's different with me."

"It's not!"

"Fuck, yes, it is!" Jon came so close that our chests almost touched. "It's not too late for you to stop this shit now!"

I laughed at his hypocrisy. I was tired of people expecting me to be better than them.

"Fine, then don't help me with this." I shoved him away, slipped into my shoes, and dashed out the door. The darkness swallowed me up within seconds, and I could only pray I wouldn't get lost on the streets again.

Chapter 25

Welcome to Narnia

Paul

As we taxied to the gate, people immediately stood up, clutching their carry-on luggage, and waited in cramped positions to get off the plane. My father and I looked at each other funny but rested comfortably in our seats. My foot hurt terribly when I got up. Like too much exertion, too little could cause it to hurt. The doctors warned me that even though they'd tried to stabilize it with screws, it would remain a bit broken forever.

My father yawned out loud as we strolled through the airport's halls. He had snored into my ear the entire flight while my brain rumbled more than the aircraft itself. Yet, I was wide-awake because I had landed in freaking Europe. We were 7 hours ahead of the time now, the morning sun bashing through the windows of this airport. I watched suitcase after suitcase slide by, but my breath got shorter with each passing. I inhaled so much air my chest almost traveled below my chin. I was in freaking Germany, with my father, not with Emily, about to meet her mother, her brother . . . the life she knew before me.

"There it is!" Dad's as always exciting voice slapped me back into motion. I grabbed my suitcase, knowing there was no return, not after an eight-hour flight halfway across the globe.

Wordlessly, Dad and I made our way through the airport, following the crowd, as the signs written in German were no help. We passed some federal policemen that looked like they hadn't slept in days, and then my focus shifted to a woman standing by the exit of the building. She panted, resting her palms on her knees as if she had been running. She spotted us and waved, causing her swarthy hair to twirl from side to side. I held tighter onto my suitcase—*that's Emily's mother.*

"I can't say why, but she looks exactly like Emily!" Dad cackled and quickened his step while I remained in his shadow. The prominent features showed no way she was her mother; even her eyes shined in a darker color, but it was apparent from how she carried herself. Her roundish cheeks lifted up her entire face, expressing warmth and kindness, smiling exactly how my Babycakes did. My heart burned as I got closer to this woman that was a stranger but gave me a vibe like I'd met her before. "You must be Paul," she said with a heavy accent after greeting my father. I extended my hand, but she pulled me into a hug. "I'm Susanne. I'm happy to meet you!"

"Es freeeut mih Siie kennen zu leernen." I tried to say *It's nice to meet you* in German, one of the few lines I had learned in those sleepless hours on the flight.

"Sehr gut!" *Very good!* She chuckled. "You two hungry? Emily said plane food not good."

Susanne used common words, and I realized how advanced Emily was at speaking English. She asked for a word here and there, but in only five months, she'd become so fluent I sometimes forgot English wasn't her native language. Her accent had slowly faded too, which saddened me as I liked it.

"Starving!" Dad expressed when I still stared at Susanne like I was a goldfish. *Ugh, why am I so uptight?*

"Great. I prepared Currywurst!" Susanne trilled, patting my shoulder.

"Currywurst..?" Dad repeated, and we followed her out of the airport.

In the car, my father and Susanne did most of the talking. She sighed a few times when describing a word instead of using it, but I was impressed. I was in her country, yet she communicated with me in my language. I should've started learning German way sooner.

"Emily made me this CD with German songs!" Dad rambled on.

"Ohh!" Susanne giggled, but I could see her clutching her chest right after. She missed her daughter, I knew, because I already missed her too. With my phone pressed tightly, I let my gaze fall out of the window. I wanted to let Emily know I'd landed and was experiencing the Autobahn for the first time. The cars swooshed by us, going at a speed I had never seen before. I exhaled, shoving my phone back into my pocket. This week was supposed to be a break from communication. Plus, Susanne didn't drive as fast. I wasn't sure if it was her driving style or because she didn't want to scare us with this cultural difference because—

Hold on! Was that . . . I looked back out of the window. There were those turbines, turning and twirling from the wind. The ones from the book Emily gave me. They were taller than a ten-floor house, impressive and solid. I fell back in my seat. *I was in freaking Germany.*

"Welcome to our home." Susanne fiddled with keys as she slid them into a red wooden door of a half-timbered house. I'd only seen places like this in movies before, large white squares framed with black trim. It was something almost witchlike.

"It's not big, and Richard, um . . . collects. I'm sorry for chaos." She opened the door with her shoulders turned in. Emily had mentioned Richard's name once, so I knew he was her mother's boyfriend. *That's it.* I wasn't aware he was living with them. We walked into an inner courtyard. Christmas decorations were scattered wherever you looked, but not like the ones we used in America. Those were more subtle. Little fairy lights with tiny sparkles. Pine branches. Candles and a star made out of woven wood. I could tell this was put together with lots of love and care.

"I tried making it Christmas." Susanne smiled at the little lights, which lit up this cloudy, cold day with no snow. Then she turned to face us. "But it didn't feel like Christmas without her."

I immediately nodded, knowing exactly what she meant. Dad stared at everything as if he had entered Narnia.

"Wow!" he gushed. "This place is awesome!"

Susanne giggled at his positive reaction, and I could tell her body relaxed by her neck growing longer. "I'm glad. Come inside."

We crossed another red door, and I was almost afraid to straighten my body because the ceiling was only a few inches above my head. I looked around and knew what Susanne meant about Richard collecting things. Books covered every surface on the wall. There were even stacks on the floor in front of the shelves. Next to the shoe rack were cowboy boots that barely left enough room to walk through the hall. Bows and arrows were squeezed into another corner, and this was only the entrance. This place had potential, but it was so crowded I could hardly breathe.

"Oh!" my father expressed, more stunned this time. "Those are a lot of books."

I looked at him, shaking my head with a pressed-together mouth.

"You like reading?" he asked Susanne, not getting the hint.

"I do." Susanne sighed while taking off her coat.

"But she can't match my reading pace." A man in a bent posture stepped through the door. His hair was faint, already wholly white. He wore a grey turtleneck shirt and glasses that blurred his eyes. "It's so nice to meet you, Paul and Henry. I'm Richard, Susanne's significant other." He waved and articulated with a charming undertone. His English was flawless. He greeted Dad with a handshake and held out his hand for mine. I looked at it, baffled, before my eyes wandered to meet his. He crooked his head a little when I didn't immediately follow his gesture.

"Hello, thank you for letting us stay at your place."

"Of course! Emily is like my own daughter."

I pulled my hand away from him, feeling this cold shudder. *How come your own daughter didn't even mention you?*

"Come on, Susanne has prepared her famous Currywurst. It's delicious," Richard coaxed and threw Susanna a smile at which she blushed like a little child. I couldn't deny this weird taste I had in my mouth. Something was off.

After having my third Currywurst, I understood why it was famous.

It was a taste I'd never closely experienced before. I would need to ask Susanne for the recipe and surprise Emily by making it.

Richard had been going forth and back, challenging Dad to a historic battle.

"The Investiture Controversy from the 11th and 12th century—" He lost me there, the jet lag kicking in.

Emily told me about the stereotype that many Germans believed Americans sucked at history and geography. The way Richard talked to us, it was obvious he was one of them. I snorted out loud when he asked us if we knew when World War Two ended. Sure, there are stereotypes, but this couldn't be generalized. I also didn't assume Germans would be in Lederhosen eating pretzels 24/7. Susanne had been hurrying back and forth from the kitchen to the dining room while Richard didn't even lift his little finger. I took my plate and got up, following her into the kitchen.

"Oh, Paul, you don't have to help." She flinched and took the plate out of my hand.

"I don't mind." I ignored her protest and helped with anything I could. Dad quickly joined us, but Richard remained idle. My distrust of him grew even more. If he was so good at history, surely he should know women's emancipation had already had its breakthrough in the French Revolution. Moreover, it was not Susanne's job to serve him!

When everything was clean, Susanne pulled me to the side. "You jet lagged from the flight. Let me show you her room."

I nodded fast, grabbed my suitcase, and followed her up the red stairs. I almost hit myself on the bookshelf covering the staircase hall. Emily's room was the first one, and my pulse raised with each step closer. Susanne stood at the door, about to push down the handle, when she turned to me again. "Emily doesn't call often. I try give space, but . . . is she good?"

She looked at me, pleading, as if she could tell even from far away that something was wrong with her little girl. I rubbed my temple. "You should ask her."

Susanne gave me a long stare before sighing. "I'm worried . . ."

Suddenly, a wave of guilt hit me. I was partly the reason Emily wasn't doing well, yet I was about to sleep in her daughter's bed at her house. I couldn't keep this from her, at least not entirely.

"Truthfully . . . um." I let go of my suitcase and scratched my nose, looking away. "We're going through something right now."

Saying this out loud felt so strange. So far, I hadn't even told my dad what was happening. No one, actually. And saying it now, to the person who loved Emily the most in this entire world, was like a reality check. Slowly, I dared to look up. Susanne chewed the inside of her cheek like Emily often did, and at first, I thought she would be mad, but then she pulled me into her arms. "Thank you for honest. I see you care about my daughter. I know you get through this."

She brought some distance between us and brushed my cheek with the back of her hand in a sweet motherly gesture. I swallowed down; Susanne had a heart out of gold.

"Pani should be in her room."

"Oh, I'm supposed to give him a million cuddles from her."

Susanna laughed and opened the door. I stepped into the little room that was hers but would be mine for seven days. But it didn't feel right . . . she was supposed to be here with me.

Chapter 26

Something Right

Jon

IT'D BEEN TWO DAYS SINCE LITTLE GERMAN HAD BARGED INTO MY Christmas and tried to use me for pills. I was fucking angry at her, but I fought myself not to reach out . . . even though I stayed up all night, wondering if she was still craving pills. I exhaled my smoke, sitting on one of my favorite playground benches. My phone buzzed.

> **Dave:** Yo, man! Long time no see. Watcha doing for New Year?

Dave, an old friend I knew from kindergarten who I only saw on special occasions because he went to a school out of town. His friend group was okay; I might start hanging with them more often to give Paul and Little German space.

> **Me:** Nothing so far, wyd?

I rested back on the bench and popped a pill. It was sunset time. Pink, puffy clouds were scattered all over the sky. If Emily were here, she would relish it. She delighted in these dumb little things when this world was a little less ugly. I spluttered and averted my gaze from the sky. *What the hell is going on with me . . .*

My phone rang. I expected it to be Dave, but it was Marna, *that bitch*. The last time I was at her place, she had tried climbing me again, but I told her I had to go as it was Christmas, and I would make up for the free pills another time. Another time, meaning never. I shoved my phone back into my pocket, but a few seconds later, it annoyed me again. I turned it to silent like this city had been muted over the last few days. For most people, the Christmas break was a time to get cozy with the family, rub their stuffed bellies, watching sappy movies. But I didn't have a stable family, plus I also hated those stupid movies that always ended with a cheesy happy ending, giving away this illusion that this would be life, but stupid life didn't follow a three-act structure.

Except for Brandon, everyone in our friend group, "the fam," went away for the holidays. I hated that name. We didn't know shit about each other. *Why pretend we're a family?* I'd hung out with Brandon yesterday, hoping for some guy talk and distraction. Maybe a party we could go to if we looked long enough. But to my annoyance, all he talked about was Hannah and their first fucking kiss, and I wasn't in the mood for happy love stories. I pulled out my black book but only found my keys. No pen ... except for Emily's key chain. Just great—another reason why my mind drifted to her. I pressed the pen onto the paper and went into a writing sprint.

The minor details
The laughter that ripples through the supermarket
The creaking of the trees that harbor squirrels and deer
The sunset transforms the world into a momentum of grace
I suddenly notice them.
Scary, isn't it?
Because even though I see the glory now,
I lack the eyes with which I perceived it in the first place.
Eyes I had obscured.

I lifted the pen because my phone lit up again, annoying me with its bright light. *Fucking Marna.*

"Shit, what do you want, Marna?" I growled into the phone.

"Some shit's going on I thought you'd be interested in, but if you're going to act like an ass, then bye!" Her voice boomed against my ear, but she didn't hang up.

"Fine . . ." The pill had kicked in, making me dizzy and tired. "What's going on?"

"Oh, now I got your attention?" She put on her flirty voice, and I regretted showing an interest.

"I'm not in the mood," I reminded her, clawing my fingers into the bench. The sound of loud rap music and people roaring mixed in my ears.

"This German girl you showed up with is here."

I sat up, unusually straight, my breathing quickened, and I clenched my jaw. "Who did she come with?"

"She came alone. Ted let her in. He thinks she's cute. I would've never—" She paused, and I heard Emily giggle in the background. "Gosh, she's so embarrassingly wasted! The dudes are clinging all over her. I seriously don't get what you all see in her."

I jumped off the bench. "Get them the fuck off of her!"

My feet went into the fastest sprint I'd ever made, and I regretted not running more often with Paul.

"I'm not fighting all those dudes for a girl I didn't invite." Marna put on her bitchy tone, and I swear, I wanted to punch her.

"Then stay the fuck with her until I'm there!" I bellowed into the phone and hung up to be able to run faster. *Why is Emily stupid enough to go to Marna's?!*

My chest stung as if someone had thrust a knife into it. I should've seen this coming. Out of all people, I should've noticed how far along she was. She came to me asking for pills, even though I was the reason Paul wanted that break with her. Apparently, she wasn't only sensitive to emotions but to addictions as well. I almost slipped when I turned the corner, but a part of me suddenly smiled. *I'll see her again.*

When I crashed through the back gate, I prayed those five minutes it took me weren't too long. I swung open the door, hitting a dude with it.

"Can't you watch where the fuck you're going!" he yelled at me when I shoved him out of the way with my shoulder. I scanned the room until I saw Little German slumped on the couch. The guys were drooling around her. One had her head in his lap, the other pressing his palm on her butt.

"Get the fuck away from her!" I roared as I shoved everyone who was standing in the way. The dudes' eyes traveled to me, but their cocky grins looked more amused than terrified.

"Chill, man, we're taking good care of her." cackled the dude with his hand still on her butt. His rotten teeth showed as he put on the ugliest smile I'd ever seen. My fist flew through the air right onto that bastard's grin. I wouldn't mind making it even more hideous.

"Shit, you'll do!" I threatened as he fell backward off the couch. The other dude, who had Emily in his lap, threw his hands up. The guy I hit at full force tumbled up, holding his bleeding nose.

"Fuck, man. We didn't know she was your girl! She got all drugged up when she came here. Can't blame us for trying when she's such a—"

I stepped toward him, and our noses almost touched. "I dare you to finish that sentence, and you will regret coming here for the rest of your life."

Mumbling went through the entire room. Great, everyone was watching us like a circus show. Suddenly, Marna stepped between us.

"If you want to start measuring dicks, do this outside!"

"Marna, let them carry it out. It's the best entertainment we've had all night," Ted threw in from somewhere behind me. *Is he for real?!*

"The show is over," I growled over my shoulder and scooped Emily into my arms. It would be stupid of me to pick a fight with Ted because he had resources and contacts so ruthless that my body would never be found. Emily didn't even react when I pulled her up. *Fuck, she's even more out of it than I thought.*

"How much did she take?" I asked Marna without pulling my eyes off Emily's glistening face.

"How am I supposed to know? I'm not her babysitter," Marna hissed back and stomped out of the room. I looked around, waiting for someone to tell me anything.

"Fuck, someone talk so I know what to do!" My heartbeat picked up. *Does she need to go to the hospital? Do I need to plug my finger up her throat? Maybe a shower?* When I got no reply, I squeezed my eyes closed. If the hospital realized she took drugs, she would be sent back to Germany. *I can't let that happen!* But what if she overdosed? Losing her would—No. I knew what an overdose looked like, and this wasn't one.

"Jon . . .?" She was squinting her eyes at me, pulling herself closer to my chest with her arms around my neck.

"I'm here. It's all going to be alright," I whispered, relieved she wasn't passed out anymore.

"I think I have to—"

Her face turned green. I ran outside with her in my arms to spare her from all those people's nasty looks. Fuck them witnessing this and not doing shit. I thought they at least had one bit of human empathy, but we live in a world now where people don't even care if someone overdosed right before them. I let her down, and she threw up in the bushes. I held her hair back and stabilized her by the waist. Something I should've done the first night we met.

"Better?"

She turned around, her eyes shooting big. "You're Jon . . ." She stumbled, falling forward. I pulled her up against my chest. Her mascara was smudged and highlighted by dried tears.

My throat tightened. Still lost on what to do, I lifted her chin up. "Yeah, it's me. Can you please answer the question?"

Her pupils dilated, and she looked at me with eyes I barely recognized.

"Do I have to bring you to a hospital?"

She let her head wander back and shook it. "Don't bring me to a hospital. I'm fine!" Her breathing got frantic, and her eyes refilled with tears.

I pulled her to my chest, whispering, "Okay."

She struggled to walk, and I lifted her back into my arms and carried her to my place. No way I would let her sleep alone tonight. Someone had to watch her, make sure she was okay. I pushed the door open, carrying her into the warmth of my place. But I couldn't let her sleep it off like this. Not with puke in her hair and dirt scattered all over her hands. I dropped her into the bathtub. She whimpered and lowered her head against the tub, not opening her eyes.

"Little German, you need to shower . . ." I shook her, but she whined little "no"s and hid her face in her palms.

"I'll wait right outside, okay?"

"No, don't go! Don't leave me alone . . . don't go!" she cried, her whines turning into sobs.

"Heck, I can't shower you!" I backed away. It wouldn't feel right to undress her in a state like this.

"Don't go!" She full-throat sobbed again. I rubbed my face, extremely overwhelmed by the situation. She needed to sober the fuck up, or she would feel like literal crap tomorrow.

"No, no, no . . .! Don't go without me!" she pressed out in between her sobs again. My shoulders dropped; this was about way more than a shower. *Paul, you motherfucker, you shouldn't have left for Germany.*

"I'm not leaving you." I sighed and dropped myself onto the side of the bathtub. She reached for my hand, and I gave it to her with no further protest. She pulled it up to her chest until my palm was pressed flatly against it. My fingers tingled from the contact with her skin.

"I'm not . . . I'm not feeling good." She opened her scattered red eyes, but they fell closed again right away. Fuck this. I would shower with her. I jumped into the bathtub with my clothes on, kneeling around her body and turning on the water. Little German's head shot up when the cold drops met her face.

"Ah!" she squealed, covering her face, but I didn't pull the showerhead away. Eventually, she closed her eyes, letting her hands fall down her body. I gently brushed my fingers through her hair to wash out all the vomit. She remained quiet the entire time, her mascara dripping down her face. Gosh, she was beautiful. Even in a fucked-up state like this. I let my thumb glide over her brows, down her cheekbone, to her lip. Even though the water removed her makeup, her ravishing lips were painted rose-colored. I dragged down her lower lip, imagining the taste in my throat from the last time we kissed. Her taste . . . its sweetness immediately built in my mouth. I could taste her again. Right now. Right here. I removed my thumb. *I shouldn't. . .*

She looked at me again. "Thank you for always being there for me, Jon."

"I'm not always there for you," I countered but then bit my tongue. Emily smiled and reached out her hand to meet my cheek. I flinched when she softly swiped away the drops.

"You were," she whispered, water still floating over her chin. "And you are."

A wave of heat coursed through me. I wanted to fight it, but she didn't let me. Her gaze was too impossible to look away from.

"It was you who reassured me I could trust Paul . . ." She whimpered at the mention of his name. "Then I called, breaking down, and you . . . you came. I didn't even ask you to come." She came closer with her face. I closed my eyes, resting my forehead on hers.

"And now you saved me from Marna's. If you hadn't come . . ." She sniffled, her hands wandering down to my neck. "You care about me. Admit it." She pressed a kiss onto my cheek, and goosebumps built on every fucking inch of my skin.

I turned my face to the side. "I care because . . ." I swallowed, getting water in my mouth. "Because you are . . ." My breathing betrayed me, making it hard to talk. "You're his . . . I can't." I swallowed again harshly, feeling my care for this girl overwhelm me with a flood of emotions. I was drowning in her. I'd fought not to go down since I'd met her, but I was running out of energy to keep myself above the surface.

"I did lie to you, you know?" she said, no whimpers left in her voice.

"What did you lie about?"

She giggled, her fingertips playing piano on my cheeks. "I did like you first, Jon. I was never just his."

I groaned, looking up at the ceiling. She was high. She couldn't think clearly. This was wrong . . . I couldn't. Or could I? I really tried . . . I stopped fighting and dipped below the surface, pressing my lips onto hers. Little German was like an addiction—but fuck, she was the best addiction I'd ever had.

Chapter 27

Mother So Daughter

Paul

I slept well in Emily's bed, partly because it still smelled like her but mostly because being in her space made me feel so much closer to her. Her fluffy cat had slept by my feet. He'd given me a skeptical eye as I crawled below the covers for the first time. Yet after some intense sniffing, I think I was approved. From her bed, you had the perfect view of the sunset. Just outside the window were huge mountains. Susanne called them the "Siebengebirge."

The night Emily and I had met, she said she'd come to America because something was missing in her life. I thought she meant an adventure, but now, being here, I could tell this was about more. Her room was the opposite of the entire house. Outside this door, the place was crammed with stuff. In here, everything was neatly put away, kept to a minimum. White furniture, one light purple wall. Nothing gave me a deeper insight into who she really was. No picture frames, no decoration. Just a few books, all romance novels I had never read before. She was much more than the girl next door . . . she was the girl with a secret, and I would discover it.

Knock. Knock. My body shot up, and Pani gave me an annoyed look as he slipped off my lap.

"Sorry, Pan." I quickly petted him. "Yeah?"

The door opened, and a dude a little smaller than me but with such muscular shoulders I knew my height wouldn't give me any advantage walked in. "Hi."

"Lucas?" I asked, a bit afraid I was wrong because ... *C'mon, that would be hella embarrassing.*

"Yes. You must be Paul."

I hurried out of bed. I could tell Lucas didn't give me his most friendly smile and puffed up his chest like a chicken instead.

"It's great to meet you," I said as I shook his hand.

Then he crossed his arms, his chest still swollen up. "So tell me, Paul ... why are you here without her?"

He skipped formalities, and his eyes, still harshly fixed on me, turned my mouth dry.

"Um ..." Pearls of sweat formed on my forehead. "I ... I always wanted to taste German beer."

His brows curved, and I held my breath. *Jesus Christ, why did I say that?* But then his face transformed, a huge grin spreading all over it.

"That's a darn good reason." He beamed and threw his arm around my neck. "C'mon. I'm here to pick you up. We're going out!"

We reached downtown by bus and train. A freaking train! Cologne's infrastructure blew my mind. In Boonville, we had one bus, which drove only every other hour, but here you could see bus stops, train halts, and subway entries wherever you looked. Thinking back on how Jon and I sometimes walked for hours to get a party, which was almost dead when we finally made it, this seemed surreal.

My jaw suddenly clenched. I wondered if he was with her ... It'd been over two days, after all. I almost called him last night but not to check if he was with Emily. I regretted punching him. Despite all the shit he'd pulled, I still cared too much about him. I ran my fingertips over my knuckles, which were still slightly bruised. I kept telling myself it was justified ...

but then again, why? He was just friends with Emily. As far as I knew, no other lines were crossed. I bit down my lip. He hadn't even fought back.

"Sorry, man, my girlfriend is always late," Lucas grumbled as he searched the street. I shook my head to pull myself out of my thoughts. New rule for tonight: no more thinking about Jon or Emily. *Neither of them.* Tonight was about me, impressing Lucas, and trying German brew.

"Don't worry about it."

I looked around. We stood in front of an Irish pub. People streamed in and out after the bodyguard checked their IDs. I guess we weren't going in there. *I'm only seventeen.*

"Ugh, I should've picked her up. I don't like it when she walks around alone, but she insisted—"

"Ich bin hier." *I'm here.* A girl dressed in a trench coat preened from behind him. Lucas rotated around and pulled her into a tight embrace.

"Oh, Kelly, endlich!" *Oh, Kelly, finally!*

Although I tried hard to pick up as much German as possible, I still didn't understand anything. She gave him a quick kiss before drawing her attention to me.

"Hello, Paul, it's nice to meet you. I'm Kelly, Lucas's girlfriend."

She was pretty but not the smeared-with-makeup type. More natural, like Emily. *Fuck, I just did it again.* I chewed on my upper lip as she pulled me into a close hug.

"I'm glad you're taking care of her. It makes Lucas calmer." She squeezed me and then took a step back with a smile. I usually would be thrown off by such affection from a stranger, but for some reason, I felt like this hug was supposed to be for Emily.

"Shall we?" she said, putting on a bit of a British accent as she pointed at the bar.

"I'm not eighteen yet . . ." I slumped my hands in my pockets.

"Oh, you could even go in with sixteen, don't worry!" Kelly waved. My jaw got so heavy I struggled to pick it up from my chest. *I'm seventeen, and I'm allowed into a freaking bar?!* I liked Germany more and more with each second.

The interior of the bar was rustic. Dark green walls were filled with pictures of old cars, people drinking and laughing, or other random stuff. The space was small, and almost every spot was covered in tables. Squeezing through the crowd, we found a free one in a corner. I peeked down at the menu.

"What's Kölsch?" I asked when I didn't know one single name of the beer. Kelly and Lucas giggled a bit, but they didn't do it in a *we're laughing about you* way.

"That, my man . . ." Lucas slammed his hand on my shoulder. "Is the local beer. It's good as a starter as it's light."

"Light beer sounds good." I smiled and approved. I didn't want to blow my head off tonight. Lucas raised his hand at the waitress.

"Zwei Kölsch bitte und—" *Two Kölsch, please, and*—He leaned toward his girlfriend. "Schatz möchtest du auch einen Jägermeister Shot?" *Baby, do you also want a Jägermeister shot?*

I understood the word "shot." That wasn't good . . .

"Ja! Und einen Aperol Spritz." *Yes! And an Aperol Spritz.*

The waitress nodded, rushing away after Lucas told her, "Danke," which I knew meant *thank you.*

He caressed Kelly's cheek for a second. She received his sweet gesture as if it was the most normal thing in the world.

"How long have you guys been together?"

"Um, a few years." Kelly shrugged.

"Two years and three months," Lucas pointed out.. I tugged at the side of the menu. I could only dream of getting this much time with Emily. *Screw not thinking about her.* It was impossible not to think about her—I was in her country with her brother, doing everything she always talked about. I already had many questions for her. Like why none of her friends had shown any interest in meeting me? If she had been in a bar like this herself. If she viewed Richard as her father . . . why I hadn't met her real father.

"I got to use the bathroom." Kelly stood up, brushing her hair over her shoulder. I knew Emily liked her deeply, adored her even. Her eyes sparkled when she said she was perfect, followed by a sigh. *But why that sigh?* I should've asked her. I bit my lip again until I could feel my teeth clenching through my skin.

"Are you okay?"

I tilted my head, seeing Lucas peeking at me with narrowed eyes. "Yeah, sorry, man. I'm . . ." I massaged my neck. "Being here, I realized there's so much I don't even know about her."

"You've only known her for a few months." Lucas shrugged, folding his hands on the table.

"I know, but I'm talking about essential things. She never mentioned Richard to me. Or her father . . . why haven't I met him yet? Does he even know I'm here?"

Lucas's eyes flew up at me, and this time, it was him biting his lip. Yet, even after a few seconds, he remained silent.

"What's up with him?" I pushed. Normally not my style, but I wouldn't make the mistake of not asking again. Lucas rested back in his chair and crossed his arms, pressing his tongue below his lip. "Let's say Emily's father figures aren't exactly father material."

I squeezed my lips together. His response was cryptic. "Which means?"

"Our father wasn't around much. He worked a lot, and when he came home, he played online card games in his office . . .while our mother—" Lucas groaned and rubbed his face. "Our mother is an angel. Even though Dad starved her emotionally, she stayed with him for over a decade, just so Emily and I would have a father. But either way, we didn't have one because when he was home, he was drinking."

Lucas loosened his arms and let them drop back to the table. He took a beer coaster and fiddled with the sides of it. His strong affection for his girlfriend . . . he was trying to be the opposite of his father.

"Then Mom met Richard. He was everything she wished for. Charming, affectionate, and he had a soft spot for Emily."

"Soft spot?" I tensed.

"Not in a creepy, inappropriate way," Lucas corrected. "I think he liked the idea of her being his daughter."

I couldn't help but notice the beer coaster was almost ripped apart.

"My mother finally dared to leave our father. For a year, we lived in an apartment so small Emily and I had to share a room. Food was always running low, mold in the bathroom, but my mother was fighting to give us everything we needed. We learned to live with the bare minimum while our father remained in the big house."

"Why wouldn't he let you stay in the house?" I couldn't understand. He should've left, not them.

"Because my father blamed my mother for leaving. Till today, he pretends like she'd done the evil. But she fought for many years to change and help him. He didn't. He only saw my mother's mistakes."

"But you were with her! He should've cared how his kids lived." My hands balled into fists.

"He said we could stay with him. But we both would've never left our mother. No matter how we lived, having her in our life was more important. She wasn't only our mother . . . she was also our father."

I shook my head. I'd always had stable parents, never appreciating how happy they made each other. I had good role models, a secure home, and I never had to worry about an empty fridge. I could barely imagine what this must've felt like . . .

"Emily is a lot like our mother. Caring, kind . . . I was so pissed when she introduced her ex, Michael, to me. He was terrible."

Lucas swiped the ripped-apart paper into a pile and then placed his hand on my shoulder. "That's why I'm glad she's with you now. You seem like a decent guy, not someone who needs to be fixed. It gives me hope she isn't repeating my mother's behavior."

My entire skin burned. *That's why she's so drawn to Jon!* He was messed up and in definite need of help. I wasn't. At least not the parts of me I showed to her. Emily had tried breaking the devil's circle by choosing me, yet I pushed her right back into it. *Well done, Paul. . .*

The waitress brought our drinks over, three shots filled with brown liquor and beer topped with foam.

"Ready for some Jägermeister shots?" Lucas raised his glass, and our conversation was drowned in the herbal liquid. But it wasn't even as close to bitter as the story I was still processing.

Chapter 28

Goodbye, Control

Emily

MY HEAD PULSATED, CREATING A SEVERE TWINGE IN MY temple. *Why does it hurt so much?* I squeezed my eyes shut and curled up in the pillow, comforted by a smoky, woodsy smell. My eyes flew open. Grey sheets. I fumbled around, trying to move, but every muscle screamed for me to stop.

I'm in Jon Henry Denson's bed.

I took three breaths as slowly as possible, my heart rumbling like it was about to escape my chest. I swallowed for air when the emptiness almost winked at me. My throat was parched. A fresh cup of water stood on the nightstand next to me. I reached for it and drank a few sips. Another wave of nausea hit me, and the glass flew onto the carpet with a little thud.

Grumbling hit my ears from right behind me. My muscles pinched; Jon was sleeping on one of the couches with no blanket. His arms were crossed above his head, his bare chest stretched, eyes softly closed. I bit down my lip. His body was new to me, different than Paul's—more of a heavy-muscle type, while Paul was more defined. A smile spread on my face. Like the last time I saw him sleeping all those months ago when we worked on the Malcolm X project, his long lashes framed his eyes, his chest moving with slow breaths.

I wondered what he was dreaming about, why he never looked calm when awake. I fiddled with the hem of my shirt, almost down to my knees. I wore one of Jon's signature black shirts and . . . I slowly lifted the blanket. My panties—*just my panties.* My breathing sped up—last night was one dark cloud. I held my body straight by pushing my palms into the sheets. Questions upon questions roared through my brain, my stomach turning upside down. I found myself next to the toilet seconds later.

"Ugh . . ." I sighed when my stomach finally calmed down. Nothing had come out except for acid. Puking was becoming way too much of a habit of mine, and my body crumbled due to it. Lifting myself up on the sink, I looked at what was left of me. I was pale, my eyes empty and exhausted from what I had put my body through over the last few days. My hair was wavy, as if it had dried overnight. I twirled around. There were still shower drops wherever you looked. *I showered?!* I ran my hands through my hair, trying to concentrate. But there was nothing about last night. I splashed water into my face, but having my eyes closed made the dizziness return. My heartbeat was still playing the drums. I turned left and found my clothes hanging over the heater, drying.

"Oh god . . ." I squealed, knowing the possibility of Jon seeing me naked was not slim. I lifted off Jon's shirt, pulled my sweater over me, and stepped into my jeans.

"I need air . . ."

As quietly as I could, I opened the door. Jon was still heavily passed out on the couch. I sneaked over to him, my hand almost on his shoulder, but then I froze. *Do I even want an answer to my questions?* I fiddled at the necklace Paul had given me for Christmas. I hadn't put it off so far. Trying to decide, with nothing but guilt in my chest, the fear of having made Paul's fears come true. The sickness returned, and I pressed my lips together. I had promised myself to be with someone good. Someone who appreciated me and wasn't only using their charm whenever they wanted something. Someone who knew how to be in a healthy relationship and didn't need to be fixed. *I'm not like her.*

I looked for my parka but was running out of oxygen, so I gave up.

I rushed up the stairs, literally praying not to run into Tim right now. I didn't feel like talking to anyone. Words couldn't give me back what I craved most—control over my decisions. And whenever I was with Jon, control slipped out of my fingers. When I smashed the door behind me, I shuddered. I'd made it. Whatever happened last night wasn't me. It was ... I don't know what it was or what even happened. But it wasn't me. I hadn't been me since he left to go to Germany.

I flattened my hands onto my face, suppressing the sobs overcoming me. Imagining Paul sitting with Pani on my bed, having my mother wash him with her kindness, and Lucas taking him to our favorite bar increased my breathing. I was jealous—jealous he got to be with my family while I was here with no one ... no one but the guy I wanted to stay away from ever since I'd met him.

I took away my hands, the frog in my throat about to jump. I walked around a little snow mountain at the end of Jon's driveway. I knew going to Marna's wasn't safe, but Jon didn't want to help me end it. Not my life *this year.* Make me get sent back home by doing something reckless. One last impulsive move before I was back to being the Goody Two-shoes. Heck, what a stupid idea to trade a few days in Germany with him for over six months in America. That couldn't have been me!

WHOOOOSH!

Something harsh hit me right on my butt. I twirled around, seeing Jon smirking at me with a snowball cupped in his hands, his leather jacket on. He'd followed me ... My lips parted as I gaped at him—a moment he used to make his second throw, this time hitting at the height of my boobs.

"Jon, stop!" I cursed. But he lifted his brows in a playful manner and leaned down to grab another pile of snow. My stomach was still sick, and my mind was dizzy, but I dodged when the ball flew in my direction. *That's it!*

I gathered snow, formed a quick unstable ball, and threw it. It landed not even remotely close to Jon. He looked at it, but my throat couldn't hold it. I burst out into laughter—what a hella sad throw.

"Here, I'll come a bit closer." He laughed, our eyes tearing up with happiness. I lifted my middle finger, flipping him off. It started to feel less weird. While walking, he reached down for the snow. I quickly squatted down, grabbed a handful of snow myself, and ran toward him. Without hesitation, I smashed the snow right into his face. He tilted his head to the side and threw his arm around me. His palm, covered in snow, fell straight into my neck.

I screamed out loud and jumped into his chest. Jon tripped, and we flew down together. But he cushioned our collision with his body, mine pressed tightly onto his.

"Are you okay?" he immediately asked, cupping my glowing cheeks with his ice-cold hands. I tried moving away, but my body didn't react to my brain's command. *Goodbye, control.*

"Yeah, this is even better than coffee in the morning."

My stomach was still unsettled, but my head had stopped pounding. The pounding was somewhere else now. It was deep in my chest, crashing hard against my rips. Jon smiled. A pure smile I had never seen on him before. I didn't even know he had those little wrinkles next to his eyes. His lashes were covered in snowflakes, his cheeks rosy red, and his lips . . . parted. I looked back up from his lips to his eyes. The smile had faded by now, and a gentle stare was pulling me in. I swallowed, looking from his eyes back to his lips, back to his eyes, back to his lips. My palms still pressed against his chest, making it impossible for him to get up. I closed my eyes, feeling him leaning up with his hot breath grazing my nose. His palm found its way to my neck again. It nestled in there perfectly as if it was always made to be placed in this exact spot. He swallowed harshly, but then his voice hit my eardrums.

"Why did you leave without saying goodbye?" he whispered, breathing in more quickly than I was used to from him. I bit my lower lip to resist the growing urge to kiss him. Instead, I opened my eyes again to find him looking at me with the fire flickering. I was about to get burned, and I didn't even mind. He pressed me closer to his body until our chests met. The energy in the air became unspeakable, almost magical even. I wanted to feel him all over me, like in my dream. Cup my cheeks, let his fingers travel over my skin, and cuddle in my lap, revealing this soft side of him I was sure was there.

"Because I . . ." I tried to talk, but my breathing got heavy; the words were only little gasps. "Jon, I . . ."

His scent switched off my brain, and I could feel the blood pulsing through every vein in my body. It muffled every sound around us, leaving only our hearts beating. I touched his forehead, pulling aside the raven curl of hair that hung almost to his nose. His bruised eye was more yellow now. My heart ached to know I was the reason he had it. His eyes followed my every move, squinting as I let my thumb slowly glide over the harmed skin.

"Jon. I'm sorry . . ." I whined, not meaning the eye this time.

"Don't be," he hushed me, and our lips met in the middle. When they connected, I felt the relief I had so desperately needed. A thousand sparks lit up in my chest. This wasn't like our first two kisses. They weren't topped with this intense care for each other. I could feel his blood pulsing up his throat, entering my mouth as our lips collided. I was afraid to run out of air. Even though running out of air would be a burden, I would gladly suffer as long as I didn't have to stop kissing him. I let go of all those denied feelings, all those pretending he was just a friend to me. And for the first time since I met him, I felt . . . free. My heart took the lead. My lips closed, and I relished looking at him. Because looking at him was almost equally as good as kissing him.

"Don't you ever dare leave without saying goodbye again." He smiled, brushing back a strand of hair that had fallen over my face.

I grinned, feeling heat rising through my entire head. "Same goes for you."

Jon twirled me around so he was leaning over me this time. And then we kissed again, less angst and more embracing of the other.

"Hey, hey. You guys do know you have a room downstairs?" I heard Tim's sleepy voice coming from the entrance. Jon continued to plaster kisses on my cheeks as he waved his father away.

I giggled out loud. "Sorry, Tim!"

But I never felt less sorry before. I heard Tim chuckling back before the door shut. Jon leaned back in for another kiss, but I lifted myself.

"You know, your father is right. There's a bed a few steps away."

Jon shook his head and rolled off me. "I have an even better idea."

I crooked my eyebrow at him. "And what would that be?"

"Patience, baby." He winked, and I swear my heart almost died.

Chapter 29

Heart Capacity

Emily

JON HAD RUSHED BACK INSIDE AND RETURNED WITH AN EXTRA black jacket. Thankfully, I grabbed it and put it on. It smelled like him.

"Have you seen my parka?" I asked. It was new and my only warm jacket.

"It's not here."

My shoulders dropped; I must've forgotten it at Marna's.

"You can keep mine. I have my leather jacket." Jon tugged at his jacket, and I smiled.

I asked where we were going two more times while walking until we finally ended up at the Crispy Biscuit. I dashed ahead to a table on the far right, as far away as possible from where I sat last time with Madison. So much had changed in those few days.

"We would like coffee, pancakes, scrambled eggs . . . oh, and hash browns," Jon ordered as we sat down to a gum-chewing waitress. I gave Jon a wide-eyed look, letting my hands fall into my lap. *Hasch Brownies* were edibles in Germany. I get Jon was more open about this topic, but this wasn't appropriate to say to a waitress. The waitress rushed off.

"You can't seriously be asking for hash browns!" I nudged him over the table, then took off his jacket. The waitress immediately returned to pour us some coffee. Her chewing irritated me. I clenched my teeth, trying not to focus on her, squeezing the gum in her mouth. I let out a sharp breath when she left again. Her strawberry gum left a chemical smell in the air.

"Why not? They're tasty!" Jon questioned, sipping on his black coffee. He drank it exactly like me. Black—no milk or sugar. Just pure caffeine.

"But we can't order weed at a diner!" I threw my hands above my mouth, covering it when I realized I talked a hint too loud.

Jon spat out the coffee to the other side, making a mess on the window, which didn't bother me when I heard the most beautiful laugh ever falling from his lips. "You think—Little German!"

"What?" I rested my elbows on the table and leaned in closer, all while having a broad grin on my face as well.

"You can't tell me Paul has never introduced you to hash browns before?!"

I swallowed and looked to the side. *Paul* . . . I hadn't even thought about him in the last hour.

"Forget what I said." Jon's jaw got tense, and the smile I enjoyed was behind the mountains. He took another sip of coffee, his look wandering out of the window. We kept silent for a few breaths as if we were grieving a lost friend. My heart turning so heavy I pressed my knuckles onto my chest. I had no idea what I was supposed to do next. I waited for Jon to say something, but he must've fallen deeper into his head than I did. I let him, staring out of the window as well. I used to hate the silence with him . . . but not anymore. His silence held something almost comforting. He knew when it was better to keep quiet. When a moment would only be destroyed by words, in either a good or bad way. And I felt a bit better knowing I wasn't alone in feeling guilty.

The waitress came flying back with a plate of what looked like *Gitterpommes*, which are fries in the shape of a mesh. But those right here looked juicier, like *Reibekuchen* with plenty of holes.

"Those, Little German, are hash browns." Jon pointed at them after the waitress left.

"Oh! Guten Appetit, then," I took a skeptical bite and shoved as much as possible into my mouth right after. My appetite had finally returned, and swallowing didn't feel like a challenge anymore. "Grease . . . exactly what I need right now." I rolled my eyes dramatically, and Jon joined my food munchies. But he ate extra slowly at first, then picked up his speed whenever I stopped putting stuff into my mouth.

"Can Jon Denson have a gentlemanly side?" I winked at him while wiping my mouth with a napkin. I think I'd never eaten this fast before.

Jon shoved eggs into his mouth. "We can't all eat like we're on the edge of starving, Little German," he said, chewing with his mouth closed, and I threw my napkin at him in return.

We walked a few streets in silence again, but even though we didn't connect with words, we were connected physically because Jon was holding my hand. Yep. Holding hands. Him and I. I had almost pulled it away from him when he reached for it, as this was the last thing I had expected. But our hands merged smoothly, and his thumb gently drew over my palm with every other step. Each time he did, I had to gasp for breath. His touches were tender and thoughtful . . . unexpectedly lovely. His behavior confused me, though. Was this all part of a game again? Or was this genuine? My head pounded.

"Thank you for breakfast." I came to a standstill when we were a corner away from the Shields' house. He bit his lip and took his hand away from me. I whimpered when our skin lost contact.

"No problem," he said with a neutral face, hard to read again.

"I think it's better if you don't walk me to the house."

"I know."

I took a deep breath. "Jon, maybe we, um . . . should talk about this?"

He stepped toward me, cupping my cheeks in his surprisingly warm hands and pulling my face to his lips. Gosh, this time, he tasted even better. The flavor of coffee and sugary pancakes were still on his lips, and they molded with mine, no tongue, the softest of contacts I'd ever felt. My knees turned into soft butter.

"Jon . . ." I gasped between our kisses.

"I know—talking," he breathed into my mouth but didn't stop kissing me. My lips parted again, and our tongues melted like the snow in the grass below us. My fingers tingled, my veins throbbed, and my heart's capacity was tested. A car honked at us out of nowhere. I jumped back, turning to see if it was Gena. But even worse . . . my worst nightmare, Mrs. Stone, glared at me with a murderous face. She stopped her car as our eyes met. Jon stepped in front of me, giving her only a view of his back.

"Ignore her." He looked at me calmly, pulling his attention back to him. I pulled in my lower lip, obliging to his wish. After another second, I heard her wheels turning again. I swallowed harshly, mad at myself for still letting her have an impact on me. I thought I was over it . . . what a lie I had told myself.

"That was . . ." I pointed past him with a shaking finger.

"I know," Jon whispered, not breaking his gaze on me. "But you don't owe her kindness, Emily."

Emily . . .

Hearing him call me by my name still made goosebumps travel everywhere. Kinda ridiculous as being called by your name is the entire purpose of having a name, but the way he did it was . . . special.

"I didn't know you knew what she did to me."

Jon snorted, shaking his head to the side. "I might don't say much, but I listen."

My face heated up again, but my mouth remained closed. This was another moment where words would only destroy. But then again, I needed words to understand what was going on between us.

"Jon . . . are you okay?"

"I'm fine." The corners of his mouth twitched, but mine pressed together. *Fine?* You feel fine when you make it through an average day. Not when you betray your best friend.

My impatience grew. "How come you can be fine in all this?"

My fingertips tingled, fearing all the question marks I would have again in minutes.

"This isn't a talk to be held here, Little German. You live right there . . ." He cleared his throat. "As well as Paul."

I nodded in understanding, but Jon furrowed his brows.

"I should go, then." He said what I wanted to hear the least and walked away without another word. All the joyous moments were suddenly overshadowed by this abrupt goodbye.

He suddenly twirled back around. "Can I pick you up later?"

I smiled. "Yes, text me!"

Even though the sun blinded me, I could see a broad smirk on Jon's face. A smirk I used to describe as cocky . . . but admired now in ways too impossible to put into words.

I had this broad grin on my face all the way down the street to the doorstep. But it faded when I heard Paul's voice coming from a laptop in the living room.

"Germany is nice. You would love the architecture here, Mom!"

A little squeal escaped my lips. Zack came sprinting around the corner, heading straight for me.

"I told Mom you took a morning walk to listen to birds or shit. Don't you dare tell her I lied!" he pulled away, giving me a warning glare. "Woah, you look like road kill!"

Zack dashed away again. I collected my thoughts. I was almost touched he'd covered for me, but then again terrified to walk in there now, knowing I looked like *a run-over animal.* But before I could escape into the basement, Gena stood in the doorframe.

"Honey! I have Paul and your mother on a video call. They want to talk to you!"

She rushed away, not noticing what Zack had seen. Looking down, I made my way to the laptop.

"Hey . . ." I sat down, my chest relaxing when I saw my mother. But then I noticed Paul right next to her.

"Hey, Babycakes." Paul grinned, and Pani's head shot up from his lap, looking at the screen. "Pani approves of me," he joked. *Of course Pani likes him. How couldn't you like him?*

My breathing quickened as an intense knot built in my stomach.

"Und ich auch!" *And so do I!* My mother placed an arm around his neck. "You were right, Emily. He is a gentleman."

But no smile escaped my lips. And Paul's dropped when his gaze fell onto my jacket. *Jon's jacket.*

Chapter 30

In His Shadow

Jon

We fucking kissed. And it wasn't a *Hey, I'm horny* kiss. This kiss was new to me—a kiss topped with so much angst I held on to every fraction of it. I'd had good kisses with Kiki before, kisses tinged with desire and compassion. But I'd never shared a kiss with someone I wished would never end. A kiss that wasn't only good, but . . . great. I flipped over in my bed, smacking my face against the pillow.

"Fuck!" I growled into it, slamming my fist down on the mattress. Her scent still hung in the fabric, and my fist unclenched as a hint of apple crept into my nose. I couldn't let that be our last kiss. I'd rather never kiss anyone in this world again than have this stay a memory. I turned over and straightened up until my back rested against the headboard. Right after I walked away from Little German, I hid back down here, trying to figure out what to do next. My head was spinning. My eyes were burning. My heart . . . *fluttered?*

"Dude . . ."

I closed my eyes and breathed deeply through my mouth. When my dad asked me how it was, I disregarded him. I couldn't tell him how great it was that, for the first time in a year, I didn't feel like total shit. That I was enjoying my time and looking forward to the days ahead. Because if I had admitted that to him, I would've become an even shittier person than I already was. It meant I was completely ignoring that my happiness meant taking happiness away from my brother, like I had at the same time last year. I sighed and banged my head against the headboard several times in a rhythm. I shut my eyes and forced myself to relive the first time I had destroyed Paul Shield's life.

I was back on the playground, feeling my skin freeze from the cold air, and my mind shouted with naivety. Paul and I were sitting on the swings, having a smoke and a few Bud Lights, tipsy but not drunk. A regular evening back in the day.

"Jamie doesn't get it, man . . ." Paul took a quick drag of a joint before passing it to me.

"What?"

I had gotten lost in my head, thinking about what I would get Kiki for her birthday in a month. I knew she liked jewelry, but heck, I still needed to learn how to afford that. Paul looked at me, slightly pissed.

"Sorry, man. I'm in my head lately." I explained, and he nodded, understanding. He always seemed to understand. I sometimes wished he wouldn't because I barely understood it myself.

"I was talking about Jamie. I think we're too different, you know?"

"Really?" I wasn't even one bit surprised. Jamie was a bitch most of the time. Even Kiki, who was kind to everyone, expressed anger about her a few times. I wondered how Paul kept up with her, but I was trying to be supportive, so I didn't ask him.

"But you're the football team's captain, and she's the cheerleader captain. Doesn't sound different?"

"Yeah, I guess . . . but we barely . . . talk?" Paul scratched his head as if he struggled to admit his relationship was purely based on sex. I snorted out loud. I would like to have his issues.

"Shit, Paul! If Kiki only cared about sex, my relationship would be much easier." I stood up from the swing and walked in circles over the snow to hear the cracking of it below my feet. When I looked back at him, he rolled his eyes.

"You should be lucky Kiki cares about who you are as a person."

I looked back down. Kiki cared so much she was mothering me to a point where I didn't feel like she liked who I was. I knew she was trying to help, bring out the best in me and shit, but I didn't need help. My family issues were something I had to handle myself. I still had time to fix my grades, and I only used Adderall for long shifts at the call center. It wasn't an addiction—nothing to be concerned about.

"Right . . . Kiki is good."

Wonderful even, but her too-big heart was getting too heavy for me to carry. I let out a long breath, watching my hot breath fizzle into the cold. Paul received a message and focused on his phone. I took a couple of quick drags of the joint.

"Holy crap!" Paul suddenly jumped to his feet, and I almost dropped the joint.

"It's Coach! He invited a couple of scouts who want to see me play my next game!" Paul bounced on the spot, rereading the message multiple times. "If they like me, I could get a full college scholarship, man!"

My eyes widened. *That was an opportunity of a lifetime!* I threw the joint away, walked up to him, did our handshake, and gave him a bro hug.

"That's amazing!" I congratulated. I never minded watching him play or the girls being crazy over him. I was in his shadow, getting pulled along to whatever party or benefits he got. This dude was the definition of loyal. But I sometimes questioned why he was even friends with me. I had nothing to bring to the table. He had the status at school. The popular girlfriend. The stable family life . . . I cracked the bones in my knuckles. What I would sacrifice for happy parents. And now, he also had a promising future. Fuck, of course I envied him, feeling like a piece of shit. All I had was a girlfriend who tried fixing me instead of focusing on herself to become a doctor. I was pulling her down with me, and my family barely survived a five-minute conversation without a fight. No matter how many nights I spent at the call center, my bank account always seemed empty. I clenched my brows.

"Yo, bro. What's up?" Paul placed his palm on my shoulder.

I inhaled the cold air. Right, I had my best friend, whom I knew I could count on even when getting off track. I hated I had to force myself to be happy for him.

"Nothing." I shrugged.

He cocked his neck to the side, looking at me with a severe face. "But—"

Honk, honk.

Our conversation got interrupted by Brandon honking from the street. *Shit, our bro got a car?!*

We both dashed over to him with giant steps.

"It's my mother's! But guess what!" Brandon held up a sheet of paper. "I got my license!"

"About time!" Paul nudged his shoulder, but I remained behind him. I hadn't gotten my license yet. Not because I was too young—I'd been sixteen for half a year—but because all I did was work to afford to treat Kiki the way she deserved. I shook Brandon's hand.

"You want to do something crazy?" I asked, feeling the effects of the joint spreading through me.

"Sure, what?"

"Hand me your keys," I commanded, holding out my hand.

"Shit, no. This is my mom's car, and you—"

"I know how to drive, dude." I glared at Brandon. I was tired of being reminded of what kind of loser I was.

Brandon snorted. "Fine, but I'm sitting in the passenger seat."

Paul was about to go to the back, but I held my arm in his way.

"You don't sit there."

"Why not?"

"Because you're sitting in the front row!" I pointed at the car's hood, grinning proudly about this stupid idea.

"Shit, man. But go slow, okay?" Paul rushed and jumped on the hood while Brandon and I got into the car. I did go slow at first, and Brandon, Paul, and I had a blast driving around the neighborhood with way-too-loud music and the windows down, even though it was dark and freezing. We were young, stupid teenage boys that didn't think anything through. Driving high. Unexperienced. And foolish. My skin shivered, thinking about what happened next. I didn't focus for one second. For one second, I forgot Paul was sitting on the hood, one second in which my feet turned heavy.

I pressed down on the gas, causing the car to slip on the frozen streets. I tried getting it back under control, but when I hit the brakes, Paul fell off the hood, and his foot ended up below the wheel. The sound of his breaking bones, painful screams, and torturing silence for months after created my bed of self-hatred. Sleep became a treasure, rare for me to achieve. His football career was blown away by the wind. That night, I had lost him . . . for months, he barely even looked at me, saying it was his fault too, but I knew he blamed me. He always sent me away, giving me this hateful look. But I kept trying until I lost my job because I often came in late. This also resulted in my insufficient money to buy a Valentine's present for Kiki. I ended things with her before she could find out, leaving me with absolutely nothing . . . for months. Until the night he asked me to hang out again, the night he met Little German.

I swiped over my still-cracked phone. I was picking Emily up tonight, but I couldn't wait. I had to kiss her to stop this war in my head. My heart made a weird double beat when I opened my messages.

Paul: Dude, this shit is so good!

Attached was a picture of him drinking German brew. I stared at the screen; he had reached out. Not with an apology for beating the shit out of me, but heck, I didn't even need that. This was way more than I could've asked for. I began typing, but no matter what, I couldn't form one line without thinking about telling him I kissed his girl and that I was planning to do it often from now on. I jumped onto my feet, running at my punching bag. Even though my head pounded and my muscles were sore, I punched it with all my strength. Paul was everything I had. And now that, finally, something great was happening to me, I would have to trade him for it. As if I was only granted one good thing in life.

"Ahh!"

Left, right, jab, punch. I screamed and destroyed my punching bag until sweat ran down my forehead. I couldn't make a decision. I beelined to my nightstand, searching for a plastic bag of pills, but I only found a bottle of whiskey. I lifted it, taking a large swig as if the elixir would carry all my answers.

Chapter 31

A Meal for Pani

Paul

WHEN I SAW JON'S JACKET ON EMILY, I CLENCHED MY TEETH so hard that the muscles in my jaw squirmed with tension. All my suspicions were true—I was right, no matter how much I had wished I was wrong. I had forced the most painful smile in front of our mother's, reminding myself I had left, to give her this chance to sort through her feelings for Jon. How was she supposed to do that without spending time with him, right? *I don't know what I was thinking . . .*

My grip around the blender tightened as the potatoes got cut into little pieces. First, I wanted to shout at her for repeating her mother's mistakes. Shake her for believing he could make her happy instead of me. But after everything Lucas told me, I understood that her emotions for Jon were rooted in her desire to help him. She had to try to pull him out of the shithole he had thrown himself into. It was against her nature not to try. Just like a hurricane strives to merge with the ground. I'd been there myself. I tried, Kiki tried, *heck* . . . his father even gave up on trying. Jon wasn't capable of accepting any help. We knew that, but she didn't. At least not yet. So, I acted like I hadn't noticed her new addition to her wardrobe and repeated to myself that in a few days I would be her only choice. To Jon, on the other hand, I'd sent a picture of me with German beer—to shove my face into his, to trigger guilt because fuck, he deserved feeling shitty for destroying something great in my life—again. I pressed the blender even deeper into the pot. *Ugh, I don't like this manipulative side of me.*

"Paul?" Susanne was standing next to me in the kitchen, carefully taking the blender out of my hands. "The mashed potatoes are soup now." She laughed, not angry about me messing up dinner. I let her take the blender from me, and she immediately cleaned it in the sink.

"I'm sorry!" I trembled back, crashing against the kitchen trash can. Sharp pain rushed through my big toe, ending up in every nerve of my body. I jumped on my healthy foot, holding my fucked-up one with my hands. I could run on it again, but one false load or push against it, and my stomach twisted and turned. Susanne immediately grabbed frozen peas out of the freezer.

"Here!" She held them out to me.

"I'm fine."

Susanne curved her brows. "Paul, you're white and sit on ground."

It was then I realized I wasn't standing anymore. Leaning on my palms, I chilled in the middle of the kitchen. I took the peas, pulled down my sock, and placed them on my foot. It sent another shiver through my body but one way more welcoming than the pain. Richard had left earlier to eat with some colleagues, and Henry was out for a walk. He loved looking at the mountains and Germany's nature. I went with him the other days but didn't want to leave Susanne alone with dinner preparation.

"What happened to your foot?" Susanne asked while looking at the scars that spread all over my skin from my ankle to my toes.

It was a question Emily had also asked me when we were at the caves with Breana. I didn't like talking about my slight disability, so I pretended it was nothing, but it wasn't nothing. For months, I was locked to the bed, unable to go to the bathroom, and a successful career as a football athlete had slipped away. I was high on pain pills, playing video games twenty-four seven. Eventually, I counted the minutes until I could pop another pill—and I realized how much control I had given those monsters. I asked Jon to hide them from me. If I couldn't find them, I couldn't take them. Especially when I couldn't even walk through the room on my own. It was a shit few weeks, but I managed to fight the addiction. In the end, Jon's hideout was swallowing them himself. I never understood why. It was me with the injury.

"A friend of mine, Jon—"

"Oh, Emily mentioned Jon!" Susanne's face lit up with joy, and a genuine smile spread.

"Oh, did she . . .?"

"Yeah, she told me how he annoyed her. That she spoke German because she got angry. But she sound so excited." Susanne laughed out loud. "I think Jon made her speak up?"

I opened my mouth but closed it again. Finding confidence was part of Emily's list; she spoke up the most around him. I'd never considered this.

"I guess . . ." My shoulders dropped, and I pressed the peas onto my foot. I had saved her, but he had built her. Even though I was furious at her, I kept forming these explanations to defend her actions. The power she had over me. . . it was insane.

"Sorry, I interrupted. What happened with your foot?" Susanne asked again.

"Um . . ." I suddenly didn't feel like telling the entire story anymore. "A car rolled over it."

"A car?" Susanne gasped into her palm.

"Yep, stupid accident."

Emily didn't want her to dislike Jon, and I wouldn't be the one to put him in a bolt of bad lightning.

"Why are you sitting on the ground, dude?" Lucas stood in the doorframe, his girlfriend behind him, peeking over his shoulder. I quickly lifted myself and handed Susanne the peas.

"I slipped." I tried shrugging it off, and Susanne turned back to the freezer, keeping our secret. Lucas nodded and glanced into the pots.

"Potato soup? You knew I was coming. Why would you make soup, Mama?" Lucas said with sincere confusion.

Susanne spun around. "I thought today we get a miracle you eat soup." She winked at me, and I couldn't help but smile wide.

"Well, I love soup." Kelly beamed, and she and Susanne exchanged a hug. Lucas joined them, throwing his arms around both their shoulders. "Oh, it feels good to be here again."

They held still for a couple of seconds, and I felt unnecessary. I scratched my arm, but Susanne waved me to join them. I hesitated but then walked into their embrace. I would've loved an exchange year with Susanna as my host mother and become part of this family like Kelly did. I held my breath . . . It could've been so perfect. I could've lived here for a year, and then Emily and I could've decided which country we would like to live in. I would've been fine with whatever she wanted, ready to support us through college before proposing. But now, if my assumptions were correct, this wouldn't be my story to live. It would be his.

I quickly wiped my face. Yet there was something I couldn't understand in all this . . . They were great, amazing even. *How could Emily leave them behind for such a long time?*

"Plates and silverware." Susanne pointed at a cupboard, and I reached into them. Kelly took care of the glasses while Lucas searched for some pot holders. While setting up the table, Lucas talked about his day. He studied social work and had to write an exam about a book he hadn't even read. For ten minutes, he created a story about analyzing the tree on the cover instead. I almost laughed to tears again. He knew how to tell a story. This was my fourth night but the first one Lucas and Kelly were here.

Susanne came in with a roasted chicken in a casserole dish. "I hope you hungry because I cooked for ten!"

"Oh, please! Paul and I would be able to finish this alone!" Lucas pointed out.

"Definitely!" I agreed, feeling the water already doubling in my mouth.

"Paul, do you know when your father will be back?" Susanne asked.

I heard a door opening and falling closed. "That must be him."

Susanne turned around, the casserole dish still in her hands. But it wasn't my father. Richard walked in, wearing a long dark coat and black hat, giving detective vibes. I threw up my hand to greet him, but his face immediately landed on Lucas, and his eyes got so dark my hand froze in the air.

"*Was machst du in meinem Haus!*" he screamed at Lucas, and Susanne let go of the casserole dish in her hands. With a loud thud, it crashed to the ground, the porcelain smashing into multiple pieces. Pani, who was resting on a chair, jumped down for the chicken. My hand was still frozen in the air. Lucas was on his feet, Kelly covering her mouth in dense shock. Richard kept screaming words I couldn't understand. Susanne ran up to him, pleading with him to calm down. Or at least I assumed because she almost kneeled before him. He slapped her hand away, and I shot up in my chair.

"Paul, don't!" Kelly looked at me with desperation. I panicked as the two grown men rushed at each other. Susanne tried to stand between them, but Richard shoved her. Her head crashed against the table. Lucas went for Richard's neck, choking him. *Heck no, I won't stand here watching this!* I squeezed through the dining room and tore them apart. Kelly rushed over to Susanne, placing an arm around her. Lucas and Richard ignored me, getting back at each other with words. But the way the spit flew between them, I knew it was a matter of time until the first punch would fall.

"Stop! I don't know what is happening here, but this isn't how to solve conflict!"

I pressed my palms on both their chests.

"You stay out of this before I kick you out too!" Richard's eyes were red as he glared at me. Kelly cupped Lucas's cheek and gave him an intense look while whispering in German. I held Richard one arm's length away.

"Thanks for your help, Paul." Lucas gave me an apologetic look. Then he glanced down at his mother. "Mama, wir gehen lieber. Es tut mir leid."

They rushed out of the dining room. I held a firm stare on Richard until I heard the door closing. He snorted at me, but I didn't let him intimidate me. Instead, I checked for Susanne, leaning down to her. She was bleeding, the blood flowing down her forehead.

"Are you okay?"

It wasn't a lot of blood, but enough to get mine boiling. *Who does he think he is to push her?!*

My fingers clenched into fists, but Susanne held me by my arm. "Paul, I'm okay. Please, give Richard and me a moment alone?"

I heard Richard mumble something with disgust, still spitting his words in full rage.

"I'm not leaving you alone with him."

She looked at me with tears still flowing silently down her cheeks, but eventually, she nodded.

"Okay, wait there." She pointed back at the chair where I had been excited for tonight's dinner minutes ago. I disliked stepping away from her side, but I didn't know what was happening. I gave Richard another glare before getting out of their air. Richard immediately gesticulated with his hands, not even worrying about Susanne's head injury. She continuously said: "Es tut mir Leid."

I eventually realized this must mean she was sorry or something. But what the heck was she sorry for? She was only having her son and his girlfriend over for dinner. Richard stormed out, slamming the door into Susanna's face. She remained frozen, sobbing into her hands.

I immediately circled the chicken Pani licked at as if nothing had happened. *Oh, Pani, you better not throw up in my bed later.* When I reached Susanne, I pulled her into my arms, and she sobbed into my chest.

"I understand why Emily left." Susanne sobbed louder and louder. "She's better off without him."

"You would be better off without him as well," I said. I could understand how Emily could leave her family behind after all . . . she had left them because there was poison. Poison named Richard.

Chapter 32

What I Want vs. What I Need

Emily

My heart was still fluttering when I rushed down to the basement. I swiped Jon's jacket off and dropped it on the bed just to pick it up and throw it against the wall. Tears crawled out of my eyes—Paul recognized it. I leaned down for the charger because my phone had been dead again. I plugged it in with a snort, impatient for it to turn on. I had to tell Paul what had happened, but whatever this was with Jon, my heart barely even sent all the information to my brain. It made no sense . . . all I had were feels. I fell on my belly, nose pressed into the mattress, and mewled. Paul's shocked face traveled back into my brain when his familiar smell reached my nose. It was a matter of seconds, and then he smiled. Smiled as if my wearing Jon's jacket was standard. *Shouldn't he care?* I knew Jon would've freaked out, lost it even—it wouldn't have mattered if our parents were present. That was the big difference between them. Paul avoided the uncomfortable while Jon embraced it. Except for talking—neither one would win a medal for that. With fumbling hands, I reached for my now turned-on phone. I checked my notifications, and Paul's name popped up for the first time since he left. My heartbeat escalated into my throat as I read the message.

Paul: Hey. You looked a bit sick. Are you alright? Mom told me you were down with the flu, but I didn't know it was that bad.

I stared at his message, my entire body shaking now. Here I was, clearly hurting him, and he was worried about my health. He was too good for his own good. The knot in my stomach inflated, forcing the contents to creep up my throat. I sprinted to the bathroom. There went the hash browns and pancakes. Down the toilet, with all the respect I'd left for myself. Paul was a great guy. Even now, he didn't dare to hurt me. I clamped onto the toilet seat, struggling to hold myself on my knees. A loud sob exploded out of me. *Paul deserves better than me.*

I jumped into the shower, scrubbing my skin and shampooing my hair like this could eliminate the guilt in my heart. But no matter how hard I scratched my skin, it didn't make me feel any better. I was crap . . . *no!* I was shit, pure shit! My sight fell onto the razor, which I had cut myself with accidentally a few days ago. I grabbed it, letting my finger slide over it sideways. I never understood why people hurt themselves. Why would you want to feel pain on purpose? But I had to do something to make myself pay for what I'd done. For not even thinking about him when it happened. For even feeling happy when it did. I shouldn't feel happy about kissing Jon. I should feel . . . pain.

I crouched in the bathtub until the bleeding stopped and wandered back to the basement. I took Jon's jacket and folded it in my hands when suddenly, a plastic bag fell out of its pocket. It carried little pink pills, like the one from Marna's. I closed my eyes, running my fingertips over the plastic. I'd experienced a few nights of being high now, and those were the only nights I could sleep without my brain screaming at me. I was exhausted, my veins itching to take one of these to get a good afternoon nap. I had told Gena I still didn't feel good and would lie down anyway. She wouldn't notice. Nobody would. Maybe Jon, but he wasn't one who was allowed to judge. I took out two and threw them down my throat. Then I grabbed my phone to text Paul back:

Me: We need to talk.

"Ugh, stop . . ." I mumbled, sweat pooling down onto the sheets.

"Please, don't . . ." I twisted and turned, but my body was too heavy. "I said no!"

I inhaled my spit, causing me to cough. I let my head fall back into the pillow. *It was a dream.* They weren't here touching me. Something suddenly vibrated below my back, pulling me out of this stupor. *My phone!*

I quickly grabbed it, and the light crawled into my eyes like acid. I lowered the brightness, but it took a few seconds till the blurry screen turned sharp for my eyesight. I expected it to be Paul, but his name was nowhere on the screen. Instead, there were eight missed calls and twelve messages written in capital letters from Jon. My head was still tumbling from left to right. I must be dreaming. I checked the time. 11:30?! *I slept over twelve hours?!*

My thumb moved to the messages when I received another call from him.

"H-hi!" I tried to talk, but my throat was raspy, and only cracking sounds escaped. I reached for the water bottle beside my bed.

"*Why the fuck did you go to Marna's!*" Jon roared into the phone, and I accidentally dropped it into my lap. He continued yelling, but my ears were weirdly muffled from the sleep coma I had awoken from.

"Jon, hold on . . . I dropped my phone," I said while picking it up. *Silence.*

When I pressed it against my cheek, I swallowed to eliminate the lump. "Jon, what's going on? Did something happen?"

My voice was back, still sounding raspy but better than before. I was startled that he mentioned me going to Marna's; I thought we had successfully ignored that.

"Are you fucking kidding me, Little German?! We kissed!"

My entire body tensed up. Jon regretted the kiss. He had time to think about it, and now he wanted to backpedal!

"Um . . . I . . ." I exhaled way too many times. I couldn't pretend it hadn't happened . . . not again.

"You know what? Fuck this shit. I'm coming over!"

"No!" I stood up so quickly that the little moonlight in this room turned dark. I was unprepared, and it was too late to go out. Gena would notice.

"Too late. I'm on my way." He hung up.

"Fuck, fuck, fuck!" I covered my mouth. Saying fuck three times was a new first. I put on the closest clothes I could grab and sneaked down the hall. Gena was sitting on the couch, eating popcorn and watching a horror TV show. She was off work for the first time since I'd moved in, and I barely spent time with her. I tugged at the ties of my sweatshirt. I had to make sure Jon wouldn't burst through the door and declare whatever this was, like in a drama movie. I brainstormed on how I could sneak out without Gena noticing. *The garage!* I could walk to the basement door, pretending I wanted to sleep there. I walked out of the secured shadow.

"Oh, honey!" Gena beamed, with popcorn still in her hand. "You want to watch some ghost detecting? I think they might have something there!"

I swallowed, looking at my hands. "I'm still not feeling well . . ."

"Oh, you do sound sick." She put down the popcorn and muted the show. "You want me to make you some tea? Soup? I don't know how to cook the ones you taught Henry, but I'm good heating up a canned one." She got off the couch.

"I wanted to head down and sleep." I pointed at the stairs, my brain ticking like a watch.

"Honey, you slept all day . . . and you're wearing your clothes." Her eyes fell to my jeans.

"Um, yeah. This sickness is really tiring me. My fresh pj's are downstairs . . ." I mumbled, but she looked at me with a crease on her forehead. "I put them in Paul's closet."

Her confusion faded, and she nodded. "If you need anything, I'm here." But I couldn't help but hear the disappointment in her voice. I forced a smile and dashed downstairs. *Tomorrow I will spend time with her, for sure!* I pulled open the garage door and froze when the lights were on.

"Hi!" Zack peeked around a wall from his haunted house labyrinth, which I had sadly missed as I was still living at the Stone house.

"Um, what are you doing here?" My voice was shaking. Zack let out a loud laugh as he walked in my direction, circling buckets of paint, spiderwebs, and dolls with wounds painted onto them. I shivered. This would be Danielle's deathbed.

"I'm always down here." He shrugged, irritated I even asked this question.

"But Halloween was two months ago," I reminded him.

"Yeah, I'm planning for next year." He made a face. "Why do you look like a minion who has gotten into trouble?"

I looked down at myself. In my rush, I had picked out blue denim jeans and a bright yellow sweatshirt my mom got for me at a thrift shop.

I laughed out softly. "I don't know what I'm doing, Zack . . ."

I let myself drop onto the next chair and let my fingers glide over a clean paintbrush, feeling suddenly calm. Lying to Gena was one thing, but lying to Zack . . . it was getting out of hand. I didn't say anything until he had taken a seat on the ground himself. Him placing himself below me gave me a weirdly comfortable feeling . . . as if he was letting me have the upper hand.

"You were sleepwalking or something?" He chortled loudly; like Henry, he had this sense of lightness about him.

The air poured out of my throat. "I wish it would be that . . ." I leaned back in the chair, letting go of the brush. "It's all fucked-up, Zack."

My eyes teared up, and I kept my stare on the wall.

Zack cleared his throat. "If I'm supposed to play counselor, I'll need a little more. Because, yeah, humanity is fucked-up, and the world is fucked-up. Nothing new."

I had to laugh again. Zack always focused on what made him happy, like zombie slaughtering, food, and his haunted house obsession. Even though he had a daily fight with his ADHD, he didn't let it affect his happiness. He embraced it, pulling out the positive by exploring his passions. I couldn't help but admire that.

"It's about Paul, isn't it? I noticed some tension at Christmas."

I nodded, unsure if talking to Paul's little brother about my love life was a good idea. But I liked Zack. He was different . . . a bit like me.

"I want Paul. He's good to me. He makes me happy . . . but yet I feel like I do everything to sabotage it." My lip trembled. I'd been swallowing up this entire break since it happened, my head feeling like it was exploding. I sobbed into my hands.

"Sometimes what we want and what we need are two opposite things. You want him, but he's not what you need if you do everything you can to smash it." Zack lifted his body, dropping his hands into his pants as if he had read the weather aloud.

"Zack . . . how?"

"You think I'm blind? I saw how you and Jon looked when I came out of the bathroom. Heck, another second, and you would've kissed, which would've made it hella awkward." He made a vomiting gesture. I laughed wearily and shook my head. How come someone on the outside could see it while I couldn't? I had tried so hard to find someone who would treat me lovely. To not end up in a trap like my mother. Unaware that I had built my own prison this way . . . but now I held the key in my hands. I could get out, find out what I want. . . and need.

"How do I know if Jon is what I need, though?"

"Crap, how should I know?" Zack walked up to me, placing his hand on my shoulder. "I get you're lost. But let my brother off the hook . . . he doesn't deserve chasing after a girl that is in love with his best friend."

I wanted to fight his words, saying I wasn't into Jon. But there was no denying anymore—I had feelings for Jon, whether I liked it or not.

"I'm in love with your brother as well . . ." I stammered instead.

"Then you got some shit to figure out." Zack shrugged, walking toward the door. When he got there, he turned around.

"I didn't see you coming through here. This is your mess—don't pull me into it . . . however, if you don't make a decision soon, I will tell Paul."

I swallowed harshly and nodded, entirely understanding his siding with his brother.

"Good." He turned off the lights as if he hadn't seen me and closed the door behind him. I reached for the wall and navigated myself outside soundlessly. After letting down the garage door, I checked the window. Gena was concentrating on her show, munching popcorn. I sprinted down the street. The call had ended at least twice the time

Jon would need walking here. My run was cut short when I found him on the same street. He was tumbling, a bottle of something in his right hand. Adrenaline shot through my entire body at seeing him.

"Fuck, I told you I would come to your place!" Jon cursed when I reached him. I caught my breath.

"J-Jon . . . be quiet."

"Oh, screw those nosy neighbors!" Jon roared even louder, shaking the bottle filled with brown liquid. He was drunk. Not just tipsy but full-blown drunk.

I set my hands on his shoulders to attract his attention and shot him a warning glare. "Jon, I'm serious."

He looked at me calmly, but then his brows furrowed, and the edges of his lips quirked. "You're high. Why would you do that shit again?! Wasn't yesterday enough for you?!" A vein pulsated on his neck, and his grip around the bottle tightened. But so did my patience with him.

I pulled my hands away and crossed my arms. "At least I care about what's happening around me. You're entirely wasted!"

"And exactly, that is your issue." He smiled broadly, lifting the bottle for another sip. He grimaced as he swallowed it. "You care so much about everyone around you. It's sickening." Jon twirled around, throwing the bottle to the ground. It splintered into a thousand pieces, causing me to flinch back. "Sorrrrryy, neighborhood!" Jon laughed loudly, throwing his head back like he owned this street.

I shoved him as harshly as I could. "Stop this, Jon!"

"You want me to shut up?" He made a provoking step toward me, placing his hands on my neck and pulling my face to his. Just by his touch, his dark brown eyes entered my soul and spread through every vein in my body, electrifying me with this bliss of excitement. Something I never felt with Paul.

"Kiss me, Little German. Right now, right here, and I promise I'll shut up."

I pulled in my lower lip. The urge to kiss him was tremendous, but Gena could still see us looking out the window. Plus, I didn't want him to think I would accept this type of behavior from him.

"Jon . . ." I tried to back off.

"Right . . . you still want him, don't you?" Jon growled, not breaking his eye contact with me.

I heard a door opening behind me, followed by a male voice. "You kids, it's the middle of the night!"

My gaze flew over to the Shields' house, seeing the TV light wasn't the only light coming from the living room anymore. "Let's not . . . not here." I tried to drag Jon with me, but he remained put.

"Why not? Are you afraid someone could see us? Because you're embarrassed about being with me? Guess what, I'm not perfect Paul!" Jon's face hardened, and he finally walked down the street. I followed him.

"I'm not embarrassed about you, Jon! I don't want Gena to find out I'm not with her son at the moment. Paul and I didn't talk about if we—"

I crashed into Jon's back as he suddenly stood like a statue around the corner.

"Ouch." I tumbled back.

"At the moment?"

He turned around with furrowed brows, and I clutched my hands against my chest. *Why did I have to say that . . .*

"I . . . um. I . . . I don't know." I stumbled, turning away.

"Wow, I'm just your replacement until he returns. You suck that much at being alone?" Jon snarled at me, and my confusion lit up into ashes. I wouldn't let him put any words into my mouth.

"What do you even want from me, Jon?" The heat crawled from my neck into my cheeks, and I glared at him. "Last time I checked, you told me you don't want to date! Then you get with Kiki. Then you kiss me. Then break up with her. Then you're talking to her on the phone again, and who knows what else!" The words spiraled out of my throat, and Jon's sight dropped. This wasn't a moment where silence was better than words. No, this was a moment in which it was now or never.

"What Paul and I had . . ." I swallowed harshly, feeling my eyes turning into a blur again. "It was perfect! He was a great boyfriend, and I felt safe with him. Protected and calm. But then you . . ." My breathing became hectic, and I could barely form any coherent sentences. "You . . . you did you!" I pointed at him and bit my lip harshly until it hurt. "Get out of my head!" I shoved him, letting out all this anger at myself for having let him crawl under my skin.

"No." Jon shrugged.

"No?" I shook my head in utter confusion. "I poured my heart out, and all I get from you is a no?" I snorted, finally coming to my senses. It was impossible to talk with him. Or be with him, for that matter.

"You know what, Jon? A no is not enough . . ." I turned around, ready to go back.

"No, I can't get out of your head because I fucking fell for your ass, Little German. And I fucking hate it."

I twirled back around. "What?"

Jon's eyebrows pinched together as he stepped to get rid of the space between us, and he cupped my cheeks.

"I said that I fell for you, Emily."

I gasped for breath. I got the pure version, with no fucking, no ass, and no hate. Words I thought weren't even a part of his vocabulary. *Jon fell in love with me?*

"You . . . I . . ." I didn't know what to say, so I stared into those eyes that had now not only entered my soul but were burned into it. Jammed with glue, staples, and so much duct tape impossible to tear off again.

"Good to know that this is how I can get you speechless." He pressed his lips onto mine, and I turned the key out of my cell. I had felt dizzy before, but this was a new high. And I swear, for a moment, I was flying . . . okay, maybe it was because he picked me up, and I clasped my arms around his neck. I was unsure if I felt like crying or laughing. Jon had fallen in love with me. Just like I fell for him. We broke the kiss.

"You better remember this tomorrow, or I'll be freaking mad at you." I glared at him.

"Aren't you always mad at me anyway?" Jon grinned, and I leaned in to shut him up with another kiss but got distracted by red and blue lights. A cop car had parked next to us, and the doors slammed shut.

Jon's eyes widened in panic as he let me down. He grabbed my hand, ready to pull me away with him, but the cocking sounds from a gun made me stiffen.

"Hands where I can see them!"

I threw my hands into the air. Just two nights ago, I would've given anything to get sent back to Germany, but now, after hearing those words . . . *I fell for you* . . . going back was not an option any longer.

Chapter 33

Without a Speed Limit

Paul

"DID YOU KNOW THIS CAR IS THE GERMAN SUPRA?" LUCAS asked, avoiding the awkward space from last night.

"You did." I sat on the passenger seat on the Autobahn in Germany, staring at Emily's message about having to talk. I couldn't bring myself to reply to it.

"Oh . . ." By now, Lucas had told me every little detail about his car—"after Kelly, Emily, and Mom, my biggest treasure," he said. A black number 3 BMW 335I. No idea what those numbers meant. The stereotype of Germany having fancy cars was an understatement; they had nice-ass cars. I put my phone away. No matter how excited I was to drive fast, my thoughts were still on Susanne and how Richard had shoved her. How desperately she cried and how I couldn't understand a thing. I had sat with Susanne for a while. We didn't say anything until Dad walked through the door. His mood crashed when he saw shredded porcelain and her bleeding head. I got sent to the room so he could have a grown-up conversation with Susanne.

I had received a hint of something Emily had grown up under for years—and I already wanted to get away from it. Susanne said she would understand if we wanted to take a hotel room, but my father and I shook our heads at the same time. As long as we could be there for her, we would. Who would we be to leave her alone in this mess if we could help her get through it, even if it was only for a few days.

"Why isn't Susanne leaving him?"

I didn't know where we were going, but I didn't question it either. I was glad to have a moment with him alone.

"It's complicated." Lucas shrugged. "Did you see that car? Guess how many PS this has!"

"PS?"

"Horsepowers."

"Ah . . . but why is it complicated? Does it have to do with why he went crazy on you?"

"Richard and I have a history." Lucas sighed, and I could see the speedometer flying. It wasn't a good idea to start this topic on the unlimited-speed Autobahn. 150 km/h . . . about 90 miles per hour.

"Richard wasn't always like this. He used to be charming, gave Mama many presents, and treated us, especially Emily, like his own. She was about twelve. I was sixteen."

160 km/h. Lucas's eyes remained stoic on the street. I didn't say anything, not daring to make him stop this story.

"For about a year, we grew closer. Receiving support and affection. I was thankful he supported our mother after all the shit she had to endure with our father."

170 km/h. I bit my lip. Emily never told me about the divorce. If it was ugly or if she got pulled into it.

"Then he bought the house you're staying at right now." Lucas swallowed, and I couldn't help but notice how he made sure to not use the word *home*. "And when we lived there together, it all changed."

"How?"

"He revealed his true colors." Lucas hit the gas even more. *180 km/h. 190 km/h . . .*

My body pressed into the seat, and I held on to the armrest. Lucas's fists were wrapped around the steering wheel.

"Lucas, you don't have to tell me if you don't want to . . ." I reminded him, my fingers digging deeper into the seat's leather. *200 km/h. 205 km/h. 210 km/h.* But Lucas didn't notice this speed wasn't my everyday life.

"He became jealous of Emily and me because we are close to our mom. He had no one except for her . . . I should've questioned earlier why."

My heart crashed hard against my rib cage. Never in my life had I felt so much speed. I wasn't sure if I was terrified or amazed. Either way, I would rather hear the rest of this story with both feet on steady ground.

"How fast can this car go?" I yelled because the outside noises had gotten loud.

"Oh, up to 250. We're not at the limit yet!" He smiled again. "But maybe we will do that another time. We're taking the next exit."

We stopped at a rest stop with only parking spots and a toilet house.

"You ready?"

"Ready for what?" I asked as we stepped out of the car. Strong wind hit me, and I dropped my body into it. Lucas pointed behind me. I shivered as I realized we were standing next to a wind turbine. My mouth dropped. I imagined them being tall, but not like this. They were gigantic, close to touching the clouds gigantic.

"Wow . . ."

"I don't know what is fascinating about them, but I promised Emi to show you." Lucas cackled, clearly confused as to why I couldn't pull my eyes from those turning wings of the wheel.

"Emi?" I asked, eyes still not drifting away. The wheel was turning fast, by its own produced energy.

"Yeah, that's what we call her."

Emi . . .

"So what is fascinating about these things?"

I smiled. No one understood it. "I think it's crazy how something like this can produce energy and barely causes any harm to the earth. Don't get me wrong, I love cars, and I could never stop driving mine, but I believe if we all would work together and make some changes, we could keep the beauty of nature alive." I turned to Lucas. "I want a world where my children can enjoy it as much as I could. Going fishing, lurking between trees to see a deer, and has Emily told you about the squirrels? She's obsessed with them." I grinned from ear to ear, picturing how she always watched them out of the car.

"Damn, Emily made a good catch with you." Lucas placed his palm on my shoulder with an approving nod. I swallowed harshly, not telling him what had been going on felt wrong, but I didn't want to worry him about his little sister. He let go of me and placed his hands in his pockets, watching the wind turbines with different eyes than before. I wiggled my toes. I was on even ground now.

"So what happened when Richard got jealous of you two?"

Lucas's shoulders stiffened. "He made sure to remind us daily how terrible we were. Nothing we did was good enough. Everything we said was analyzed and twisted against us. I could handle it. But Emily let him reduce her entire worth, losing every ounce of confidence, her voice . . . her opinion. Eventually, she fought with depression."

"Depression?"

I heard many people saying, "*Oh, I'm feeling depressed,*" and I knew from Zack how tough it was when your body decides your mood. When I was chained to the bed for a few months, I thought I was depressed as well. But as soon as I could walk again, I felt better; it wasn't depression. If Emily was dealing with mental health issues . . . *fuck, that's bad.*

"Emily had to be submitted to mental health care for a few months when she was fifteen. The feeling of never being good enough . . . she was acting impulsively. Unpredictable. One day, she was full of energy, and the next, we could barely get her out of bed."

My fists balled. Richard had destroyed her, turning toxic into normal behavior for her . . . her self-sabotaging . . . her liking it when Jon argued with her . . . her impulsive decisions.

Lucas continued the story. "One day, I went crazy on Richard, told him what a bastard he was and that he was responsible for Emi struggling this much." Lucas kicked the pathway with his foot. "He threw me out of the house, saying I wasn't allowed below his roof any longer. He wasn't supposed to come home last night."

Lucas slumped down on the pathway, his head hanging between his shoulders. I sat down next to him. *That fucking bastard!* I would've done the same as Lucas. I took a few breaths to let it all sink in, but there was something I still couldn't understand.

"Then why is your mother with him?" I kept my stare on the ground.

Lucas inhaled and exhaled heavily. "He's a manipulative asshole. He knows what he's doing, giving enough for my mother not to be able to leave him but too little to make her feel appreciated. She's like a dog jumping for every treat."

He wiped a tear away, and I joined him in seconds. Fucking unmanly to cry at a rest stop, *but screw that!* I was tired of hiding my emotions and feelings. I wanted to scream them out, cry like a child if my chest was bursting open, and not run. I was done running.

I rose to my feet again. "We have to get Susanne out of there!"

"You think I haven't tried? She thinks she's worth nothing, man! Every time she tries to leave him, he lures her back in. I'm helpless in this."

"How could you let Emily go to America, then? If she struggled with her mental health . . . wasn't it kinda risky to let her do this on her own?"

"Because I knew she would live in a safer home. A home in which she wouldn't feel like crap. But it's like those narcissistic people are pulling in Emily. When I heard about Mrs. Stone, I bought a plane ticket."

"You came to America?" I shook my head. "Emily never mentioned you were here!"

"Because she doesn't know." Lucas shrugged. "I was close to walking into the Stone house, ready to pull her out and get her back home. Here I could at least be there for her. But then I saw her with you. I was used to seeing her tense and afraid, but with you, she was happy. I knew she wasn't alone anymore, so I left again."

My heart suddenly turned heavier, pulling down my entire body. "But now I'm here and not there."

"Yes, now you are here," Lucas whispered back, and my urge to get back to my girl doubled.

"We have to do something to help your mother!" I had to use my time here if I couldn't be there for her.

Lucas smiled. "That's my job. You take care of Emi when you return, okay?"

I nodded hectically. I would make it right. We would start over, and everything would be perfect.

"So, do you want to drive this time?" Lucas stood up and held up the key to his BMW.

I startled. "No shit?"

"I trust you enough with my sister. I can also trust you with my car." Lucas grinned and threw me the key. My stomach twisted into knots. I shouldn't be trusted because I had failed. I had pushed her away when I should've pulled her close. I opened the door to the seat of control. I had to prove to my brother's girlfriend I could be trusted—by not crashing his BMW . . . and returning to Emily as soon as possible. Because yes, Emily would be my girlfriend again.

Chapter 34

Sugared Coffee

Jon

I'D WOKEN UP IN STRANGE PLACES BEFORE. BEDS OF GIRLS I DIDN'T remember meeting, the bathroom floor, or my neighbor's front yard. One of my most glorious moments was when I woke up naked in a pool . . . I had a talent for living in a scenario people had weird dreams about. But nothing, and I mean absolutely nothing, was as twisted and messed up as when I realized where I was this morning. I heard some whispers in front of the door. One was the voice of this annoying little girl, and I smiled. I pointed my ears to listen to her, but another familiar voice pulled me out of this comfy state—the voice of my mother—and my eyes burst open.

Although my head was banging and I felt like I was going to gag, I sat up. With one look to the left and right, I realized I was in the room my mother had created for me when she'd moved together with her *oh-so-perfect* husband. This was my first night sleeping in this bed, and heck, it was comfortable compared to the lousy old one I had at Dad's. I tried to concentrate, but the memories of ending up here were nowhere. Deleted from the archive, not even left in the trash anymore. *Fuck . . . did I drink that much?* The door opened slowly, and Emily sneaked in with her head held low. She was wearing some pajamas, probably from my sister. She turned to close the door silently, and I sucked in my breath. Emily had more weight than Lauren, so those red-and-black shorts sat tight around her waist. Her butt cheeks hung out the right amount of seductive, and . . . holy crap. She usually hid her ass behind dresses or long jackets. My cock pulsed up in my pants, and I lost all the blood in my brain. She closed the door and jumped when she noticed me staring at her.

"Oh, you're up!" she gushed.

"Just woke up."

"How are you feeling?" She swiped strands of hair behind her ear and looked at me with big eyes.

I bit down my lip and let out a heavy exhale. "I'm fine."

I wondered what she would look like in her underwear. Or what type of underwear she would even be wearing. I couldn't imagine her being innocent in bed, especially not after what Paul said to Jamie. My cock fell back down. Right, Paul had slept with her. He was in love with her. I think I was in love with her as well. If what I felt was love. I knew I wanted to be around her . . . all the time. *Argh, it's annoying.*

"I expected you to have a hangover." Emily walked to the bed and sat down like I was her patient.

"Been worse."

I wasn't surprised that my drunk brain had searched for Emily. It was almost impossible for me not to try and get close to her whenever I lost my threshold. But how on earth did we end up at my mother's place? Out of all the possible beds in this town, this one stood at the very end of my list.

"You don't remember how we got here?" Her face turned pale, and she scooched a bit away. I shook my head, which left a harsh stab rush through it.

"Do you remember anything from last night?" she pushed, but all I could focus on was the sting behind my eyes.

"I only know I need an aspirin right now."

She sighed and gave me something out of her hand. "Figured you would need it. I asked your mother."

She handed me the little lifesaver, and I popped it into my mouth, not even needing water to wash it down. "Thanks."

She looked at me expectantly, her eyebrows squeezed together.

"The only way I could remember is if you give me some starter points, Little German.."

I concentrated on saying this in a sweet tone. Emily could be sensitive—I kinda liked that because her emotions made me reflect on myself, but right now, I wanted nothing more than answers.

"You called me and wanted to see me." She blushed adorably, my cock twitching again. "You were drunk, screaming, and waking up the entire neighborhood. I was so mad at you." She smiled.

"You don't look mad." I noticed my mood lighting up.

"Well . . . you, um, told me—" She looked down, biting her lip.

"What did I tell you?" I asked impatiently. She played with the hem of her shirt, not looking up from it, her cheeks growing reddish.

"Um, I meant you were about to say something when a police car surprised us."

She shook her hand as if that wasn't a big deal.

"We got arrested?!" My hearing was muffled. I knew from the first night we hung out that Emily could never get caught by the cops, or she would have to leave the country. I glided my fingers into my hair and tugged at the roots, my face almost between my knees. "Fuck!"

I'd brought her into this situation, even though I promised Paul to make sure I wouldn't get her in trouble, and—

"Jon!" Emily shook me by the shoulders, kneeling between my legs. I looked at her with burning eyes. "Jon, we didn't get arrested."

"But you said there was a cop car?" I almost shouted.

"It turned out to be your stepfather. Why didn't you tell me he's the local police chief?"

I let out a loud growl, partly annoyed. This gave Humphrey another reason for me to owe him, but I was somewhat relieved because this story could've ended much worse.

"He wanted to bring me home, but you said you wouldn't go anywhere if I wouldn't join you." She giggled into her palm. "That's how we ended up here, but you passed out the second we lay down."

I looked down at my jeans. "Little German—"

There was a soft knock on the already opened door. My mother.

"Jon, we would like to talk to you . . . alone."

She threw Emily a straight face and left without waiting for my reply. She used to be filled with so much warmth she could lift everyone's mood. Now the temperature dropped whenever she walked into a room. *Isn't the sober life supposed to make you happier?* At least, that got preached in all those meetings I had attended a few months ago. That it would be tough for a while, but we would be rewarded with happiness and control, and the painful cravings would be worth it. But what I saw didn't look worth it: no smiles, stifled mouth, a worry line in the middle of her forehead. I prayed it was just her that felt that way.

"Jon?" Emily had placed her hand softly on my shoulder. I must've zoned out.

"Um, yeah." I swallowed and wiped over my face to get rid of the oil, my body trying to press out all the toxic elements I had put into myself. "I guess I gotta do this."

Emily swiped the long curl out of my face and gave me a gentle look. "It's going to be okay."

I jumped up without a word and pushed Emily's hand away. This felt close. *Too close.* The way she was caring for me, worrying about me. I didn't need a Kiki 2.0 situation. Not that Emily would be anything like Kiki—they were different . . . but I swear if she tried to fix me, I would lose it.

At the door, I turned around to look at her again. I didn't know why, but my heart felt conflicted about our possible future. She smiled at me, full of hope and kindness like how my mother used to smile. *It's either her trying to fix me or me pulling her down with me.* I ground my teeth and walked out of the room with a headshake. *I should've stayed away. . .*

I knew exactly where to find my mother. We always had serious talks in the dining room because the large-as-fuck table created as much distance as possible between us. As expected, I found my mother and Humphrey sitting on one side. When I entered, he extended his hand to the seat on the other side.

"I'd rather stand." I crossed my arms, leaning my body onto the doorframe.

Humphrey opened his mouth with a snort, but my mother shut

him up by placing her palm on his hand. "Please, Jon. This is going to be a longer conversation."

I snorted. I would fucking make sure it wouldn't be. I noticed a freshly brewed cup of coffee waiting for me at the spot they pointed to. Bribery—fine, I would take it. I sat down with a slump and immediately swallowed most of the contents in this tiny cup. An overly sweet taste spread in my mouth. I made a face; someone had added sugar to this.

"Jon. You know I was on the same path as you, and . . ." My mother took a long dramatic breath, her aura traveling back to those days. I could tell by the way her lips twitched. "And I wish I had someone helping me sooner."

There it was again, putting the blame on Dad. As if she didn't pull him down with her. As if he didn't fight with his last ounce of energy to help her. Mom didn't want his help, and I didn't want hers.

I stood up from the chair. "Stop adding sugar to my coffee. It's addictive,"

I remarked sarcastically and turned around.

"If you take one more step, I'll change my mind and report what happened last night to the police."

The threat of Humphrey shot me like a bullet in the back. My hands transformed into fists, and I froze. If this was just about me, I would storm out of here without looking back. But Emily was with me last night . . . I couldn't let her suffer the consequences.

"Fine," I growled, sitting back on the chair with my body facing to the side instead of the front.

"We don't want to annoy you, but you're ending up in more difficult situations. And we're noticing a pattern, which can only mean you're on harder drugs than we originally thought."

I made a loud snort. "And how do you know that, huh?"

Mom slammed her right hand on the table. "I know what a drug addict looks like, Jon! Don't provoke me!"

For once, I wasn't prepared for my mother's words. She never talked about her experience, always pretending she had this picture-perfect life.

"You're my son, and I can't let you make these mistakes." She took a sip of water.

"So what do you want to do, huh?" I used my chance to speak. My mother let her palm glide over the tissues in front of her, even though they had no wrinkles.

Humphrey steeled his voice. "We want you to go to rehab, Jon."

I was back on my feet. "Fuck no! I'm not doing that shit!"

"It's either that, or you're not part of this family anymore." He grinned as if he had been looking forward to shoving this line in my face.

"Blackmail? That's how you want to do this?" I almost laughed out loud.

My mother sniffed. "Please, Jon ... it's what helped me. I understand how your mind works, and if this is what we have to do to save your life ..." Her sniffing had turned into sobbing now. "Then it's my job as a mother to abandon you."

I laughed harder and leaned my body onto the table with my palms.

"You know, for this to work, I should've felt like part of this family in the first place."

My mother gasped and pulled at the tissue, making it all wrinkled and imperfect. Humphrey remained stoic, but I saw a tiny sparkle in his eyes. I turned around and rushed to the door.

"He doesn't care enough about us ..." I heard my mother sniffing, my neck hair standing up.

"He doesn't care about anything," Humphrey snapped, and I had to control myself not to go back and leave a juicy punch on his Clooney face. Emily was waiting in my room, all dressed and ready to go.

"What happened?" she immediately asked when I crashed the door open.

"I'm not her son anymore." I took her hand and pulled her with me. They were wrong. I did care because I cared for her. And that was a fucking issue.

Chapter 35

Connected by Disaster

Emily

"Jon! Don't walk so fast!" I stomped when Jon didn't slow down his pace after a few blocks. The houses surrounding me were all white brick, shining with fancy balconies and wealth. This was the fancy neighborhood of this town.

"Please!" I yelled when he still didn't flinch, my ears turning hot. I should've known he wouldn't listen if I asked kindly. I sprinted and crashed into him, losing my balance on the slippery street. Jon twirled around and held me tight by the waist.

"What the fuck, Little German! I don't want you to crash your head and get amnesia or some shit," he growled, but I wouldn't let him lure me in this easily.

"Then. Talk. To. Me!" I blazed, still holding on to his arms. He was pushing me away again. I already expected that when I cuddled up to him last night—I was prepared to fight.

"About how I almost got you arrested last night? Or how you let us end up at my mother's place?!" He tried to yank away my hands viciously, but I didn't let him.

"It's not like I had a say!" I reminded him with a sharp undertone.

"You're your own person. You can do whatever the fuck you want!" His eyes got empty, and mine burned with anger. Blaming someone whenever something went not their way—Richard always did that to me, and I wouldn't let Jon do the same.

"I decided to stay with you. I came out because I wanted to see you. I remained on that street because I wanted to be with you. And I got into the police car with you because I—" I pointed at myself with a slow and controlled voice. "Because I chose to do so."

My words cut the air, and Jon pressed his lips into a thin line.

He ran his fingers through his hair, looking helplessly at the sky.

"What happened in there, Jon? What did your mother tell you?" I swallowed as soundless tears rushed into his eyes.

"My mother told me I wasn't worthy of being her son anymore."

I stepped ahead, clutching my arms around him. He hauled me tight and cried into my neck.

His mother was friendly when talking to me, yet I noticed her wearing a mask. One I didn't expect was hiding something so nasty. Jon pressed his head onto my chest, and as he was too heavy for me to carry, we slowly glided onto our knees. I let my hands slide behind his neck. His body was heaving, fighting for air.

"I'm sure she didn't mean it . . ." I said because I didn't know what else to say. I knew too little about what happened and their relationship in general.

"You can't understand. No one can." Jon snorted and wiped his nose.

"Try me," I whispered, letting my fingers run over his cheeks to wipe the tears away. Suddenly, his hands found my wrist and trapped them.

"Shit, you think you can fix me by making me talk about it?! It doesn't work like that!" His face turned red. Quickly, I took my hands away and got up. I couldn't help him if he didn't let me.

"Jon, I'm not saying I could fix this." I inhaled deeply and waited until he looked me in the eyes. He finally did. "All I'm saying is if you want to try and talk to someone, then I'm willing to listen."

Jon chewed on his lower lip and stared at his shoes. Maybe he was too far gone to accept any type of help.

"Nobody knows what it's like with divorced parents, a controlling stepfather, a manipulated mother . . . oh, and let's not forget my alcoholic father. Or ex-alcoholic, whatever." He gave me a here-you-have-it look. The air got forced out of my lungs. I turned around so Jon wouldn't notice how deep that hit. I pressed my knuckles against my teeth. *Did Jon have the same family issues?*

"See, it's impossible to know how I feel," Jon huffed behind me.

"It's not," I sniveled, my eyes blurry.

"Then why don't you say anything?"

I took another deep breath, turned back to him, and sat on the path next to him. I stretched my legs and pressed my feet together.

"Scratch the ex from the alcoholic, and you have my situation," I whispered, the winter wind almost carrying away my words. I pulled my knees in and hugged them.

"Your parents are . . ."

"Divorced since I was twelve."

"And your mother gets manipulated—"

"By her lovely boyfriend, Richard. He's so cold."

I tried swallowing, but thinking about him locked my throat. Not allowing him into my head had been working well in the past few months, but I couldn't pretend he didn't exist any longer. He had bruised me, no matter how much I tried to pretend he didn't. He made me constantly afraid to say or do something wrong. I had begged my mom to leave him. To move back to the tiny apartment scattered with mold with Lucas. Anything would've been better if it were only the three of us. Yet each time she was close to leaving him, she didn't. So I fled to America, no matter how much I hated leaving her behind. Jon kept silent as if he knew I had gotten lost in painful thoughts. I drew in a shaky breath, signaling I was okay now.

"And your father is drowning in the bottle . . .?" he concluded our disaster.

"Y-yes . . . beer is his best friend." I barely knew my father when I was a child. First, after our parents' divorce, he tried to get to know me. I'd ignored how he let us all suffer to get back at my mother, pretending it didn't happen so I could still have a father. But whenever I saw or talked to him, it felt more like a chore than a loving encounter. I crushed my palms onto my face. I didn't want to make this about me, but I suppressed so much that it burst out of me.

"Well, fuck." Jon placed an arm around my shoulder and pulled me in. I grabbed his hand and held it close to my stomach.

"I understand, Jon. I wish I wouldn't, but I do." I could barely form any words. "I was torn down for years. I . . ."

I swallowed again; forming words was painful, but I didn't stop. I wanted him to hear that it was okay to not always be okay and set an example that talking helped. When my family sent me to this mental health institution, I had tried fighting it as well . . . but in the end, I was glad I went. They really helped me. Jon looked at me patiently, waiting to hear the rest of my story.

"It was so bad that I had to go to a psychiatric clinic."

"You went to a shit place like that?" Jon questioned with a grimace.

"Yeah, and I'm glad I did. Because being there, I understood I didn't have to be perfect to be worthy." I shook my head and laughed.

"What?" Jon curved his brows.

"I preached advice I had forgotten about myself."

I had tried hard to be the perfect girlfriend for Paul . . . because he was perfect, and he deserved perfect. But I couldn't be his match, not with this dark side in me that clashed around me in the most unexpecting moments.

"Then it doesn't sound like it was helpful." Jon joined my nervous laughter.

"Apparently not." I laughed so hard tears pressed out of my eyes, and Jon joined my ungrounded outbreak.

"Well, fuck, Little German!" He pulled me into his arms again, not stopping his laughter. I pressed his body even closer to mine. I wasn't drawn to Jon all the time because he was the unattainable, emotionally unstable embodiment of a bad boy but rather because his pain and mine. . . were the same.

And I didn't see his pain as something that had to be fixed as everyone else did. I saw it as something raw. I recognized his strength and how he was far from giving up. He simply didn't know it yet.

"We're not perfect. Let's screw perfect!" I pulled away, shaking him. My smile turned bright with a ray of sunlight crawling through the clouds.

This was fucked-up, but I wasn't alone in this anymore. Suddenly, Jon's laughter stopped.

"What's wrong?" I asked, still trying to control my nonsense, laughing.

"You are . . ." Jon stammered, "Your flaws—they're . . ."

His eyes paced all over my face, but he smiled again. "Fuck, you'll be my downfall, Little German."

"Just like you will be mine." I raised my brows and leaned in until our noses touched.

"Then let's fall together."

We kissed all the way to his father's place, having no eyes for the street, nearly getting run down by a car. But kissing each other was like healing our wounds. With each kiss, the pain seemed to loosen. Screw pills and alcohol. We just needed this. Two broken souls, enough to come together as one.

Jon hovered above me in his bed as he plastered rough kisses all over my neck. His tongue popped out, licking from behind my ears to my collarbone. I moaned loudly, my hips lifting from the mattress and my fingers fisting the bedsheets. He stopped when he reached my sweater, and we both quickly pulled up, lifting it off me together. I helped him with his shirt right after and kissed the spot where his heart was with soft lips. Goosebumps formed below my connection.

"Hmm. . ." He groaned as I continued kissing his upper body, his hardness poking at my belly button through his pants. My hands traveled to the bulge, pressing around his length above the fabric. Jon's eyes rolled as I continued while looking up at him. That I barely carried any experience didn't even terrify me anymore. He opened his eyes, and our looks connected again. His mouth dropped open, and a heavy exhale escaped his lips.

"Emily . . ." He gasped and pushed me back onto the mattress, and I held myself around his torso. He swiped my hair behind my ears, and my heart exploded in my chest as all he did was look at me for an endless second.

"Are you sure you want this?" he whispered, not breaking eye contact for one bit. His hot breath fell on my cheek, my entire body heating up with so much desire that there was only one possible answer.

"Yes."

His eyes sparkled. "Good. Because I want you so badly, you've no idea."

I gasped out loud as his arms wrapped around my back and clipped open my light blue bra, which ended up on the floor. My arms remained on the sides of my body. I expected him to kiss my boobs, but instead, he drew circles right above my nipples, making them hard, and my back arched again. My stomach tingled, and a pounding between my thighs clashed around me up to my eardrums. Jon lifted his body away, and his hand trailed down slowly to the button of my jeans. I moaned again as his hand slid close to where I craved being touched the most.

"I love how you react to my touch." He blew out of his lips, and I desperately nodded as I could feel my climax rising. Love . . . a word I had never heard from him before, and it was effortlessly beautiful.

"I want you now," I begged loudly because my heart turned impatient.

"We've waited so long, Little German." He glided his fingers into my pants. "Why the rush?"

His thumb pressed above my panties. I sighed, feeling my body be consumed by an elective wave. I couldn't hold it anymore. I had to—

"Jon, I . . ."

"It's okay. I will make you come all over right after."

My eyes fell closed, and my body pulsed with so much longing I was afraid I would pass out. Jon pressed his mouth onto mine, and I groaned as his throat swallowed my moans. He groaned with me, making me fall deeper into this orgasm created by one little touch. I didn't even know that was possible. He stopped kissing me when my moans faded, and I tried to catch my breath as the thumping in my body decreased slowly.

"That was fucking sexy," Jon whispered into my ear, his body still blanketing mine.

"I'm kinda embarrassed you barely even had to do anything." I covered my face with the pillow.

"That's exactly what's sexy about this." I peeked over it. Jon bit his lip, and his finger traced my chin. "I never came that fast either, you know?"

My eyes almost popped out. "Y-you . . . came?"

He nodded, pointing down his pants, which showed a wet spot. I covered my mouth with my hands to hide this stupid proud grin plastered all over my face.

"I'll quickly shower, and then we can try to last longer." He leaned in, kissing me on the cheek. "Or do you want to join me in the shower?" he asked dangerously close to my ear. Some of me wanted to say yes, but I realized I had to finish something before starting something new.

"Maybe next time," I said instead and reached for my bra to get dressed.

"What will this be when it's finished?" Jon grabbed my waist. I smiled but continued getting dressed. "As much as I would like to stay, I'm not sure what Zack told Gena. I need to get home."

"I'll drive you."

"I wouldn't mind a walk to get a clear head." I kissed him on the cheek.

"Fine. But I will pick you up tonight because we're spending New Year's together, and I'm not accepting a no."

"Then I won't even try to argue about it."

Chapter 36

Fighting Mode On

Paul

New Year's Eve. . .

I sat on Emily's bed, staring at the voice message Jon had sent me last night. I plugged in my headphones and went for another round of interpretation.

"Paul. . ."

Heavy breathing and muffled noises for a few seconds.

"Fuck, I'm sorry, Paul. I . . ."

I was unsure if the following sounds were sobbing or water splashing into a sink.

"I didn't plan on this. I wanted to make sure she's good enough for you. I . . ."

Another long pause. *Since when is Jon one who's lost for words?*

"Fuck, I love you, man. Drink some of those beers for me . . ."

That message was sitting for almost a day, but I struggled to reply. Did he hear about our breakup? Or did something happen with Emily.? If so, was it physical, or were real feelings involved? Knowing him, it was just physical, but then again . . . with Emily, he was different. I patted Pani like a support kitten. I promised Lucas to take care of her, meaning I had to protect her from Jon. I typed out a message for him.

> **Me**: If you think I'm backing down without a fight, you're thinking wrong.

My finger lingered over it before I deleted it again. This was something I didn't want to discuss while on another continent. And then again, I didn't know exactly what was going on. I called Emily earlier today, but it went straight to voice mail. She hadn't called back so far . . .

"Paul!" I heard Susanne's muffled voice coming from downstairs. "They are here!"

. . . and now it was too late to try again.

I pulled out my headphones, gave Pani one last pet, and rushed down the steps. Three girls were standing in a perfectly arranged row in the little entryway, their eyes traveling up and down synchronously.

"Hi." I pressed my lips together. They whispered in German until one stepped out of line, her hands on her hip like she was in a beauty contest.

"Hello, Paul. We're Emily's best friends. I'm Lisa. This is Sophie and Jasmine."

She pointed at her friends, who posed when their names got mentioned. They had reached out to Susanne yesterday, saying they saw I was in Germany on Lucas's social media.

"It's nice to meet y'all." I shrugged, and they giggled, even though I didn't say anything funny. Then, they waved goodbye to Susanne and rushed outside.

I grabbed my jacket as Susanne placed a soft hand on my back. "I'm sure you have great time with them." She smiled, but it didn't convince me. Since breaking down, she treated me with extra care, as if she wanted to make up for it. I hated she felt it was necessary, and I would much rather spend New Year's with her and Dad than these girls.

"Sorry, I'm late!" A guy suddenly popped his head through the door.

"Oh, Chris! Thank god you're here." Susanne let out a heavy exhale while I lifted an eyebrow.

Chris . . . I remembered that name. Emily had mentioned him to me when he commented with a thumbs-up emoji on the picture I posted from her. That Chris was the only friend she was truly missing.

"Hey, man. It's great to meet you." Chris walked up to me, offering me his hand for a weird shake I wasn't used to.

"Ignore the girls. They are a bit weird if you ask me."

"Chris!" Susanne shushed.

"What, Susanne? You know that as well as I do." Chris cackled, not even caring if they could hear him outside.

"Hm." Susanne pouted. She agreed with him.

We ended up at someone's party a few blocks from Emily's place. It wasn't crowded but not empty either. Round about thirty people, who all looked at me with judging eyes.

"So you're a football player?" Lisa asked, playing with a strand of her hair.

"Used to be." I turned away, watching Chris making us some drinks.

"Sophie, I won!" Lisa clapped, looking at her friend, who rolled her eyes.

I wrinkled my brows, leaning close to Chris. "What was that about?"

"They made this stupid bet if Emily would get herself a football player," Chris explained, throwing them a grimace when they looked our way.

The girl, who I think was Sophie, came up to me. "You said used to, so not anymore, correct?"

"Um." I hesitated. I could tell I was starting to miss football. "I dropped out a few months ago."

"Ha!" Sophie turned to Lisa, and then they argued in German. They were here to judge Emily's new life, not to get to know me. Superficial people. Chris handed me a glass.

"Vodka energy," he explained when I inhaled the sugary smell, making a face. "Made it extra strong. I thought you might need it."

"You have no idea." I took a huge sip, and the corners of my lips fought not to go down. "Thanks."

"Don't thank me." Chris took a sip himself and also made a face.

"So you're close with Emily?" I tried asking this question as casually as possible. I couldn't imagine any guy just wanting to be friends with her.

"Yeah. We've known each other since 5th grade. She's my Gürkchen."

"Your what?"

He laughed out loud. "There was this time when Emily was obsessed with pickles. Ever since then, I called her that."

"Funny." I forced a smile and took another sip. I wouldn't say I liked that he had such a unique nickname for her.

"Relax, man. She calls me Monkey. There's absolutely nothing romantic about that." Chris slapped his palm against my back, and I laughed out loud. He had a point. One of Emily's friends—I'd already forgotten her name—eyed me from afar while talking to a red-haired dude with freckles.

"What's their issue?" I nodded in her direction.

"They act as if Emily broke up with them when she left for America. Stupid if you ask me."

I was amazed at how effortless his English was. "You don't miss her?"

"Oh, I do!" Chris bit his lip. "But I know this is a great experience for her, and I'm glad she got away from those girls. They didn't do her well. I mean, they called Emily their freaking doll, you know?"

"Yeah, she told me." I cracked my jaw. Hearing it now from Chris made this story from her turn into a brutal reality. A guy across the other room suddenly glared at me as if I had stepped out of hell.

I didn't break his stare. "What's his problem?"

"That, my dear Paul . . ." Chris sighed. "Is Emily's ex-boyfriend, who still suffers from a hurt ego that Emily rather wanted to go to America than stay with him."

Michael. I knew all about him, how he only used Emily as an object. I swallowed down my entire drink as he came toward me.

"So you're her new guy, huh?" Michael snorted, judging me again from head to toe. "You don't look like her type."

All this anger I'd felt in the last few days was ready to explode. If Michael gave me one good reason, I wouldn't mind adding blood sprinkles to his stupid freckles.

"Funny, I would've said the same about you," I countered, my feet in an even stance. Chris cackled out loud, and Michael raised his brows at me.

"You know you're brave coming here without her."

"Why?"

He grinned nasty, and I rolled my eyes at myself for even asking. "Because Emily is easy to crack. One ounce of attention from a guy, and she's eating out of their hands."

I walked up to him with my chest puffed up.

"Emily told me about you . . . how badly you treated her." I was nose to nose with him now. I heard some *oohs* and *aahs* coming from all around us. But my eyes remained fixated on Michael, who looked around. He had brought himself into this mess. Now the question was if he would get himself out of it again or bring out the worst in me tonight. Finally, his eyes settled on mine, and he pulled up the sleeves of his preppy polo sweatshirt.

"I bet she's lying in someone else's arms while you're defending her honor."

My nostrils flared, and my fist flew through the air, making Michael topple back and crash to the ground. Within seconds, I was on top of him, feeling my knuckles rip open again; I'd never given them a chance to heal. I laughed out loud. The other day, I had screamed at Richard and Lucas that violence wasn't the solution, and now look at me, starting a fight as soon as I could. The issue was Michael had all his friends here, who didn't wait to drag me away. While three held me, Michael got up to land a straight fist on my jaw. But he didn't hit me harshly. The blood from his nose was already dripping onto the carpet. He lifted his arm again when Chris landed a punch right onto the side of his head.

"Damn, I've been waiting to do this for a long time!" Chris expressed with excitement. The grips of Michael's friends' hands loosened around me, and I used my chance to get out. Chris and I stood back to back. People screamed, and girls whined at us to stop. But my anger had surfaced, and I couldn't contain it any longer. Because I knew Michael could be right . . . Emily could be lying in Jon's arms. If I liked it or not.

Chapter 37

Superwoman Pose

Emily

I MET ZACK RIGHT IN FRONT OF THE HOUSE. "TOLD MOM YOU GOT an emergency girl call from Danielle. Boy trouble or something."

"Thank you, Zack." I tried to hug him, but he pulled back.

"When you lied to Mrs. Stone, I got it. But lying to Mom . . . that's not cool." He waved his hand and ambled down the driveway. He was right, and I deeply hated that I had done it, but a part of me couldn't stop. The terror of the truth trapping me again overwhelmed all my reasoning, even though I knew that Gena wasn't Mr. Stone.

Gena asked me with her usual ease how my night with Danielle had been and if everything was okay with her boyfriend. I faltered because I had no idea how things were going between the two of them. Or how her cosmetology class had gone. Maintaining friendships felt harder than it should. I pressed Danielle's name on my phone as soon as my battery was full. I had let myself be consumed by two guys I had called stupid while chopping vegetables in the kitchen of the Stone house. I still had a small scar on my thumb from that. I was bleeding so much because of them. But it was still better than how my father emotionally starved my mother and turned to the bottle instead of his wife. How Richard portrayed the perfect man, only to show his true colors when she was too invested in leaving again. I sighed. When I came to America, I had hoped that not all stories would end with a broken heart.

"Emily?"

I closed my eyes and switched to my happy mask. "Hey, girl! How has your course been?"

"Oh, great. I got the scholarship," Danielle said as if it wasn't a big deal.

"*Wha*—Congratulations!" My body tingled in pure excitement for her.

"Thanks. I was by far the best candidate!"

I smiled broadly. Danielle wanted something and grabbed it like it was nothing. Her confidence was a gift. Or was it usual to approach life without overthinking everything?

"Shoot, when I saw your name on the phone, I thought something had happened."

That line hit more than expected. "Can't I call my best friend?"

I tapped my fingers on my stomach, waiting for the seconds to pass. Danielle was the best friend I'd ever had, besides my guy friend Chris, but I'd known him since *Weiterführende Schule*, 5th grade. Danielle listened, was honest, and made uncomfortable situations easier. If I hung out with her daily, my social battery wouldn't even die. I stopped the tapping, now pressing my fingers into my belly. *What if Danielle doesn't even care about me? She must have many friends—*

"You're my best friend too! But don't let Breana hear that." Danielle cackled, and I jumped a little, sitting in the bed.

"I won't," I giggled. "How has your Christmas been?"

"As predicted, we overate, and my parents let me drink eggnog. Disgusting stuff, but after those, we were all heavily rocking to Christmas music." Danielle cackled into the phone, and I heard music playing in the background. "Sounds like fun. I haven't tried eggnog so far."

My Christmas vibes were a little cut short this year. The only time I'd listened to Christmas music was in Tim's kitchen. The plane tickets had changed everything . . . but I didn't blame the tickets. Paul and I hadn't been in a good place beforehand.

"What about you? Cuddling with Paul in the basement watching *Grey's Anatomy* or something?"

Air pulled out of my lungs. Danielle didn't know what had happened. The kiss at the lake, the breakup, the time I had spent with Jon alone. Knowing her opinion about Jon, she would say she warned me that I got lured in as all the other girls did—that I couldn't trust him. But weirdly, I trusted Jon. I just didn't have trust in the trust he had in himself.

"Um . . ." I knitted my brows, and a headache spread out of nowhere. "It's a long story, but Paul is currently in Germany."

"No way!" Danielle shouted so loud I held the phone away from my ear. "I want all the deets!"

But I couldn't give her all the deets. Not until I figured out what was going on in my heart and head.

As promised, I spent the rest of the day with Gena on the couch. Cuddled into blankets and hot cocoa, we watched some episodes of *Dance Moms,* a show where little girls compete, dance every week, and get compared and screamed at by their teacher. Their trying to reach this perfectionism was terrible, yet watching it was somewhat comforting.

Jon texted me in the afternoon, letting me know he would wait around the corner for me by eight.

Me: Where are we going?

Arschloch: To a place nobody will know you

I let go of my breath. I felt so bad we had to hide, but at the same time, I was glad he respected I needed more time before I could let anyone in on . . . whatever we were. Not while being stuck in two situationships.

"Oh wow! You saw that twirl!" Gena gasped, holding her hand to her chest.

I looked up. I hadn't. "Yeah, amazing."

Gena's phone rang, and she reached for it. When she read the number, she turned it to silent.

"You don't wanna pick it up?"

"I'm on vacation. If it's something important, it would be a number I know. I'm not giving my precious free time away for people trying to sell me crappy stuff."

I stood up from the couch. "I've got to go to the bathroom."

Gena pressed the pause button on the remote. Compared to last week, today had been a bit more mundane. Talking to Danielle and spending time with Gena reminded me that there was more to life than boys. I hadn't picked up a book in weeks, and even my diary only got touched every other day. I washed my hands and scrubbed until the dirt under my fingernails disappeared into the sink. Paul had tried to call me earlier, but he would be back in two days. It would be better if we talked face-to-face and not through a speaker. Guilty eyes, glittering with despair, looked at me in the mirror. I slapped my hands on the sink. We all played our part in this mess! Just because I was the only woman in this didn't mean it was my fault. Heck, Paul and Jon had deeper problems than me. The fact that Jon tested me proved that their friendship had an unresolved conflict. Something had changed their story, and that something wasn't me. I braced my palms on my hip bones and faced the mirror like a superwoman.

"I won't let it get me down." I used a technique I knew from my time in the mental institution. Usually, when I did this, I pictured looking at Richard. But this time, I thought of the two boys I loved differently.

"I'll do what's best for me!" My voice got louder. I didn't care if someone would say this was slutty or attention-seeking. All I wanted was a happy love story lasting close to a year and then to return to Germany, thinking back to a great year with great love and adventures. But instead, I was consumed, always on the edge of smothering happiness or staggering pain. Stuck in a story I knew I wouldn't be able to leave behind in a few months.

Tonight I would do whatever I felt like—no more overthinking and guilt. I took off the necklace Paul gave me for Christmas and placed it in my drawer.

It was cold outside, but I still wanted to dress up, so I grabbed my wool dress and thick tights. I always celebrated New Year's with friends in Germany. I was sure they were going to another superficial party, comparing outfits and discussing who had the best eye shadow. I hated the firecrackers, but the fireworks carried my heart. When bright colors covered the sky, the cheers when the clock struck midnight . . . and that I would get my first New Year's Eve kiss tonight. . My parka still hadn't shown up, so I grabbed Jon's winter jacket, which added a touch of bad girl to my whole look. I styled my hair into curls, applied dark red lipstick, and used some darker eye shadow from Gena. I couldn't stop staring at my reflection. It was a new person staring back at me, but I liked her . . . loved her, even!

My alarm went off at 7:55 pm. I walked into the kitchen to say goodbye to Gena, but she was preparing something.

"You're cooking?"

"Yeah, I thought we could start the new year with a feast and—" She turned to look at me with a steaming pot filled with vegetables. "Woooow!"

I searched around me until I realized she was looking at me.

"Emily, you look great!" She put down the pot. "Paul would love this look on you."

I smiled shyly. I expected Gena to be upset about me going out and not eating with her.

"You're not mad I'm going out?"

"Emily," she sighed. "You're young. When I was your age, I would rather spend time with friends than with my parents. Especially on New Year."

"Hold on. Watching trash TV with you is still my favorite thing to do." I pointed up, and Gena laughed with her whole heart.

"We will do another marathon tomorrow."

I nodded fast with widened eyes.

"Who are you going out with?" Gena asked, and I twirled back around.

"Um . . ."

Usually, Zack covered for me, but now I had to find an excuse myself. *Could I tell her I would be with Jon?* She knew I was hanging out with boys, her son being one of them. So it shouldn't be an issue . . . but then again, she knew Jon wasn't the best influence, and the last thing I wanted was to worry her, and—

"Just a little get-together with the usual people," my mouth decided for my brain.

"Oh, tell Brandon hi from me! I haven't seen him in ages."

"I will."

I wondered if he and Hannah were now a couple. I hadn't received any news about their first date yet. My second New Year's resolution would be to keep in closer contact with my friends. My first: to stop blaming myself. I was a piece of the puzzle but not the missing piece.

Chapter 38

Into the Sunset

Jon

EMILY LOPED OUT OF THE HOUSE, AND I HAD TO DOUBLE-CHECK to ensure it was her. Not only because of her unusual makeup but also because of how she carried herself, unencumbered and excited.

When she reached me, she jumped into my arms without hesitation. "Hey!"

"Hi . . ." I breathed into her neck. Tonight was going to be fucking great, a memory I would have when she returned to Paul. I hated that I couldn't keep up with him. But I had tonight, and to make sure I didn't forget it, I kept my daily dose to a minimum. Enough I didn't feel the withdrawal taking hold of my body. I had done some research, and the cold turkey was dangerous.

I put Emily down, and she beamed at me. I kissed her twice on the cheek and opened the car door for her. *What the hell . . .*

I had never opened anyone's car door before, but those moves came naturally to her. I wanted to do all the things I usually despised.

In the car, she asked me over five times where we were going, and I always answered the same.

"To a party of an old friend of mine. His girlfriend will be there as well, she can be a bit straightforward, but she's a cool girl."

"Natalia?" she confirmed.

"Yes." I nodded, pressing Play on the CD.

"Oh, our song!" Emily pointed at the radio as "Fix You" by Coldplay began to play.

"Our song?"

"Yeah, we sang the song together at Halloween! So it's our song!" She sang along. *We had a song.* She pulled up the volume, and even though her singing was terrible, it was beautiful. She nudged me when I didn't join her, and after some arguing, I sang along with burning cheeks. And, of course, we were driving through a stupid sunset. But I knew better than to think this would be our happy ending. I grabbed her hand and squeezed it, which made her smile so adorably that my cock pulsed. *Fuck, I never knew what a simple smile could cause.*

"Do you know why I like this song?"

"Because it's fucking predictable?"

Emily rolled her eyes. "No, jerkhead. It explains what we want is not what we need." Emily rested deeper into the car seat. This answer surprised me, and I looked at her in awe. She bit her lip, looking back at me in a playful way. My stomach dropped when she looked at me even though she could've focused on the sunset. *Maybe she's not set on Paul?* Either way, we had tonight, and I would make sure it would be the best fucking night of her life.

After singing more songs, we finally made it to the party. It was out in the woods, at Dave's parents' cabin. A long line of cars was parked in front of the house. I noticed Emily was dressed lightly in her dress. I parked the car and reached back to grab an extra sweater.

"Here. I don't want you to freeze."

"But I don't want to destroy my outfit." She bit her lip, pouting.

"You look beautiful no matter what you wear, Little German."

"Fine." She grabbed the sweater and pulled it over her, making her hair go messy in a sexy way. *Ugh, she wears this sweater better than I do.* She was mine, and everyone would know now. We walked over to the house with a group of people. I held her hand tightly and glared at anyone who looked at her for more than two seconds. She quickly drew everyone's eyes to her and wasn't even aware she was a natural beauty. Damn, I needed to make her realize how fucking stunning she was. All the way to the house, she rambled on about how exciting it was, an American house party in the woods. I shook my head but enjoyed listening to her squeaky voice. Paul had only taken her to our gatherings at Hannah's, with the same people as always, even though she craved excitement. Almost as if he wanted to keep her on a leash so she couldn't escape.

The cabin, actually a three-story house, was full of people. Red cups covered every table, every staircase step, and every windowsill. Music was blaring so loudly from the speakers I could barely hear my footsteps as we stepped through the door. Here, we were safe. The police never came this far into the woods, and since there were no neighbors, no one could complain about the noise. I noticed a few familiar faces and saw Dave and Natalia dancing. When our eyes met, Natalia brushed her dark hair out of her face.

Natalia was a girl every boy could get along with, and every girl wanted to be like her. She recognized a trend even before it started. She was the one I wouldn't dare pick a fight with because I knew I could not win it. If anyone could teach Emily about self-confidence, it was her.

"Jon, Jon, Jon . . ." She smirked, causing Dave to turn to us as well. "You have some nerve to show up here after not even replying if you would come."

She didn't say it madly, more with *you better be here for a great time* attitude.

"I missed you too, Natalia." I winked back and hugged her, not letting go of Emily's hand.

"Fuck, it's good to see you, man." Dave reached out his hand for a shake, and I had to let go of her this time.

Natalia used her chance and grabbed both of Emily's hands into hers. "So you're Jon's girlfriend . . . ?"

My ears perked as I looked over my shoulder at her.

"He wishes." Emily winked, an adorable chuckle following.

"Uhhhh, I love that!" Natalia squealed, and she and Emily hugged. My heart warmed up by her handling this situation lightly.

Dave eyed me. "You two want anything? Beer? Some pills?"

Emily's face shot to the side. "I'm not saying no to either."

My blood froze, and I grabbed her by the waist.

She mouthed, "Excuse us," when I pulled her to the side of the hallway.

"I don't think that's a good idea."

She raised her brows at me and placed her palms on my shoulders, giving me a stare. Then, with a sarcastic voice, she said, "Jon, I think it is."

"You know how I mean it. Drinking is okay, but drinking and pills? They make you lose control."

"Jon." She lowered her voice. "Tonight, I gave myself a promise. I would do whatever I felt like, with no rules or restrictions. You said the police never show up here, and I crave some pills and drinks. Let's not overthink this and have a great time."

Her answer frightened me. I knew she had taken pills a few times, but had she passed the occasional point? Or was her addiction level already kicking in after the first try?

I sighed. "I just—"

"You heard her, Jon." Natalia jumped at me from the side. "And I don't mind sharing mine with her."

"C'mon, Jon, let's live tonight!" Emily squealed like she was already drunk from her surroundings. My cock pulsed again. The way she surprised me . . . she was a fucking turn-on. But I suddenly feared what could result from that. I rubbed my face as she stumbled away with Natalia.

Dave came from the other side, throwing his arm around my neck. "Man, tonight is going to be crazy."

"I hope not too crazy," I admitted, suddenly being the responsible one for a change.

Chapter 39

New Year New Me

Emily

"YEES!" I JUMPED UP AND DOWN AS THE LITTLE WHITE BALL landed in the cup filled with the pee-like American beer.

Jon hugged me from behind, kissing my cheek and shifting us from one leg to the other. He whispered into my ear, "My little American."

I twirled around to kiss him in haste, but it ended halfway on his cheek and the corners of his lips. Natalia had given me a pill Jon had signed off on, but all I felt was this extreme rush of happiness, as if I could finally see clearly. Kinda like my focus woke up from a long nap.

"Ich liebe es, wenn du mich deine kleine Amerikanerin nennst!" *I love it, when you call me your little American!*

"Und ich liebe es, when du redest Deutsch zu mirr." *And I love it when you talk in German to me.*

My mouth fell open, and I froze. Jon said an almost grammatically correct German sentence to me.

"Did you—?" I pointed at his lips, looking at them as if they had a hidden speaker.

"I might have picked up a word here or there." He turned to the side, reaching for his beer to take a large sip.

"You learned German!" I squealed, covering my mouth with my hands, bending down. "You did!"

Jon shrugged playfully, the cup still half in front of his mouth. "It bothered me when I couldn't understand you, so I learned a few lines."

"Jon Henry freaking Denson." I took my cup and held it up in the air. Then, I crashed it against his, . "You're crazy!"

"I'm crazy about you." He leaned in for another kiss—a soft yet hungry one. I deepened the kiss by twirling my tongue around his until they danced. That he learned German made my heart light up. Jon could achieve anything he set his mind on. He just had to burn for it, and he was burning for me.

"Guys? The game isn't over yet." Dave's voice interrupted our kiss, and we pulled away with huge grins. Natalia was quiet, staring at us like a piece of art. "Wow" was all she said before throwing her ball.

I stood with Natalia on the cabin's porch as she was smoking. She'd asked me to join her while the boys chatted about some old times from elementary school.

"Can I have one as well?" I asked, pointing at the cigarette package.

"What's mine is yours." Natalia smiled, handing it to me. My hands shook a bit when I took out the cigarette or, as Jon called them, square. I wasn't sure what I wanted to call them yet. I grabbed the lighter and almost burned myself when striking it. Instant coughing stabbed into my lungs. Natalia didn't comment on it, and I took another drag until it lessened.

"So, which drug did you give Jon?" She suddenly asked out of nowhere, causing me to cough even harder.

"Excuse me?"

"Whenever I saw him with Kiki, he tried to do his own thing. With you, he clings onto you, treating you like a diamond. Jon is an old friend, and the way he is right now . . . it's a first. What's your story?"

My chest warmed up at hearing those words. If he was different with me, then maybe we could work after all.

"Our story . . ." I exhaled the smoke, feeling a rush climbing from my toes to my fingertips in the form of slight dizziness. "I don't even know how to sum up our story."

"Well, what is it you like about Jon?" Natalia sat down on the porch chair. I sat on the one next to her, taking another drag.

"The way he excites and inspires me." I exhale slowly. No more coughing.

"Inspires you?"

"Yeah." I ashed off my square. The reason why I liked Jon, why no matter what he did, I couldn't keep my mind off him. Why our souls connected with one touch, one look. Why he had the power to make me feel the happiest and the saddest. Why I fell in love with him . . .

"He inspires me to figure out who I am and what I need. With him, I don't feel like I need to hide my imperfections."

Natalia nodded, impressed. "Why that sad look, then?"

I hadn't realized my lips were hanging down until she said it. I sighed, taking a final drag of the cigarette. "Because I'm kinda with someone else."

"Holy shit!" Natalia squealed. "Break up with him, then!"

"It's not that easy." I pressed the cigarette into the ashtray.

"It is easy. You love Jon, you don't love the other dude, or you wouldn't betray him like that."

I bit my lip, not replying to what she said. *Is it that easy?*

"Not to destroy the moment, but I got to pee, and I like my privacy in the bathroom, so . . ." Natalia chuckled and got up. I remained in my seat for a while, watching the night sky. Then I lifted my body as well, but I didn't follow her inside. Instead, I rushed down the steps with a mission to finally do what I'd been dreading to do for way too long. *It's time. . .*

My view was like a tunnel as I passed all the people to find a spot I could be alone. Eventually, I found a tree stump on the other side of the house. I pressed Paul's name on my phone screen, but he didn't pick up. Then I remembered it was like six in the morning for him, and the voicemail beep occurred. This wasn't a conversation for a voicemail, but I didn't want to carry it into the next year. No more excuses. It was now or never.

"H-Hey . . ." I took a deep breath, my voice shaking, my heart skipping many beats. I was afraid I would pass out.

"I'm calling because . . ." My eyes burned as the tears dwelled in them. Finding the right words was an impossible task. I hurt him, I betrayed him, I played him . . . didn't matter that I didn't mean to do so. I did it, and I had to learn to live with me being the villain in someone's story.

"You were right. You were right from the very beginning." I sat down on the snow-covered tree stump, feeling my dress soaking in.

"There is something between Jon and me, something I didn't understand, which was why I couldn't admit it, but it's there, and it's . . ."

I could barely talk as the tears streamed down my cheeks, every muscle in my body feeling heavy.

"I'm in love with him, Paul."

My head exploded into a thousand fireworks. "You were the best first boyfriend I could've ever asked for, but—"

I exhaled again to get out the following line in between my sobs. "I can't give you what you deserve. I can't be the perfect girlfriend. I'm sorry . . ."

I hung up and clutched my hand onto my chest. I could no longer breathe; the air had become too heavy. I squeezed my eyes shut, and my mouth tightened into a soundless cry. I loved Paul. I loved him so much that my knees buckled at losing him. But the love I felt for Jon was different. It was like an invisible force pulling us together. Every part of my body yearned for him. It wasn't perfect. It was messy. It was harrowing and frightening, . . . but it was real. Natalia was right. It was easy to know who I wanted more, but to throw my principles overboard and hurt someone I cared about so much was not.

"What did you do . . ." Jon's voice appeared out of nowhere, and he kneeled down in front of me.

"I told Paul the truth. He deserved it." I cried and Jon's fingers wiped away my tears.

"What kind of truth?" Jon breathed, and I could hear his heart throbbing. I hated he was still fighting the obvious.

I looked Jon straight in the eyes, my heart flickering in heavy flames. "I told him that he was right—that it's been you all along."

Jon's eyes twitched and blinked like he was close to a panic attack. "All along?"

I nodded, tasting the salt on my parched lips. "Yeah, since the moment I saw you in US History."

His face didn't even flinch. All he did was look at me as my heart exploded.

"What if I can't give you what you need?" he turned away, and the thin ice we were moving on cracked. Jon held the power to shatter me with a snap of his fingers, but I wasn't afraid to drown. I could actually check off #3 now, experience *real* love. This was real, because I loved him for everything he was, not only his good qualities.

"You're already giving me all I need, Jon."

His head fell onto my chest. "I hate that we're hurting him . . . he's my best friend."

"I know," I sniffled, wrapping my arms around him. For minutes, we sat there together like idiots on the cold ground, in the dark, with a party happening a few feet away from us. Jon's grip got tighter, and we held each other until our sobs quieted. Finally, he pulled back and lifted my chin with his thumb.

"Fuck, who would've thought I would be bawling my eyes out to this little girl who one day stumbled into my US History class," he whispered, leaving chills when his hot breath met my skin. I rested my forehead against his.

"And I never would've thought this cocky smirking boy, who annoyed me by calling me little, would ever get my permission to call me his little one."

"*I'm not your little one* . . . I think that was the first thing you ever said to me."

"I couldn't have been more wrong." I smiled, feeling my heart lighten up.

Jon sighed, and he bit down his lip. "You're my little one."

People were screaming out loud, counting down from five, and with each decreasing number, we moved closer to each other until our lips almost met at one.

"New year, new me." I smiled.

"New year, new us," Jon corrected, and then we kissed as fireworks exploded in the sky, highlighting this unforgettable moment like the happy ending in a movie. We were official.

Inside, we found an empty bedroom. Jon slammed the door closed, locked it, and checked every closet.

"Someone is a bit paranoid?" I giggled.

"Hey, I'm doing this for a reason! People are perverts."

My smile faded as he said that. "Sounds like that happened to you before."

The anxiety crept in again and plucked at my nails. I hated the jealousy about Jon's past romances. Jon was in the bathroom, and I could hear the shower curtains moving. Then he stretched his neck out of the door.

"Little German, everything is my first with you because I'm not high as shit while doing it." He smiled, and my nerves calmed down. "We are alone."

And my nerves were back up. Slowly, he walked up to me as I leaned on my elbows. He reached down low to kiss me and guided me onto the bed. He pulled away when my head rested on the pillow and looked at me while caressing my cheek.

"I liked you first, and I will like you last," he whispered, his hot breath kissing my skin. My heart trembled, and I exhaled heavily.

"Jon . . . before we, um, there's something you should know."

"What is it?"

"I, um. . ." I bit my lip. "I did some stuff with Paul . . ."

His aura immediately darkened, and his face turned tortured.

"But we never went all way."

A devilish smirk returned to his lips. "What an idiot."

"He's not an idiot!" I nudged him. "It never happened because . . . I guess because we knew it was wrong."

"No, that's not what I meant," Jon tried correcting me. "But let's not talk about this right now."

He leaned down again, kissing me with such gentleness my head turned dizzy. This felt right, no matter how wrong it was.

"Um, as this could be your first time, are you sure you're ready for it? Especially when there's a party right outside?"

More fireworks exploded in the sky, and I pointed at them. "We're alone. We have fireworks. This is special."

I grinned. After all, I did get a special first. Tonight, I had escaped my prison. I was free, and I wanted to fly to the highest point of happiness I could—together with Jon.

Jon caressed my cheek. "If it hurts or you want to stop, tell me, okay?"

I liked how important it was for him to make my first time an experience I wouldn't regret. But how could I regret it when eyes that made me swoon were looking at me? I was sure of him and the choice I'd made.

"Okay."

Jon swiped my lip with his thumb and kissed me, my mouth covering his entirely. Gently, our tongues glided over each other, my heartbeat picking up in a rush as this gentle kiss let me float onto cloud nine. He lifted me and glided his sweatshirt off, followed by my wool dress. The music booming at the door turned muffled. It was him and I, our heartbeats, and this moment. My bra was off next. He kissed my neck, chest, and breasts with butterfly kisses, and his long black lashes tickled my skin. I closed my eyes, my entire body relaxing against his mouth. Swiftly, his fingers moved over my stomach and pulled down my tights. I lifted my butt to help him get me out of them. I rested back, and my eyes closed as he kissed me right above my panties. It felt marvelous. But then he stopped.

"What's wrong?" I opened my eyes and propped myself up on my elbows. His fingers outlined the fresh scars I had caused with a razor on my thighs. My body tensed. I had forgotten about them. With guilty eyes, he looked up at me, the worry in every crease that formed on his face.

"Was that me?"

"No," I replied, ashamed I did it but not ashamed he saw it. "It was the side of me I hate the most."

He sighed. "I promise to make sure this side will never feel the need to show again."

I gasped as he kissed my scars like they were as sacred as the unburdened parts of my body. I let out a whimper. This was it.

"Jon . . . I think I . . ."

He glimpsed up, and as he took in my face, his lit up with a smile. "I know. I love you too, Little German."

I swung my arms around his neck and pulled him in for a kiss, showing him all my love with my mouth. Words weren't meaningful enough to give this moment justice. He would never expect perfection from me as Richard did from Mama. He would never be emotionless, like my Papa with Mama. No, Jon was carrying more emotions than anyone I'd ever met. Anger, sadness, love. They flooded strongly through him, so strongly he acted impulsive and unreasonable for some. But I loved how heavily he felt because it was the same way I felt. A dangerous combination to pair two like us together, but I'd rather blow up with him than keep pretending for one more day he wasn't holding the key to my heart. Jon was entirely undressed now as well, only his boxers and my panties stopping us from becoming one. He pulled up my back again and let my panties glide down my legs. I was thankful I'd shaved, as if something in my mind had hoped for this to happen. He kissed my lips before dipping his head between my legs and doing what I had dreamed about weeks ago.

When his tongue tasted me, I let out a strong gasp. It felt hot and juicy as he slid over my private parts. When he touched me, my hips flew off the mattress, trying to travel closer to the ceiling. Unlike Paul, Jon put his hands behind me, letting me explore the lift and desire inside me. Multiple moans clashed around me, the fireworks nothing compared to that. He glided in a finger but never broke away with his tongue, and I came. Gosh, I came for such a long time I was afraid he would pull out and make it stop. But he didn't. He never decreased his pace and let me enjoy this high for every mind-blowing second. When my hips lowered, he reached over to the nightstand, where he had placed a condom, and ripped it open with his teeth.

"Everything okay?" he checked in first.

I nodded almost hysterically with heavy breaths—I wanted more. Jon smiled and crawled out of his boxers. His penis looked different compared to Paul's. A vein was pulsing in the middle of it, proof of the intense blood flow. I wanted to bend over to take him in, but Jon shook his head.

"Right now is all about you," he whispered and pulled on the condom. He returned his fingers to my wetness and groaned as my liquid spread over his fingers.

"Fuck!" he cursed in the most positive way I had ever heard the word "fuck" from anybody. I grinned almost proudly, not one bit terrified of what would follow next. He lifted his body over me and placed himself between my spread legs. Then he kissed my cheek, my nose, and my forehead.

"Thank you for your trust. I love you."

Those words made me whimper. "I love you, you idiot."

He grinned and kissed me. He tasted different this time, but I liked the combination of our bodies. Then he pulled away and looked at me as something slowly poked inside me. He went slow, really slow. But I was thankful he did because it was painful. The saying *there's no love without pain* became almost ironic to me.

"Ouh . . ." I gasped, and Jon immediately pulled out, even though only the tip had entered so far.

"Do you want to stop?"

"No." I brushed my fingers over his cheek, breathing out heavily.

He nodded and slowly dipped in again. With slow movements, back and forth, he made his way into me until he filled me up entirely. I exhaled as the pain slowly transformed into a new feeling. Jon and I had become one. Not physically, but like a part of my soul flew into his, while I received a part of his in return. That no matter what happened next, we would always be connected, carrying each other wherever we went next.

"I love you," Jon whispered in my ear.

My mind and heart were full of love and fulfillment. I prayed this wasn't another dream.

"I love you too."

A few minutes later, he shuddered, and I wasn't a virgin anymore.

Chapter 40

For a Minute

Paul

I WAS OUT OF THE PICTURE FOR A WEEK. A WEEK IN WHICH EMILY realized I wasn't the one she wanted. While I fell even more in love with her, she fell out. If she ever really loved me.

I sprinted up the mountain streets. I'd been running through the first rays of sunshine with no destination other than going up. After Chris and I had gotten kicked out of the party, he walked me home, undermining Michael's words that Emily would never do anything to hurt me on purpose. I knew she wouldn't do it on purpose, but that didn't change the fact that she did. All this time, I had figured that it would be me she truly wanted, but no, she wanted a dickhead like Jon. I should've seen that coming . . . Even though the sweat was already dripping over my body, and my foot stabbed so much that I should probably stop—I kept running.

Her voice message played on repeat in my headphones, spurring my anger.

"You were right. You were right from the very beginning."

From this first line and how her voice broke, I knew I got trapped in my worst nightmare. I wanted to throw my phone at the wall and destroy this message to make it invalid, but I couldn't ask my parents for another new phone.

"There is something between Jon and me, something I didn't understand, which was why I couldn't admit it, but it's there, and it's. . ."

Her sobbing hurt me almost as much as her words.

"I'm in love with him, Paul."

I had thought having her admit it would make it easier, but it was like someone cut open my chest with a rusty knife and ripped out my heart with their bare fist.

"You were the best first boyfriend I could've ever asked for, but—"

But not perfect for you . . .

"I can't give you what you deserve. I can't be the perfect girlfriend. I'm sorry."

I was confused when she said that she wasn't perfect for me. Heck yeah, of course, she was perfect to me. I always made sure she knew how damn wonderful she was. I punched the wall so hard the entire house shook. This violent behavior didn't suit me—Emily had brought out the worst in me. Yet, they were my decisions. Still, I was so pissed that she had gotten the vibe I wouldn't accept her the way she was. I knew she had flaws. I knew from the first night we met when she'd impulsively choked down the rum. I knew when we ended up on the couch together that she wanted our first kiss to be a drunk one. I saw them each time she turned quiet instead of loud when she disliked something. But I accepted those flaws as a part of her because nobody was perfect, and neither was I. She made me out to be such a good guy. *But I'm not a fucking good guy!*

I arrived at the top of the mountain at a dead end.

"Ahh!" I shouted as I stood on this platform overlooking the Siebengebierge. My scream echoed through the first seconds of the morning on the first day of the year in freaking Germany. I had come here for a girl who had simply swapped me for my best friend, as if everything I did meant nothing. I laughed out loud. I was such an idiot! With a racing heart, I got out my phone and dialed his number.

"Hello?" Jon's voice sounded muffled, and I heard a door closing behind him.

"Are you alone?" I asked because the last thing I wanted was for Emily to listen to our conversation.

"Hold on. I'm walking outside."

I waited about a minute until I heard a lighter strike.

"Okay, I'm alone now." Jon exhaled, and I immediately got pissed that he had to have a smoke right now. He knew this wouldn't be a Happy New Year call.

"I'm done with you," I said slowly to make sure there was nothing to misinterpret about this.

"Paul, I understand you're angry, but I didn't mean to—" He took a break to hit his square, an opportunity I used to get the upper hand.

"I don't want your apology, Jon. You know as well as I that you can't put this burden on Emily. Not being able to help you will break her. She won't be able to give up. That's simply not in her nature, and I fucking know what I'm talking about because I met her mother. I know who she truly is. She's holding on to the good moments, preaching them, forgetting how she felt in between, and people like you misuse that. And heck, if you pull her down with you, I will make sure you will regret it!" I spat into the phone, like an angry fighter at his opponent.

"Paul . . ." Jon growled; no more hitting a square.

"No, fuck you, Jon. I'm not done yet!"

My veins pulsed, and I gasped for air as if I were still in my final sprint.

"She might be with you now, but it won't take long until she realizes what a fucking loser you are. Yes, I think you're a loser. I always thought so, but you were like my brother, so I didn't care. I loved you and believed for a long time that I could help you. But you make it fucking hard, and I'm tired of your shitty excuses. We all go through shit in life, and I'm done with you pretending you're the only one with issues!"

Silence. I had him listening entirely, and I was on a roll.

"You can't even go through one day without being sober. The happiness from others pulls you down. You went beyond destroying the lives of others to feel better about your own. Not only mine but Kiki's, your family's . . . heck, you even messed with poor Breana to suffocate your feelings. Have you even thought this through? Emily deserves someone willing to follow her to Germany! That's what this entire trip was about, to figure out if I could picture myself here. And guess what! I fucking love it here and would transfer in a heartbeat if she wanted me to. What will you do? FaceTime once a week when you feel horny?"

I heard him swallow. My mouth becoming unfiltered was strangely satisfying.

"I haven't thought that far ahead," he finally mumbled.

"Of course you haven't! Because you never think, just like you hit the gas when I was on the car's hood. It was my call to get on top, but you forgot I was sitting there! I should've dropped you entirely after the accident. But you know why I didn't? Because I felt guilty for giving you my medication back then. But I won't carry the blame anymore. You decided to take them. I gave them to you to hide, not to consume." I took a long breath as my body shook with furor. I could barely draw a line between my sentences.

"I know," Jon said, so neutral I couldn't point out if he cared about my words.

"Now, back to Emily. Spare me with any apologies about you not planning to fall in love with her and bullshit. You decided to come between us when you knew I liked her more than a hookup. I don't know what I did to you, that you made it your mission to mess up everything good in my life, but I'm done. Done with you. Done with your crap, done with letting you get away with everything. Screw our years-long friendship. Screw the Dragon Ball blanket. Screw the thousands of hours of conversations on playground swings. I'm done sharing my happiness with you, and I don't care if you fry your brain with drugs. You're a lost cause, and don't think I would give up without a fight. Emily still lives at my place. I have access to her whenever I want. She's more to me than a fling, and she will soon realize this is all you can ever give her."

I hung up the phone; I had finally cut him off, saying all those things that had been burning on my tongue for over a year. I'd never had an emotional outburst like this before, and fuck, it was like a heavy weight was taken from me. *For a minute.*

Because then the worry returned. I knew how impulsive Jon could be. I hated him, but I didn't want him to hurt himself. I quickly redialed his number, but he didn't pick up.

"Fuck . . .!"

I was a hypocrite for being done with him one second and worried about him the next, but Jon was like a rising storm, coming in slowly, hitting at full speed, and calm as if nothing had happened right after. When taking another step, my foot suddenly sent such a stinging pain through my entire body that I fell to the ground. *Shit, did I break some of the metal in it?*

I tried getting up, but it was impossible.

My phone rang. "Hello!"

"Paul, where are you? We have to catch our flight!"

It was my dad. I swiped the sweat off my forehead.

"I'm sorry. I went running and . . . could you pick me up? Something is wrong with my foot. I'm having trouble walking."

Gosh, I wished it was only the foot that was wrong with me right now.

Chapter 41

Regretting Him

Emily

MY HEART FLUTTERED AS I STRETCHED MY BODY TO THE SIDE, reaching for him. All I hit were soft sheets though. I scanned the room. I was still in the bedroom of the party Jon and I had basically missed because . . .

"Because we slept together." I held up the covers to hide my stupid grin. I had sex with Jon Denson, and even after a night of sleeping over it, I didn't regret it.

"Jon?" I shouted, guessing he was in the bathroom. I threw my legs out of bed, waiting for his reply. *But nothing.*

"Jon?" I said more eagerly this time, my steps increasing the closer I reached the bathroom.

"Jon!" I peeked into the room—he wasn't there either. The smile I wore drifted away in a heartbeat. *Do I have to regret it?*

I twirled around, looking for his stuff, but everything was gone. I covered my mouth to dampen the squeal escaping my throat. He left. Why would he leave? A sheet of paper was on the nightstand with the key chain pen. I picked up the note, soaking in what got scribbled onto it.

I'm sorry.

I crashed onto my knees, scratching them open on the woody floor. Holding onto this note until it wrinkled, my eyes fixated like laser pointers on those two little words. Thousands of theories roared through my brain, but one stuck out. A rational one, one I didn't want to believe was true. It couldn't be true because it meant everything was a lie. That Jon was still playing the game, the game of who could screw over the new girl first . . . *and he won.*

I ripped the note into a thousand little pieces, feeling like screaming and shouting, but I couldn't because there was so much pressure on my throat. My vocal cords lost their ability to work. The tears ran down, my mouth pulled up, and I couldn't breathe.

I was stupid to assume the one who said he couldn't give me what I needed would throw all his life philosophy over the pile because I'd spent some time with him. I wasn't the main character in his story—I was just the play toy. I crashed my fist onto the ground, the first crying sounds finally escaping. It couldn't be true—there must be an explanation for this!

I got up, clinging onto the last string of hope. I had to talk to him and get answers. He owed me that. I grabbed all my stuff and got dressed until I held his sweater in my fist. His woodsy perfume was still reeking from it. I wiped the tears off my face and wrapped the sweater around my waist. Depending on his answer, I would be crazy enough to do a witchy ritual with it. I lifted the sheets, noticing some blood on them. My cheeks heated up, and I ripped them off to throw them into a basket. I sneaked down the stairs, over still passed-out people, heading for the door. He wouldn't leave me alone in the woods. I mean, we drove almost an hour last night. On the porch, I crashed into Natalia.

"Oh, morning." She looked hungover, a cigarette already hanging out of her lips.

"Morning," I mumbled under my breath.

"Couldn't sleep because of the pills either? That's what I hate about Adderall. It robs all your sleep."

"You gave me Adderall?"

"Yeah, you struggle sleeping if you don't have ADHD but consume them. Comes in handy when you're planning an all-nighter."

"Oh . . ." Now I knew why I didn't feel high like the other times. I even felt calmer and actually slept better than in a long time? Probably because of Jon. My lip trembled, and I couldn't make it stop.

"Are you okay?" Natalia put the cigarette down and got up.

"Um, yeah. Have you seen Jon? I can't find him anywhere." I tried pretending I was okay.

"Didn't you sleep in the master bedroom together?"

I tangled my fingers into my hair. "We did, but when I woke up, he was gone, and we . . . we . . . ah, fuck!" I stomped with my left foot as the tears returned.

"He slept with you," Natalia stated, which I couldn't put into words. I nodded and wiped my face. She patted the chair next to hers, and I let myself fall into it because my knees couldn't hold me any longer.

"Here." She handed me the cigarette pack with one square left. I looked at her, confused why she would give me her last one.

"You need it more than me."

I picked it up., "Thanks."

I needed something to numb this aching. But smoking turned out to be harder than expected as my chest was still heaving with sobs.

"Listen, I also believed him when I saw you together last night. He played his act strong. No need to beat yourself up over being played by him."

She didn't understand. For her, it looked like I was just his date for the night, and we hadn't soul-stripped each other before getting physical. I didn't say anything to her. Explaining this was my first time would make her feel even more pity for me . . . and if she pitied me, I would never be able to stop crying.

"Is there a chance you will go to the city in a bit?" I pressed out between my sobs.

"I'll kick out hungover people and clean this place all day. Dave's parents will return tomorrow, and we promised them no parties." She got up, ready to bring her plan into action.

"You should call someone to pick you up. Those people here are not safe to get in a car with."

"Can I use your phone? Mine is dead."

My phone being dead felt like a running gag.

"Sure." She nodded in the direction of the cabin, and I took one last drag from the square. The nicotine in my veins made me feel dizzy, but every symptom that made me think a little bit less about Jon was welcomed.

In the kitchen, I called Gena. She didn't pick up, just like she hadn't with the other number that had called her yesterday. I prayed she would listen to the voicemail eventually.

"Hey, Gena, um . . . I know this is a surprise, but I'm not at Hannah's, and I could use a ride."

Natalia mouthed the address, and I crossed my fingers it wouldn't take long until Gena heard this.

"As long as you're waiting, would you mind helping me clean?" Natalia smiled, acting like my problems were solved by one line of comfort and a phone call.

"Of course." I forced a smile.

"Great. You start with the kitchen. I will walk around with a plastic bag."

Dave wandered in. "Morning, Little German."

I pressed my teeth together. That nickname sounded wrong from his mouth.

"Great, you can start getting all those people out of here, Dave! We need to hurry up to have enough seggsy time later." Natalia poked his nose.

"Gosh, Adderall is still kicking in for you, isn't it?" Dave rested his forehead on her shoulder, overly dramatic.

"Yeah, yeah. You were right. I took too much. That doesn't change the fact I'm motivated now, so hush!" She pushed him away and stormed outside.

"This girl." Dave smiled while looking after her. "I'll marry her one day."

I swallowed. That came as a surprise. Dave turned to me, placing his palm on my shoulder.

"And she liked you! She normally never likes any girls Jon brings. Who knows, maybe you will even become her bridesmaid."

I highly doubt that.

"I like her too." I shrugged instead, bringing my best acting game.

"Well, it was nice to meet you, Little German. We should hang out more often. You're fun!" He waved and left the room.

After dumbing multiple red cups with beer into the sink and emptying an overly full ashtray, I wiped the counter. I picked up some playing cards, and below them was a bag. A plastic bag filled with little pink pills, looking exactly like the ones I had from Marna's. I searched the place around me. No one was there, and I heard Natalia shouting at Dave to be rougher with the people on the first floor. I used my chance and stuffed the bag into the pockets of Jon's sweater.

Gena was furious. I would've never expected her to be able to freak out like this, and I didn't interrupt her.

"Going to a party in the middle of the woods?! What were you thinking, Emily!"

I didn't mention Jon to her. I wasn't ready to answer any questions about why I was spending time with him.

"And you look hungover! I mean, Henry and I know you occasionally have some beer or wine, but this?! I thought you were smarter!"

I didn't have any hard liquor, but being heartbroken apparently looked the same.

"God knows what could've happened to you! You could've been abused or hurt. Oh gosh . . ." She covered her mouth. I tilted my head to the side, so she couldn't look at me. If she knew what had happened—yeah, I couldn't tell her.

"You're grounded. At least a week!" She glanced over at me. "Or make it two."

I still got off the hook too easily. If I could, I would ground myself for the six months I had left here.

"What about Paul, Emily?! Have you considered how he would feel about you being alone at a party?"

I was surprised she brought up her son. She was always careful talking about our relationship because she didn't want to snoop. But no more lies. I was done lying.

"Paul and I aren't together anymore."

Gena gasped and turned quiet for the rest of the drive, giving me the space to be alone with my thoughts. After showering and changing clothes, I went straight into the basement, through the garage, and out on the streets—ignoring that I was grounded. I would follow her rules, starting tomorrow. *But now I needed answers.*

Chapter 42

Rather Now Than Later

Jon

W*hy am I such a fucking coward?* I fucking left. I left when she was most comfortable, and all I could come up with was *I'm sorry*. I punched the punching bag till I could hear a bone in my knuckles crack. My head was still spinning, and my chest hadn't stopped stabbing since Paul ended the phone call. I was a dickhead for thinking he would accept it. I wanted his stable family, which I knew I couldn't have. I envied his promising future, but I didn't have the drive or talent. I desired his status, sneaking into it by being his best bud . . . and then I wanted *his* girl.

Initially, I went after her to prove I could finally get something he couldn't. I was a loser, even thinking my fucked-up self would be enough. It wasn't enough. No shit I did was enough. I let myself drop onto the couch.

"I can't take this sober."

Last night I had said no to pills. I felt hopeful I could escape them until after the phone call. Instead of crawling back in bed with her, proving to Paul I could be everything she needed, I went into the kitchen. I befriended people who were high on shit, took a few belly shots with random girls, and licked the pills off their necks. My spine shivered when

I stumbled back into the bedroom, seeing Emily peacefully breathing in and out with a cute little face, hugging my pillow. I couldn't even stay true to her for one fucking night. Then, on the left, I saw blood stains on the sheets. I knew she was a virgin, but this sight made me realize what I had taken from her even more. I felt sick immediately. I ripped a piece of paper out of my black book, used the pen she gave me for Christmas, and wrote the only two words I had time for before throwing up. I vomited in the front yard seconds later. I gagged until I could taste the acid in my throat, and then I drove. I fucking drove a car, high as fuck, not caring if that would be the end or not. But it wasn't supposed to be the end yet because I parked the car without a scratch. It'd been a few hours since I returned home, and the pills' effect was leaving my system. I wondered if she found the note yet . . .

I crossed my arms and rested them above my forehead, boxing gloves still on. I wanted Little German to hate me, be disgusted by me even. She couldn't love someone who did something that cruel. This way, she would return to Paul, go with him to Germany in a few months, and build a future with him. With me, there wouldn't be a future because Paul was right. I wouldn't go to Germany with her. I got up and showered, but it didn't help to wash it off this time.

On the contrary, I lost her smell, the last thing I had left from last night. *Our story ends in tragedy, as predicted.* We had one night . . . but fuck, I already craved her more than anything else. I rushed upstairs, sneaking to my father's jacket hanging in the wardrobe. As expected, I found his wallet. I took a twenty, hoping he wouldn't notice it was missing. I needed money because I doubted Marna would let me get away without paying for it . . . and I preferred paying with cash than becoming her fucking sex servant. I never stole from my father, my mom, or her stupid husband. *Sure,* they had plenty of their own, but my dad—I respected him. Something I still did now, but I had lost respect for myself. I had put the wallet back in his pocket when a soft knock sounded on the front door.

"Jon . . .?" It was her trembling voice.

My body froze, and I struggled to breathe, unsure if I shouldn't open the door, apologize, and beg her to forgive me or if I should open the door and continue this act as if she meant nothing to me.

"Jon, I know you're there . . ." She shook the handle, and I was relieved I'd locked it. It would hurt for a few days, but then Paul would be there to repair the damage. I turned around and walked down the hall.

"Jon!" Her knock at the door got harsher. "Let's talk about this. I know it can't be a lie."

I stopped, taking a deep breath. She didn't believe it. *Fuck!* Dad suddenly came around the corner while Emily continued knocking.

"Oh, is that Little German?" He chewed on a sandwich that was still halfway stuck in his mouth. I pressed him into the kitchen by his shoulder.

"You've got to tell her that she has to leave!"

He swallowed. "Why? I love that girl. She's good for you."

I sighed. "I'm not good for her."

"I saw the way you looked at her, son." Dad placed a palm on my shoulder and gave me a wide-eyed look. "You wouldn't hurt her."

"I already did. Tell her I'm gone, or even better, tell her I'm at Kiki's," I whispered, making sure my voice wouldn't cross the hall.

"But—"

"I beg you, please do this for me, Dad."

He sighed and put his sandwich on the dining table and walked to the door to open it.

"Hey, Little German. I just ate a sandwich and told myself Gutin Appetit." He tried cracking a terrible joke. I hid behind the wall of the kitchen and listened.

"Oh . . . nice."

Only from those two words, I knew she was crying. I clamped my hands on the kitchen counter.

"Is Jon here? I need to talk to him."

"I'm sorry, but he hasn't returned yet," Dad said as if he had opened the door for Paul asking if I had time to play football and I told him I wasn't there because I wasn't in the mood.

"Oh."

I closed my eyes, praying she would believe him. "Do you know where he is?"

"He said something about going to Kiki's."

I swear her sobbing in the next second tore me apart more than I expected, and I glided down the kitchen wall.

"Oh, Emily, I don't know what happened, but it's okay. You will get through this."

I peeked around the corner, seeing my father hugging her. "My son is an idiot. Not worth shedding a tear for, you hear?"

Absolutely correct.

"Someone else will treat you better, I promise."

I closed my eyes and pictured her in the arms of someone else . . . but I had no right to be jealous. I had made my choice not to get better.

"I'm sorry for disturbing you, Mr. Denson. I wish you a happy new year."

I still heard her footsteps sprinting off when Dad sat down at the kitchen table, giving me a lost look as I crouched against the wall on the ground.

"I deserve to know why I had to break that girl's heart," he said, determined, his sandwich not getting an ounce of attention anymore.

"Because . . ." I breathed. "Because I can't get sober. Not even for her."

He sighed. He knew about my addiction, but like everyone else, I had ensured he wouldn't know how far gone I actually was. But I wasn't oblivious—he knew I was deeper into it than ever.

"You sound like your mother." He snorted in disgust, grabbed his plate, and left to the door. But before leaving, he said, "And I don't mean that as a compliment."

I didn't expect him to hold me, but I didn't expect him to give me such an ice-cold answer either. I guess I got that from him. We added another spoonful of hate whenever things turned tough. It stunk in my heart—we had just gotten closer again, and I thought things would finally get better. But for things to improve, I also had to bring my share to the table. I couldn't let the others bring in the steps. I had to make some myself. But with taking steps came the risks of falling even deeper.

Chapter 43

Lost

Emily

"MORE COFFEE?"

My body shivered, and my eyes flew open as the waitress shook the coffeepot in front of me with her smelly bubble gum. The way she chewed, it looked like her jaw would pop.

"Yeah," I mumbled, lifting my face off my arms. *I fell asleep at a diner?* I stretched my body up, leaning onto the booth seats. The waitress poured me the cup with a grumpy face. I was sitting at the same table as last time. The window still had some sprinkles of the coffee Jon had spilled there. I was so happy being here with him. But it was a lie—*everything was a fucking lie.* And now he was back with Kiki. My toes curled in. I knew from the phone call they'd remained in contact. He was probably sleeping with her as I cried my eyes out about him. With her, he didn't have to be gentle, not some sunflower sex like we had last night. The pain then was nothing compared to the pain now floating through my veins.

"Something else, or will you continue sitting here and block a table?" the waitress snarled at me.

I looked around. Except for two teenage girls slurping milkshakes at the counter and me, no one was there. I cracked my neck and gave her an annoyed look. "Do you take your gum out sometimes? Or is this part of your act to play the annoying and trashy waitress?"

Her eyes widened, and her chewing stopped.

"I was just asking!" With her nose held high, she walked into the kitchen. I downed the cup and got up, losing my balance, and I had to clamp onto the booth. *Those pills are strong.*

I had taken a few of the ones I'd found in Dave's kitchen because I had no alcohol this time to increase the effect from them. I wasn't sure if that would work, but I wanted to be 100 percent certain it would numb me. I would do anything to stop this sorrow in my heart, where one second turned into ten minutes, and an hour felt like an entire day. I'd been walking for minutes. *Why am I still not by the door?* I jumped, hoping this would make me move faster, and finally got a hold of the handle.

"Hey, you didn't pay yet!" The waitress stood by the kitchen door with her hands shoved onto her hips.

"Right!" I pointed up, agreeing with her, but I couldn't find my wallet. I closed my eyes, praying my body wouldn't betray me.

"I'm sorry."

I'm sorry. Two little words that can be used for such small things, like asking to get through, apologizing for forgetting to bring out the trash, or . . . *for fucking someone to win a bet.* And in my case, to rush out of a diner without paying.

I woke up on a bench. I tried to remember how I got here, but my mind was blank. My head was pounding. It was dark by now. I searched for Kiki's place, not even knowing where she lived. My phone vibrated in my pocket, and I took it out, feeling my stomach turn when I saw the name on it. *Gena . . .* I hated sneaking out again and breaking her trust. I couldn't talk to her. I couldn't tell her I broke the heart of her perfect son, that I slept with his best friend, and had been lying to her on every occasion I could. That I wasn't this innocent girl they'd taken into their place anymore.

My phone vibrated again.

Danielle: Hey, girl! I hope you had a great New Year! Can't wait to hang out soon. Are you free tomorrow? I will return around noon.

I would've been thrilled about Danielle's message yesterday. But now, I didn't want to see or talk to anyone. I couldn't act strong while listening to the *I told you so. I warned you he's bad news. You should've chosen Paul.*

I know I should've chosen Paul. And I did love Paul, but it wasn't the same way I loved Jon . . . *still love Jon.* Paul wasn't a pity prize; he was the jackpot. But I didn't need the jackpot. I needed the thrill in my heart only Jon was able to cause.

"Oh my gosh!" I looked up. I was at the fairy-tale-looking house on the outside, but nothing so fairy-tale inside. The place I'd spent the first two months of my exchange program, where I'd felt lonely and misused. I had tried fleeing from a feeling I tended to return to. I laughed out loud. I left Germany to get away from someone who abused me mentally. I gave up everything, even left those I loved behind, out of an act of selfishness. But I knew I had to go. A bit longer and I would've lost it again . . . It was so ironic I ended up in a family where the circle repeated. Just my luck, and when I finally found some peaceful walls, I searched for a way to screw up this security again, falling for someone who threw me away like a wet, used towel.

I pressed the doorbell multiple times. That would stop today. I wouldn't let anyone carry any power over me anymore. Not Jon, not Richard, and especially not Mrs. Stone!

They want to abuse me? They've got to fight me first!

Mrs. Stone opened the door in a white gown and with messy hair. She looked like she had already had her sleepy good-night tea.

"Emily?" She squinted her eyes as if she struggled to see me.

"Fucking right," I spat, ready to provoke and attack to get my revenge.

She startled, holding her palm onto her chest. "Are you doing alright?"

"If I'm alright?" I laughed out loud, even louder. "I don't know. Why don't you tell me? Apparently, you always knew better what was best for me."

"Emily, I don't understand." Her hand wandered to the door, ready to shut it if needed. My nostrils flared. She had no right to be afraid of me.

"I needed a safe space! That's all I wanted. A place where I didn't feel like I had to walk on eggshells! A home where I could speak my mind without worrying about being judged or talked down to!" I pointed at her with squeezed-together brows.

She sighed, her hand dropping down. "I understand. I did a lot of reflection after you left. I can't express how sorry I am for the way I treated you."

I snorted out loud. "Yeah, right."

If she had felt terrible about how she treated me, she could've written me a letter or found another way to contact me. This was her way of talking herself out of this, how they always did it. An apology to make us quiet till the next big catastrophe.

"The lies, they all started with you! Did you know I couldn't lie without giggling? You made sure I practiced, and now I'm lying without a second thought." My breathing quickened, and I had to gasp for air with every other word, tears burning in my eyes again.

Madison came to the door. "Mom, what's going—"

She turned stiff when she saw me, and her eyes wandered, panicking from her to me, me to her. But I didn't care she was here.

"So congratulations!" I wiped my face, feeling nothing but hate in my chest.

"What are you congratulating me for?" Mrs. Stone asked carefully.

"You won! Just like he did!" I balled my hands into fists and screamed.

"Win in what? And who is he?"

I cried-laughed, my emotions all over the place. Irony because I was what Mrs. Stone said I would be: pain because, against all my trying, I got abused again; anger because I couldn't understand why it was always me.

"Because you were right!" I fell onto my knees. There was no one to blame than me. Mrs. Stone knew what would happen if she loosened the leash. The only thing missing was the pregnancy. *Gosh, I can only pray the condom didn't rip . . .*

"I'm a hormone-controlled teenager. I went down the wrong path!" I screamed into my hands, crouching on the ground. "I had a perfect boyfriend, and you know what I did?" I looked up at her, Madison covering her mouth to suppress her tears right next to her.

"I slept with his best friend! Gave him my virginity instead of him! I'm taking drugs and say I got it under control, which I clearly don't because as soon as I'm feeling emotional, my brain finds an excuse for why it's okay to take them. I ran away from home, even though I got told minutes before I was grounded. And the guy I love doesn't love me back. I'm a joke, a walking joke, and I don't want this anymore . . . I want it to stop! Why won't it stop!"

I cried out loud, squeezing my eyes closed while lying on the ground like a fetus. And I cried—I cried heavily, even more than when I'd found Jon's letter, when I told Paul I loved Jon, when Richard hit my mother for the first time.

"Yes, hello." I heard Mrs. Stone talking to someone.

"Mom, there are other ways to solve this!" Madison's voice.

"She needs help, Madison. But, unfortunately, help neither you, me, nor her new host family can give her."

Help . . .

Because I got broken, I let them break me. Each time I tried to fit in, I molded into what they wanted me to be. I was never able to be who I was except with Jon. I could be myself with him, feeling ultra-familiar yet distant and strange when it happened. But being myself wasn't good enough. I was only good enough to win a bet. I opened my eyes, my face still in the muddy snow. My heart was bleeding on the doorstep of the hell I had tried to escape. I felt warm hands trying to lift me, but everything turned dark. I didn't feel anything anymore. Not even pain.

Chapter 44

Searching for Redemption

Paul

"DRIVE FASTER!" I YELLED TO DAD BECAUSE I KNEW THIS was bad. It was like I had loaded the gun, but the bullet didn't hit Jon—it lodged in Emily's chest. My lungs clenched. I should've known Jon would do something stupid that would make me regret being bad for once.

"I know you're worried, son. I am too, but the ground is covered in snow, and going faster won't be safe."

I shook my head. "She's missing, Dad!"

This speed was like a turtle compared to Germany.

"Should I call the police?" My mom's upset voice came from the speakers of Dad's phone. It broke her that Emily ran away instead of talking to her.

"Don't call the police, Mom!" I took the phone from the holder into my hands. "She will get sent home if she has any records, and I'm sure she's not sober. We will be there in twenty!"

I hung up the phone.

"Son, we need at least 40 minutes to get home. Gena should call them. Emily's safety is a priority."

"No, she has to stay! She needs more time away from him." I glared at my father, and after a second, he nodded, knowing I was talking about Richard. I didn't know what Dad discussed with Susanne . . . a part of me didn't want to know because I feared he couldn't change a thing either.

I held on to my crutches. After returning from my run, the pain in my foot hadn't stopped, and Susanne found them in their basement from the time Lucas had broken his foot. Having months of practice from back then, I could almost fly with them over the ground. I reached for my phone to call Danielle, but she was still not in town and didn't know where Emily could be. Same with Breana. While my father drove, I called everyone I could think of who had even the slightest contact with her. Kiki only asked about Jon and why she hadn't heard from him by now. I didn't tell her. I was done cleaning up Jon's mess. I dialed Jon's number for the eleventh time, but it went straight to voicemail. Frustrated, I hung up the phone, folded my hands, and looked at the car roof. The second the car halted, I jumped out of it with the crutches. Mom was already waiting in front of the door. Her face was all puffed up from her crying.

"I drove around and asked everyone I saw on the streets. No one saw her!"

Her voice broke while talking, and I pulled her into a hug. Zack came out of the door as well, but when our eyes met, he looked to the ground instead, not saying one word.

"I didn't know what to do. I called the police. I'm sorry, Paul."

"What?!" I stepped back. "Mom, they will send her back to Germany when she's drunk or high!"

"I know, Paul . . . but you should've seen her this morning. She didn't look like herself anymore. Something happened to her, and maybe it's better if she has to go back."

I shook my head and stumbled backward. "You want her gone?"

My father suddenly put his hands around me from behind. "Of course, we don't."

"We love Emily as if she's our daughter," my mom added. "But if something happens to her, we're responsible, and she doesn't listen to us."

I shook my father's hands off. "I'll search for her before the police find her," I hissed and hobbled down the road.

"Paul, wait!" Dad called out.

"Let him, Dad." Zack finally spoke, but I was already too far gone to hear what he was saying next.

A few feet away, I called Brandon. I knew he could take his mother's car if she didn't have it, and I couldn't drive with my foot. He was the only hope I had left to help me search for Emi. His car found me on the streets five minutes later.

"Hey, man!" he greeted me when I hopped in.

"Hey!" a girl squealed from the back seat. Light freckles and fiery hair welcomed me. Hannah. I looked at Brandon, realizing I had missed a hell of a lot in his life lately.

"I brought Han because we were hanging together," he informed me with a proud grin, and I gave him a wordless fist bump, knowing he would tell me everything in way too much detail some other time.

"So Emily is missing? What happened?" Hannah asked, and I suddenly minded he had brought her along. It would spread like wildfire if she knew about Emily being with Jon. I had to extinguish the fire because I wasn't ready for pity yet.

"I don't know. I just returned from Germany, but let's pick up Jon to help." Brandon nodded and hit the gas to drive to Tim's place.

When we arrived, I told them to wait in the car. I knocked on the door like a tornado hitting the ground. Tim opened it seconds later, and I stormed inside.

"Paul?" he asked, a bit startled about my rushed entry.

"Is Emily here?" I looked left and right.

Tim sighed. "No . . ."

His shoulders were hanging, and he scratched his ear.

"Well, is Jon here?"

"You missed him."

I turned around without saying thank you.

"Paul, wait!" My hand froze at the doorknob. "Jon is in a bad episode right now. I tried to make him stay, but you know how he gets when he's in a dark place. Be easy on him, okay?"

My body tensed even more. Tim had never intruded into our business before.

"I've been easy on him my entire life, and see where this got me."

I eyed him, and he slumped his shoulders. So he knew about Emily and Jon doing—ugh, I didn't even want to think about it. I walked out, slamming the door behind me. I knew exactly where to look for Jon next. His heaven on earth: Ted and Marna's place.

I told Brandon to continue driving around, to search for Emily, and I would call him whenever I needed him for another ride. I smashed the gate with my healthy foot and walked through the muddy path to the house's back door. I didn't even knock when I burst into the smoke-filled living room with its usual lack of oxygen. The stupid crutches made my entry look a little less badass, though. And then I saw Emily's light blue parka, dirty on the ground, my hope to find her blooming. But the only heads here were Jon, lying on the couch with Marna's body all over him. I wasn't even one bit surprised. He was dressed with his arms resting over his head., Marna's puffed-up lips pressed onto his neck, sucking on it. It was disgusting. He jumped from one girl to another like they were his trophies. My fist balled up again. *Emily isn't a trophy.* She deserved respect, and no matter how much I hated them being together, her respect was something I would honor.

"You fucking bastard!" I roared. Marna lifted her body, but Jon remained silent.

"Fuck, Paul! What are you doing here?!" Marna walked up and shoved me, not caring I was on crutches. I almost lost my balance. I looked back at Jon, who I suddenly realized was unconscious. *Did she want to rape him?!*

I walked past Marna, pushing against her shoulder harshly, and she snorted. Jon didn't even react when I shook his body.

"What is he on, Marna?!" Panic rose in my chest. I lifted his eyelid to look into his eyes, but they didn't react. "Marnaaa!"

"Fuck, I don't know. Oxy, Xan, weed. He wanted it all." Marna shrugged from behind. "He's fine. We were just having a great time."

I slapped Jon's face—not even a growl. "Marna, does this look fucking fine to you?!"

I got my phone out of my pocket and pressed 911.

"My friend overdosed. Please come to—"

"Fuck, if you say the address now, Ted will kill you!" Marna threatened. I gave her a nasty look and said the address loud and clearly into the phone.

"Please, come fast!"

Marna screamed and sprinted around the room, gathering all the drugs she could find. Because that's all she cared about, not Jon, her friend who was on the edge of dying. That's why I hated her and this place. Each time I came here, I pictured Jon becoming like them, and in some ways, he did. He acted as if he didn't care about anything, but I knew he was still my best friend on the inside. I placed Jon in the stable lateral position and checked his pulse. It was weak, too weak. *Fuck, what else can I do?!* I hobbled into the kitchen to get a wet towel to dab his forehead.

When I returned, Marna stood by the door, giving me one last nasty look. "You will regret this, Paul Shields."

"You caused this yourself, Marna. You wanted to rape him! You deserve to be fucking locked up for this, you bitch!" I hollered at her while pressing a cold towel into Jon's neck. Sirens—the ambulance was here, and Marna disappeared.

"C'mon, Jon . . . stay with me. I need you. I fucking need my best friend."

Chapter 45

Feeling Fine

Emily

HANDCUFFS SLICED INTO MY SKIN, AND I GASPED FOR BREATH. The taste of stale sweat and worn leather coated my tongue, making me nauseous. My pleas for fresh air mingled with the police sirens blaring in my ears. *I have to get out of here . . .*

I whirled around, but the burning pressure on my wrist robbed me of control, leaving me trapped in the back seat of the police car.

"Nein . . ." *No . . .*

My breathing accelerated as I felt the gradually mounting panic in my chest. I kicked my feet against the front seat. "Let me out!"

The policeman, long past his prime, covered in wrinkles and grizzled hair, shot me a sour look through the rearview mirror.

"Shut up," he spat.

"No!"

I kicked harder and harder, battling my instinct to surrender. But the seats didn't even budge; I couldn't fool myself. I was weak. *Pathetic, even.*

"You can give up, little girl." the policeman mocked and triggered this new rage. I balled my fists, fueled by that flicker of hope in my heart. *A fight isn't lost until it is over; this one has one round left.*

"Stop. Calling. Me. Little!" I screamed, attempting to squeeze my hands out of the cuffs. The policeman slammed the brakes at the red light, and my head crashed into the passenger seat. My vision morphed into a vignette filter, and my body fell silent.

"There's more if you don't keep your annoying mouth shut!" With my flickering sight, I squinted at the police officer twisting in his seat. "I know exchange student brats like you! They come to America, want the high school movie experience, but take drugs because . . . agh, I don't even know why!"

He slapped the armrest and pointed at me. "You're just like everyone else, so don't think your story will have a happy ending. You'll never get to come back to the US after the stunt you pulled tonight!"

I gulped so hard my throat hurt but gave a slight nod. He shifted his focus to the now green light while I tilted my head so he couldn't see that he had hit me where it hurt the most. Searching for comfort, I let my eyes wander over the night streets of Boonville. Seeing teenagers run into the secured shadows of the woods, fleeing from the scraps they had left behind in their haste not to get caught by this police car.

But I was caught because I'd given my heart to the wrong person. My lips trembled as a fresh tear rolled down my face. *Goodbye, America . . . it was nice to meet you.*

My legs and arms were as heavy as cement. I turned over, but the other side was just as hard. *Where are my pillows*

The last thing I could remember was being at the diner and thinking how disgusting it was that the windows weren't cleaned. But this place didn't feel like a diner. It was colder. Deadly quiet.

I rallied my strength and opened my eyes, a white electric light blinding me. I raised my heavy arms to cover my vision. In a hospital, I would not be lying . . . on a bench made of metal!

Light-headedness overcame me, and my stomach flipped as I pushed my body upright. Out of the corner of my eye, I spotted a trash can. I went for it and immediately threw up. *Gosh, I'm so tired of throwing up.*

"Rise and shine," a virile voice startled me. I glanced around and caught sight of a man leaning against the wall on the other side. He had leftovers from dinner in his beard, or maybe it was throw-up. His clothes were covered with holes, but his eyes gave me a friendly impression. A bit like Hagrid from *Harry Potter*.

"You really slept late. The worst should be over now," the man explained as if he were an expert on the subject. I wiped my mouth with the back of my hand.

"What is this place?" I asked before noticing bars separating us from a corridor.

"For me, it's heaven because I have a place to sleep. For you? Probably hell." The man shrugged, and a shiver ran down my spine . . . I got arrested.

"Let me guess, you tried drugs for the first time?" His voice was scratchy. It reminded me of a raven. I rolled my eyes. No matter where I went, people judged me. Not that I wanted to look like a drug addict, but I was tired of hearing I looked like a Goody Two-shoes.

"Not my first time." I groaned and wiped my face to remove the sweat and dirt. It was sad I felt the need to point it out. The smell of vomit made my nostrils pinch. I needed a shower, but instead, I was in jail. My last stop before returning to Germany.

Tears brimmed in my eyes . . . this was it. My story wouldn't have a happy ending.

"Don't blame yourself, little girl. You'd be surprised who I've shared this place with. It happens even to the best of us."

I wearily smiled at him because at least he was trying to cheer me up, but nothing could make me feel better because I wouldn't be able to walk home. I would have to fly home with no return. The click of a clock caught my attention. It was 12:30 . . . but I couldn't tell if it was night or day because there were no windows.

"Is it day or night?" I asked the man who was my only source of information.

"It's past noon." He yawned. "They usually let us out earlier, but there's been a lot of yelling."

"Yelling?"

" Someone was here to see you, but they didn't let him through to you."

"Someone? Who?" I leaned forward.

"A boy. He sat by the bars and tried to touch you, but you didn't wake up. I offered to shake you, but he gave me a scowl and said he'd make sure I never got out of here if I got too close. The guy looked even more destroyed than you."

Jon . . . that sounded like Jon. It had to be Jon! Jon was here?

"What did he say? Was he okay?"

"He didn't say much. And when he did speak, he used a different language. A stubborn boy, if you ask me."

I wiped the corners of my eyes. He'd spoken to me in German.

"He left you this letter." He pointed under the bench. And sure enough . . . an envelope was there. I quickly reached for it but stopped when I saw it was open. I stared at the man.

"I was bored," he defended himself as if that would make things better.

I glanced at the envelope again. My heart was pounding inside my eardrums. That letter . . . it had far too much power for me to remain calm. Even though I was angry with Jon, my love and care for him had not weakened one bit. My hands were shaking, the letter trembling in them.

"I can tell you what's in it if you want." The man chortled childishly.

I took out the note. "I can read it myself."

Little German,

I'm a fucking idiot. Jerkhead. Arschloch. Or all the other words you like to call me. They are true. I've always been selfish, looking for the next high, adrenaline rush, or whatever I could find that made me feel alive. And those were the things that were slowly killing me. I didn't realize how fucked up that was because I never considered how that would affect the people around me. At least until I met you. Because you made me want to stop being selfish. And I tried. I tried so damn hard not to be. I tried to pull back so you could achieve your goals and dreams. Like your #3 reasons, car rides after school and cuddles whenever you need them. Yes, I remember, and no, I will never forget your first drunken outburst.

You deserve someone who won't leave you in the middle of the night. Someone who would cross the damn ocean without looking back. Someone who would fill your heart with happiness, not just for a few months, but for as long as you wanted. That someone couldn't be me. I couldn't give you stability, and I wasn't even willing to try . . .

I freaked out, and I screwed up, and I'm sorry . . . and I hate myself for having to tell you this in a letter. You changed everything, Little German. You didn't force your help on me. You gave it to me in small doses, and I got hooked. Addicted to you. Because whenever I was with you, I didn't feel that urge in my brain to feed it until it shut up. When you smiled, I could almost laugh at my problems. You once asked me how I was feeling and I said I was fine. You made me feel . . . fine. And while fine is a feeling for many so normal, I was almost overwhelmed by it, because I hadn't felt fine in far too long. Feeling fine reminded me I have something to fight for. From now on, feeling fine will be the new thrill I'll chase.

You believed in me, and if you can believe in me after all this shit, I want you to believe in yourself. Believe the way you are is good enough. Your soul is the most beautiful place I've ever been privileged to experience, and if I made it dwell, I could never forgive myself. Laugh loud until you cry tears. Sob when you feel this world is not good enough. Yell like there's no tomorrow when people talk over you. Your feelings are there to celebrate, not to swallow. Stop swallowing . . . please.

I love you, meine kleine Deutsche.

—Jon

I had trouble catching my breath because I was sobbing so much. His words . . . it was not a lie. He was feeling the same; tears burned my eyes, and the words blurred. My throat stung as I tried to suppress the emotions, but then I remembered his words and let them drip onto the jail floor.

"I've never been a fan of cheesy love letters, but this one. . ." The man cleared his throat and shook his head. "That boy really knows how to use his words."

"He really does." I sobbed, but my mouth twisted into a slight smile.

"Oh, what the hell." The man reached into his pockets. "Here."

He handed me Jon's black book.

"Why do you have this?" I jumped up and snatched it out of his hand.

"I thought I could sell some of these poems. But now I know how much you feel about him, I don't want the money anymore."

I wasn't sure whether I wanted to beat him up for stealing it in the first place or thank him for giving it to me. But I wasn't granted either because Humphrey abruptly unlocked the cell. He looked tired but composed. I had been frightened when I met him in the police car that night, but this time, he frightened me even more because he held the key to my freedom.

"Emily, you can go." He waved his hand for me to go outside.

"Oh . . ." I gasped as I stood up, still feeling like I had been hit by a truck. I stumbled out of the cell but then turned around.

"Thank you," I said to the man who had witnessed what I hoped would be one of the lowest moments in my life.

"I hope I never see you here again," he growled back.

"You won't."

Because I would have to go to Germany anyway, and secondly, I would never let the drugs get the upper hand over me again. I had fallen low, but I would rise again. Because I wanted to feel fine together with Jon. I clutched his book and letter tightly.

"Where's Jon?" I asked Humphrey as we walked through the hallways of the building. He stopped in his tracks.

"Didn't he tell you in his letter?"

"Told me what?"

"Emi!"

I whirled around and saw Paul waving at me from down the hall. *Is he calling me Emi?*

"You can go." Humphrey indicated I was free to go to Paul.

"I c-can go . . .?"

"Yes, but Bred was right. I never want to see you here again."

"But—"

Humphrey gave me a wary leer. "Don't become like him, okay?"

I clutched Jon's little black book tighter. I hated that Humphrey only ever saw the worst in Jon, especially since he was one of the reasons he had fallen low. I should've seen the resemblance to Richard right away.

"Becoming like him isn't bad." I refused to let him manipulate me into being nice just because he had bailed me out. Without faltering, I ran to Paul. Standing before him, I hugged myself and looked at him from below.

He was on crutches, and his foot was in a cast. But that wasn't all . . . his eyes were surrounded by blue bruises, and although they were swollen, they dilated when they caught a glimpse of Jon's book.

"What happened?" I swallowed hard and resisted the urge to hug him. I wasn't sure I had the right anymore, and I wanted him to set the rules.

He pulled his gaze away from the book and back on me. "We'll talk about everything later. But for now, I'm glad you don't have to go back to Germany." He hauled me into his arms and dropped the crutches to the floor. My breath hitched as he did so, and tears rolled down my cheeks again. But not tears of sadness . . . Paul didn't hate me. I hadn't lost him.

"Thank you." I hugged him back and smelled my home on him. I was safe.

"I was worried about you, Emi." He stroked my hair and pulled me even closer to him.

"I'm sorry . . . for everything," I whispered into his chest.

"I know . . ." Paul mumbled onto my hairline. We pulled apart from each other.

"Mom and Dad are waiting for us outside."

I was confused as to why he was understanding and didn't hate me with every fiber of his body. I had broken not only his trust but also the trust of his parents. However, another question burned in my chest.

"Where's Jon?" I ventured to ask.

Paul bit his lip and reached down to pick up his crutches. "He's gone, Emily."

"What do you mean . . . gone?" I took a step back. Paul placed his arms into the holders, taking his sweet time before finally replying.

"He made sure you didn't have to go back to Germany. He did a good thing."

I shook my head in confusion. "I don't understand."

Paul sighed, and even though his hands rested on the crutches, I knew he would rub his head if he could. Instead, his lips twitched. "He made a deal with his stepfather. You'd get out with no criminal record, if he went to rehab."

"He's going to rehab?!" I let out a yelp, and my heart shook violently.

One part of me was happy about it and the other wholly devastated because it meant my time with him would be shorter than expected.

"I have to say goodbye!" I stormed past Paul, but his crutches blocked my way.

"You don't understand. I need to talk to him before he leaves. I have to . . ." I stepped over them, but Paul let them drop to the ground again and grabbed my arm.

"Emily!" Paul spun me around roughly, and I was surprised by his dominance. "Jon's already gone. You can't say goodbye."

I let out a quivery whimper. "He's gone?"

Paul sighed. "Yeah, he left about two hours ago."

I dropped into the nearest chair, shaking my head. "He's getting sober . . ."

Paul nodded and sat down next to me. "Honestly, I didn't expect him to when Humphrey gave the ultimatum. But he didn't even hesitate when it was either you or him. He chose you right then and there." Paul gave me a pained smile, my chest tightening. We still had much to talk about, much to sort out. But I was grateful he accepted my love for Jon.

I grabbed his hand. "He didn't just choose me, Paul. He chose you, too."

Paul snorted loudly and looked up at the ceiling. "I could've been a better friend to him. But you . . ." He craned his neck to look directly at me and smiled. "You saved him from getting lost, Emily."

I breathed through my teeth, suppressing saying out loud what I was really thinking. It wasn't me who saved him from being lost; it was him who saved me from trying to be someone I was not. *Screw perfect!* I finally knew who I was, and even more importantly, I knew not only what I wanted but what I needed.

Acknowledgments

Writing this book was a greater roller coaster than expected. I was so swept up in the development of Emily, Paul, and Jon that I put off deciding who was better for her until I was already two thirds of the way through the book. That's when I realized . . . it's not about who's better but who you can be your true self with. Someone who not only loves your perfects but appreciates your hardships. Growing up, I played the role of the perfect, innocent girl. This expectation turned me into a perfectionist with constant self-doubt, who would rather hide than speak her mind. I reduced my value to my accomplishments for a long time—not anymore! When I picked up on this behavior with Emily, I could reach deep inside myself, and I am no longer ashamed of not being perfect. Mental health is a topic that is thankfully being brought more and more into the light but unfortunately is still a constant battle in so many people's lives. That's why I included ADHD, addiction, abuse, self-harm, and anger issues. As a current psychology student, I am still learning about it, so if anything isn't portrayed correctly, I apologize. I certainly don't mean to offend anyone.

Drug addiction, or addiction in general, can destroy lives. As Jon said, *drugs are not cool; they are a cry for help*. In my experience as an exchange student, I witnessed firsthand the impact pills have on youth. Often, the addiction developed after an accident until the prescription was dropped, and the teens found other ways to access them. It's not your fault if you get addicted. It's their side effects, but if you find they're taking you over more than they should, you should seek help immediately. If you are suffering from mental health issues, addiction, or abuse from authority figures, reach out, no matter how hopeless the situation may seem. Ask for help, accept help, and don't run away. You are not lost. You can find your way back. This is my promise to you!

I want to say thank you to my family. We are not perfect, but we are us. A beautiful disaster I can count on. I'm lucky to have this close support system, and I do not take you for granted. Thank you for listening to me and encouraging me when all I could think and talk about was this book. Thanks to my longtime partner, Philip, who never doubted me and loves my quirks as much as my good qualities. To my friend Shanen Ricci, who gave me feedback on every chapter of the manuscript and listened to my overthinking rages. To Kellie Storm for beta reading and for giving me confidence in my creation. To my editor Sandra from One Love Editing, my cover designer Danielle from Vixen Designs, and Stacey from Champagne Design for formatting. And last but not least, to each of you who support me and shower me with kindness on my social media. My writing career began with the reading app Episode, and it's only thanks to your passion for these characters that it's turned into not one but now two novels. And we're not done yet! There will be another part, *The Lucky One*, which will be released in 2024. Until then, stay lovely . . . or go wild. Be yourself and embrace everything you feel inside because you are great the way you are. Feel *fine* :)

About the Author

Naemi Tiana is best known for her interactive mobile stories The Lovely One, Best Woman, The Bucket List + YOU, and Bad Reputation. Her work has been featured multiple times on the award-winning reading app Episode, and she has garnered 40+ million reads. Now she's exploring writing novels and fell in love with creating complex minds on paper. Naemi lives in Germany with her boyfriend, two fluffy cats, and a family she loves deeply. Her path is guided by Shakespeare's words: "Love all, trust a few, do wrong to none."

Naemi's stories can be found on the app Episode. For more, check out @naemitiana.writes on Instagram and TikTok.

Printed in Great Britain
by Amazon